The Only Child

The Only Child

by guojing

schwartz & wade books • new york

Acknowledgments

I would like to give my gratitude to my parents, who always supported me and who helped me recall my childhood memories for this book. Thank you to Isabel Atherton and Lee Wade for all their assistance and suggestions, and a special thanks to Raju Chowdhury, who gives me such encouragement, advice, and support. I could not have completed this book without all of you.

Copyright © 2015 by Guojing ∗ All rights reserved. Published in the United States by Schwartz & Wade Books, an imprint of Random House Children's Books, a division of Random House LLC, a Penguin Random House Company, New York. Schwartz & Wade Books and the colophon are trademarks of Random House LLC. ∗ Visit us on the Web! randomhousekids.com Educators and librarians, for a variety of teaching tools, visit us at RHTeachersLibrarians.com

Library of Congress Cataloging-in-Publication Data
Guojing. The only child / Guojing. — First edition.
pages cm ∗ Summary: In this wordless graphic novel, a young girl traveling from her city apartment to her grandmother's country home becomes lost and enters a fantastical world in the clouds. ISBN 978-0-553-49704-5 (hardcover) — ISBN 978-0-553-49705-2 (glb) — ISBN 978-0-553-49706-9 (ebook) 1. Graphic novels. [1. Graphic novels. 2. Lost children—Fiction. 3. Adventure and adventurers—Fiction. 4. Stories without words.] I. Title.
PZ7.7.G9On 2015 741.5'973—dc23 2014026977

The illustrations in this book were rendered in pencil and adjusted in Adobe Photoshop.

Book design by Rachael Cole

PRINTED IN CHINA
1 3 5 7 9 10 8 6 4 2
First Edition

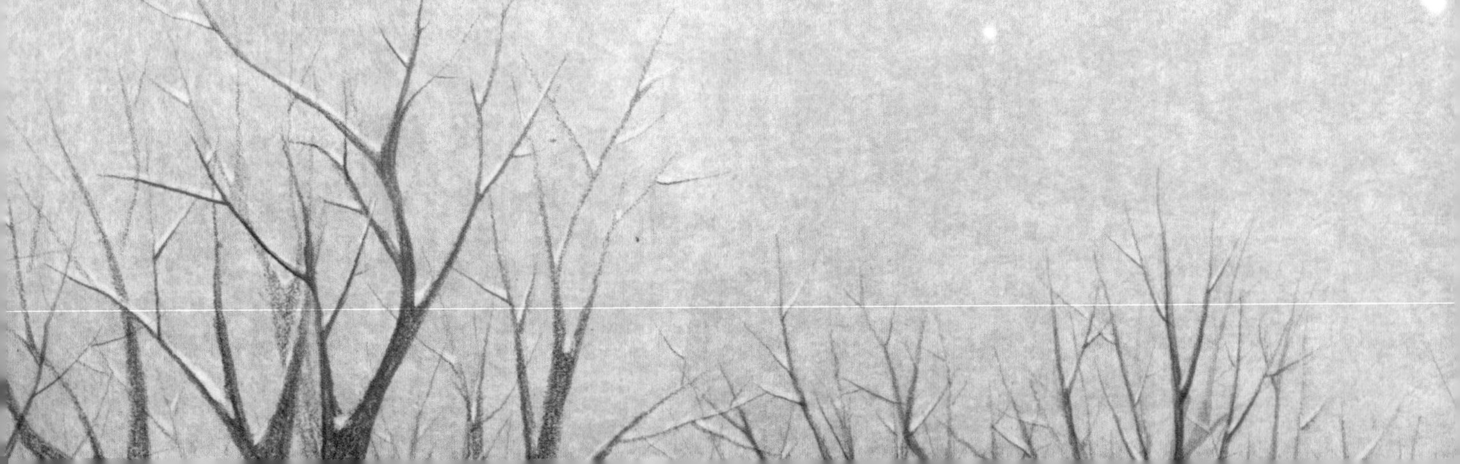

For my mom and Raju Chowdhury,
who encourage me to dream

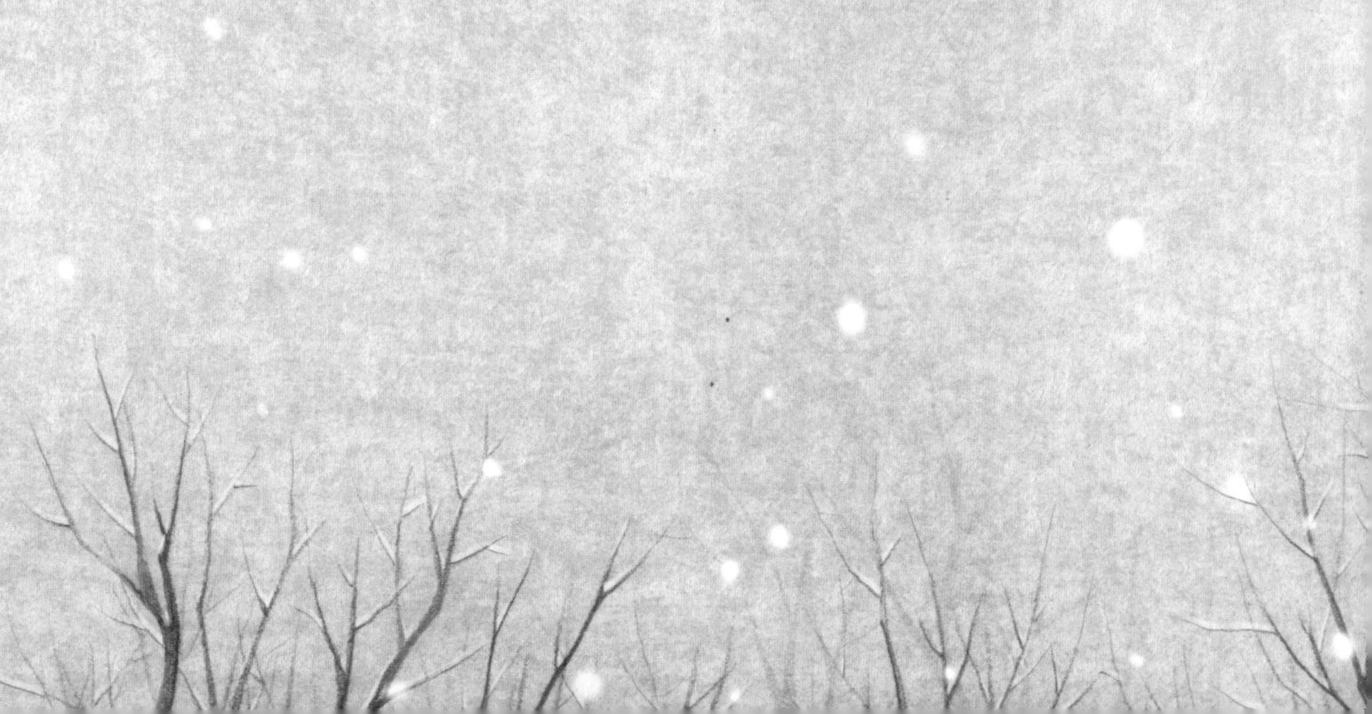

author's note

The story in this book is fantasy, but it reflects the very real feelings of isolation and loneliness I experienced growing up in the 1980s under the one-child policy in China.

When I was young, both of my parents had to work to support our family, so during the day, my grandmother would take care of me. But still, sometimes—if they had to rush to work or if Nai Nai was busy—they would leave me home alone. This experience was common in many families at that time. I belonged to a very lonely generation of children.

Once, when I was six years old, my father put me on a bus to my grandmother's house before he left for work. I fell asleep, and when I woke, the bus was almost empty. I panicked and ran off. There was no one to help me, so I started walking. I cried as I walked, following the electric lines of the bus. Luckily, I found my way back to a road that looked familiar and eventually reached my grandmother's house three hours later.

As I've grown, I've realized that it is easy to become lost, but if I look hard enough, there is always a path—like the electric bus line—guiding the way back home.

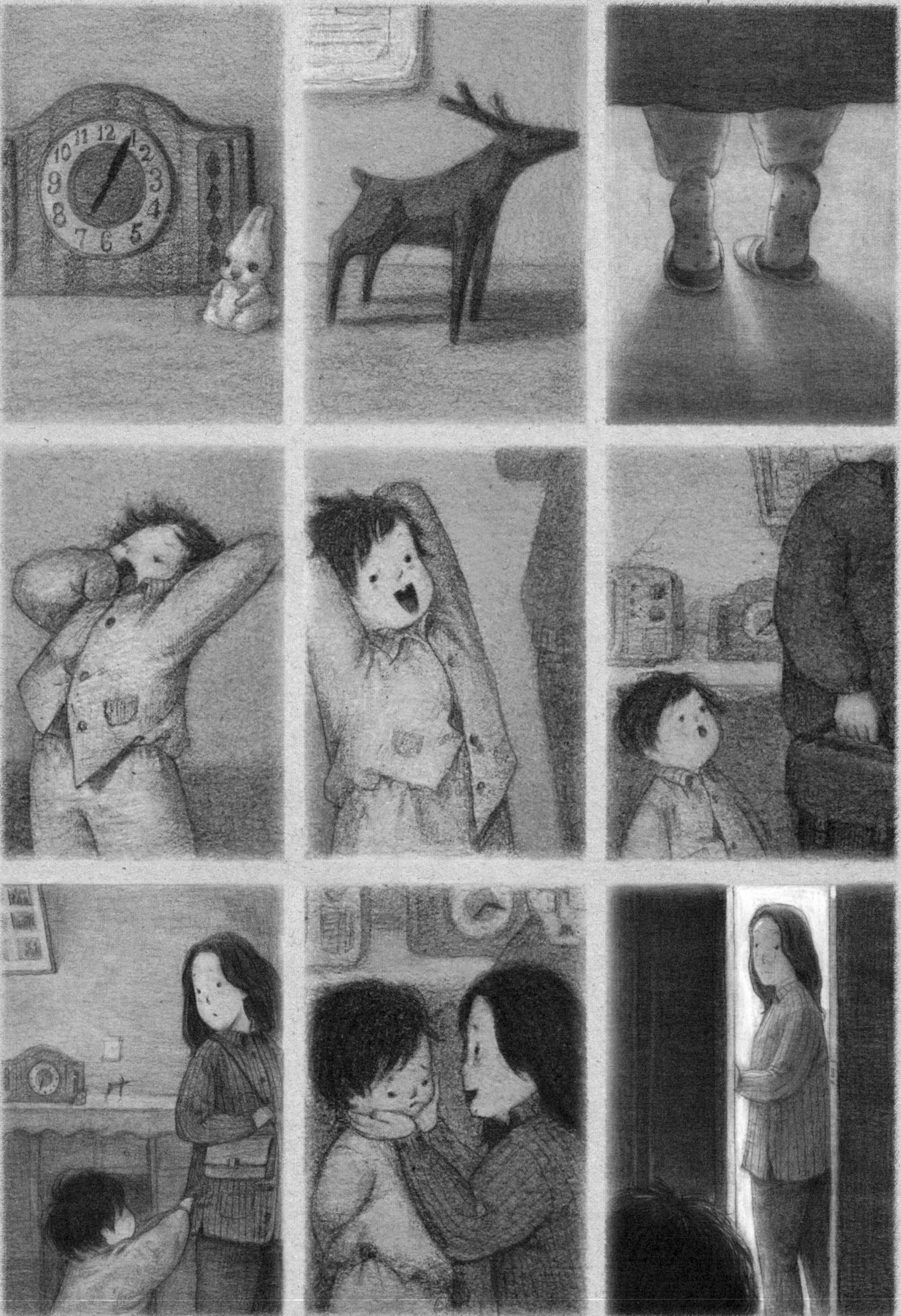

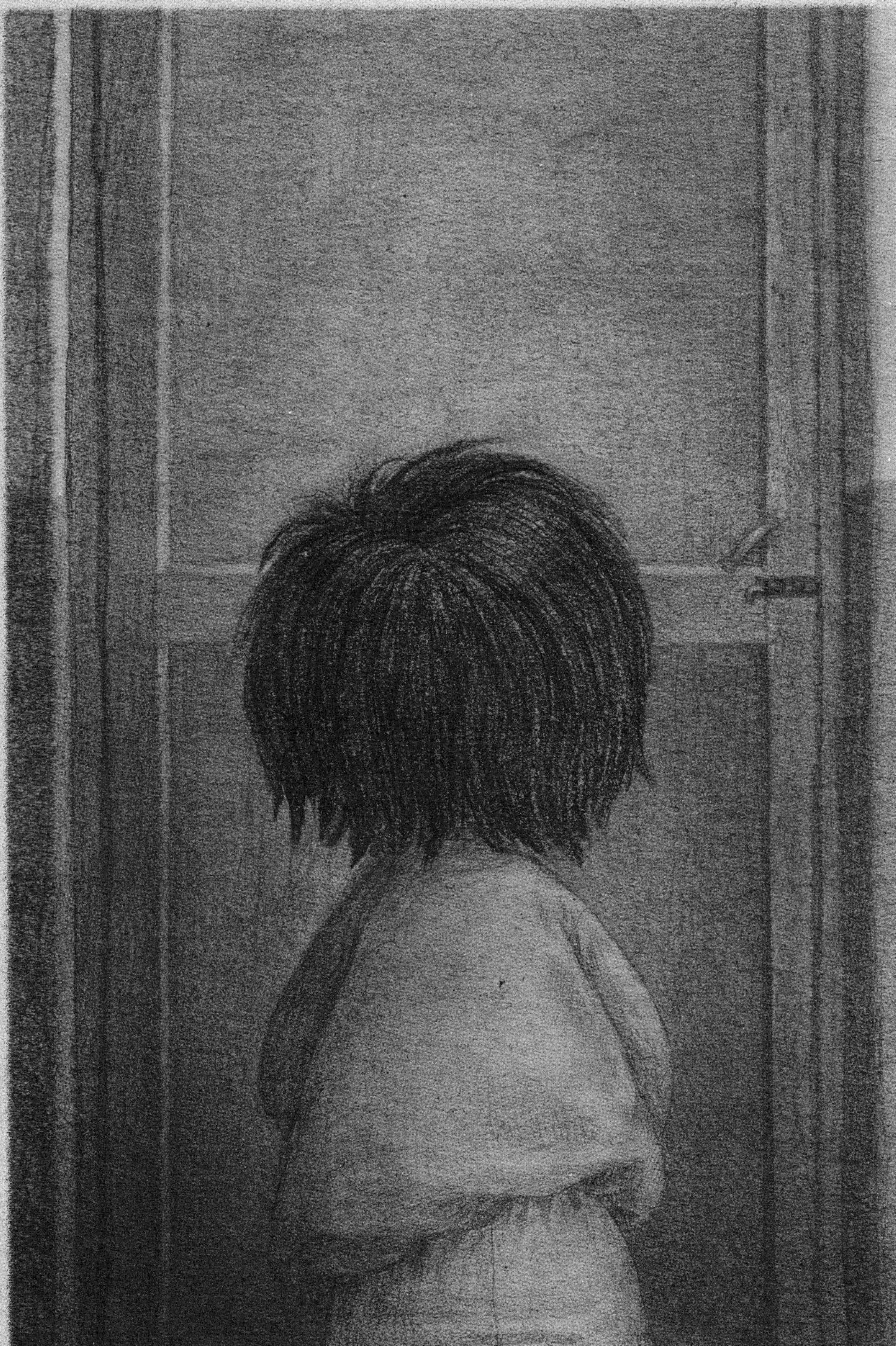

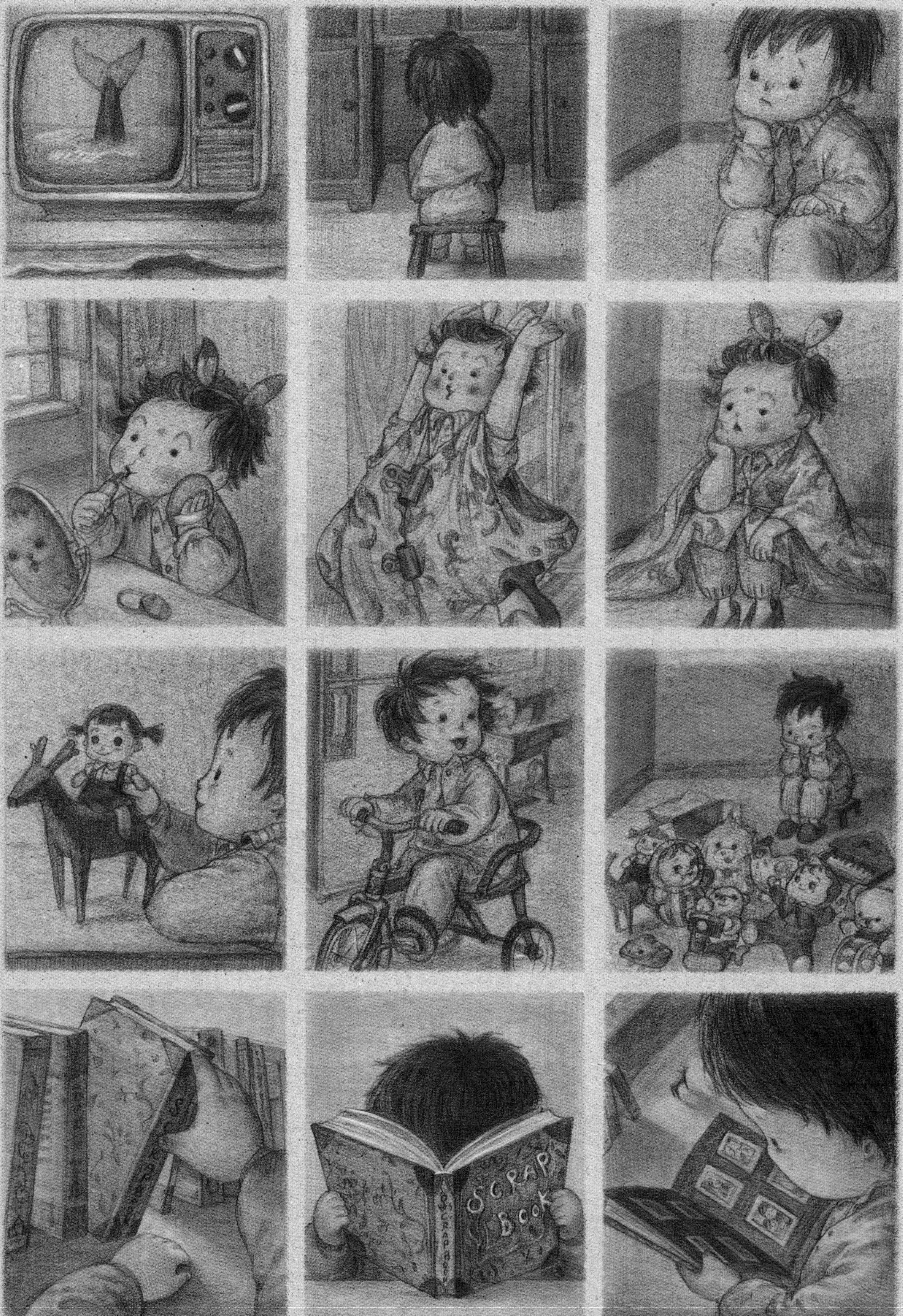
SCRAP BOOK

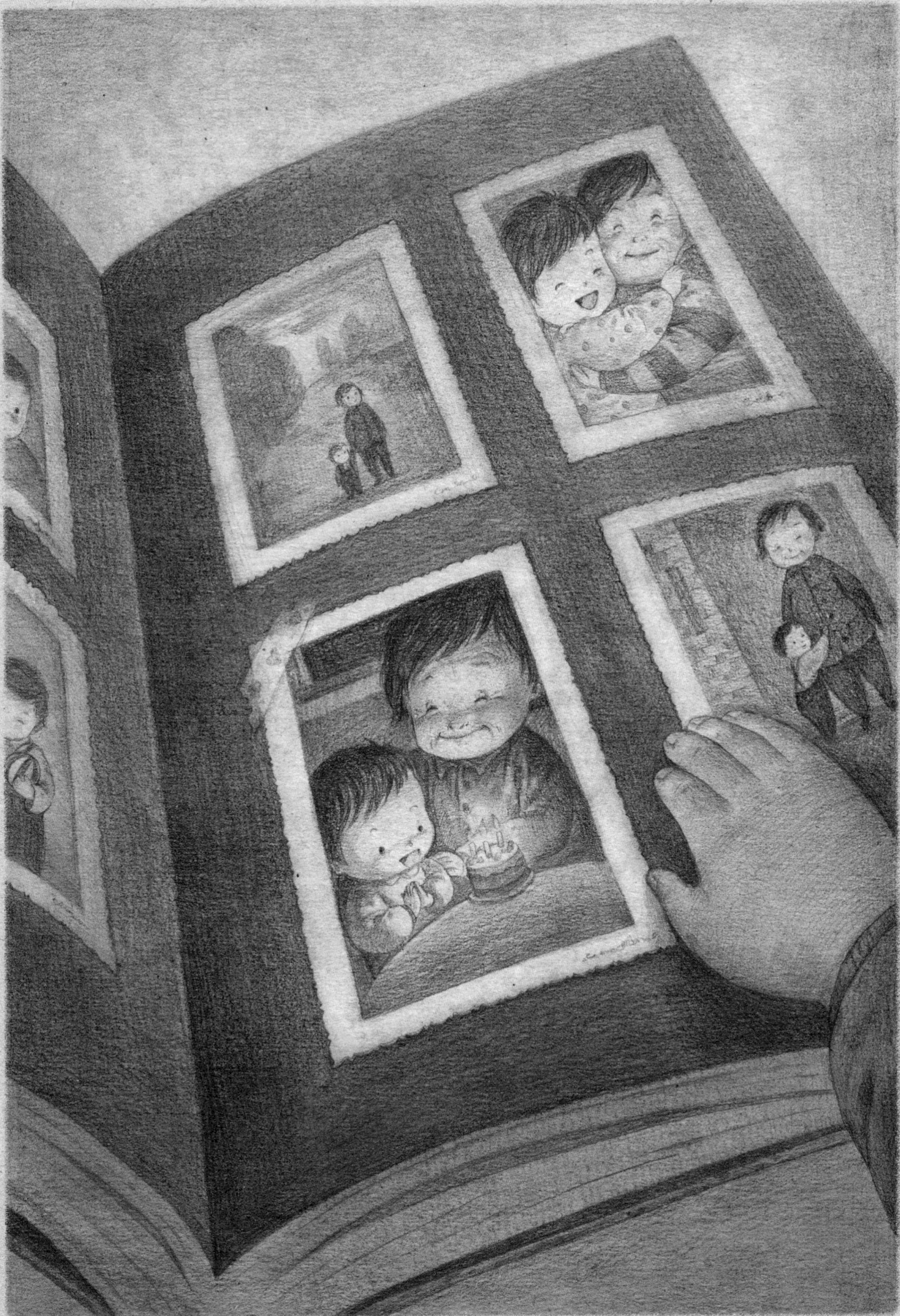

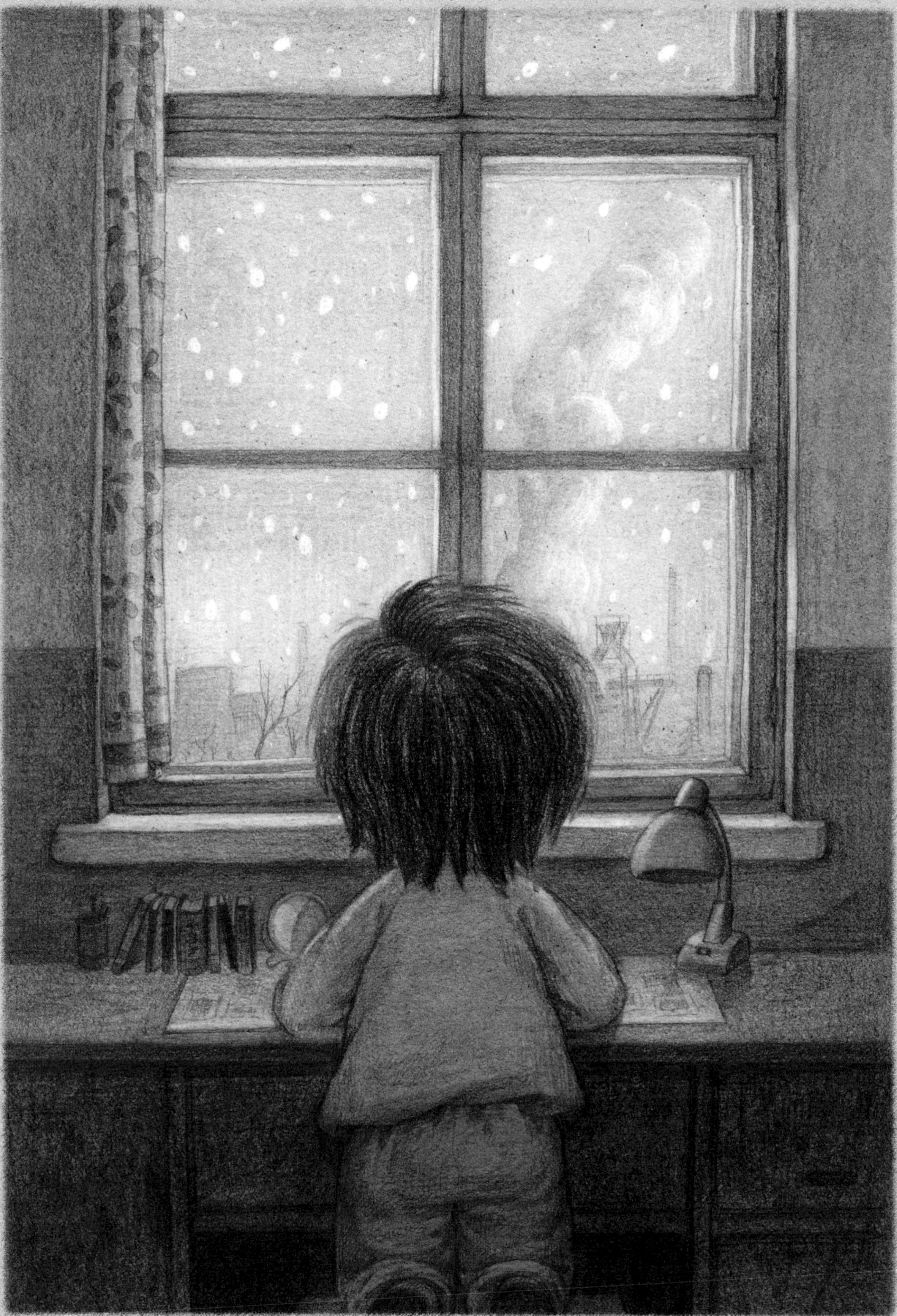

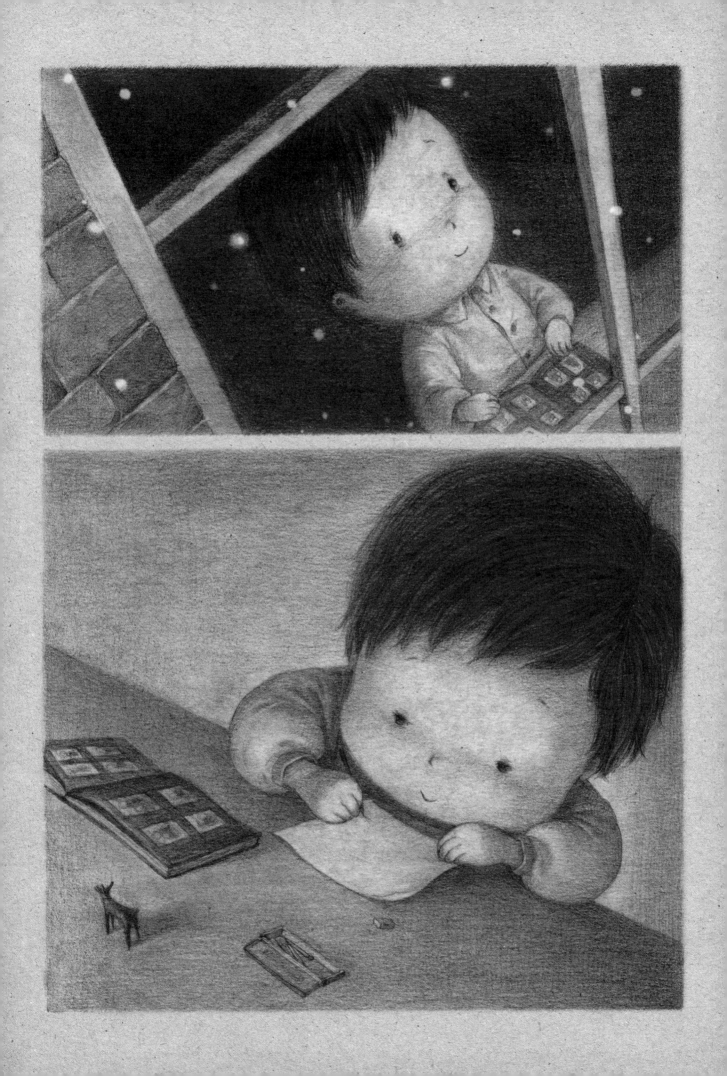

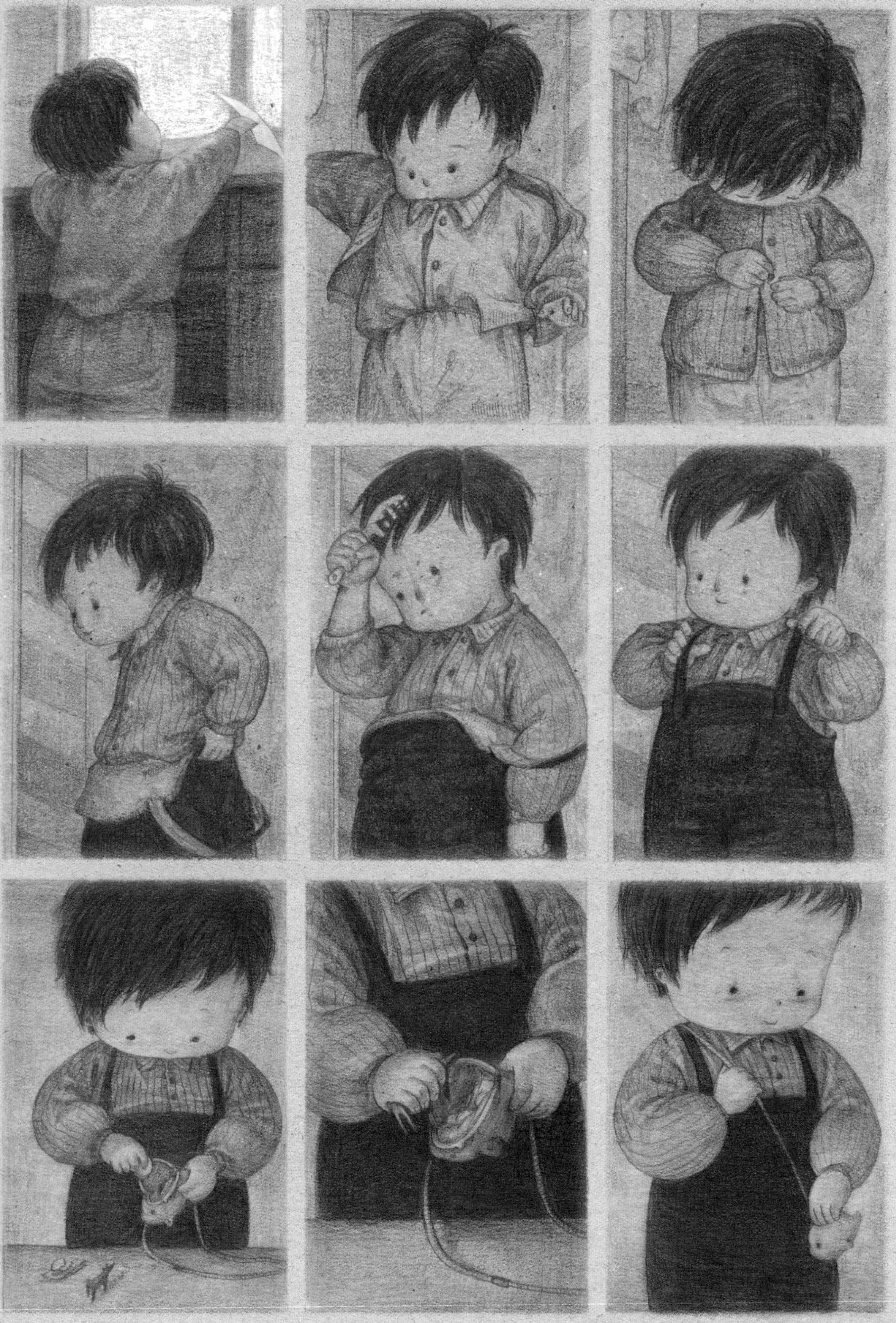

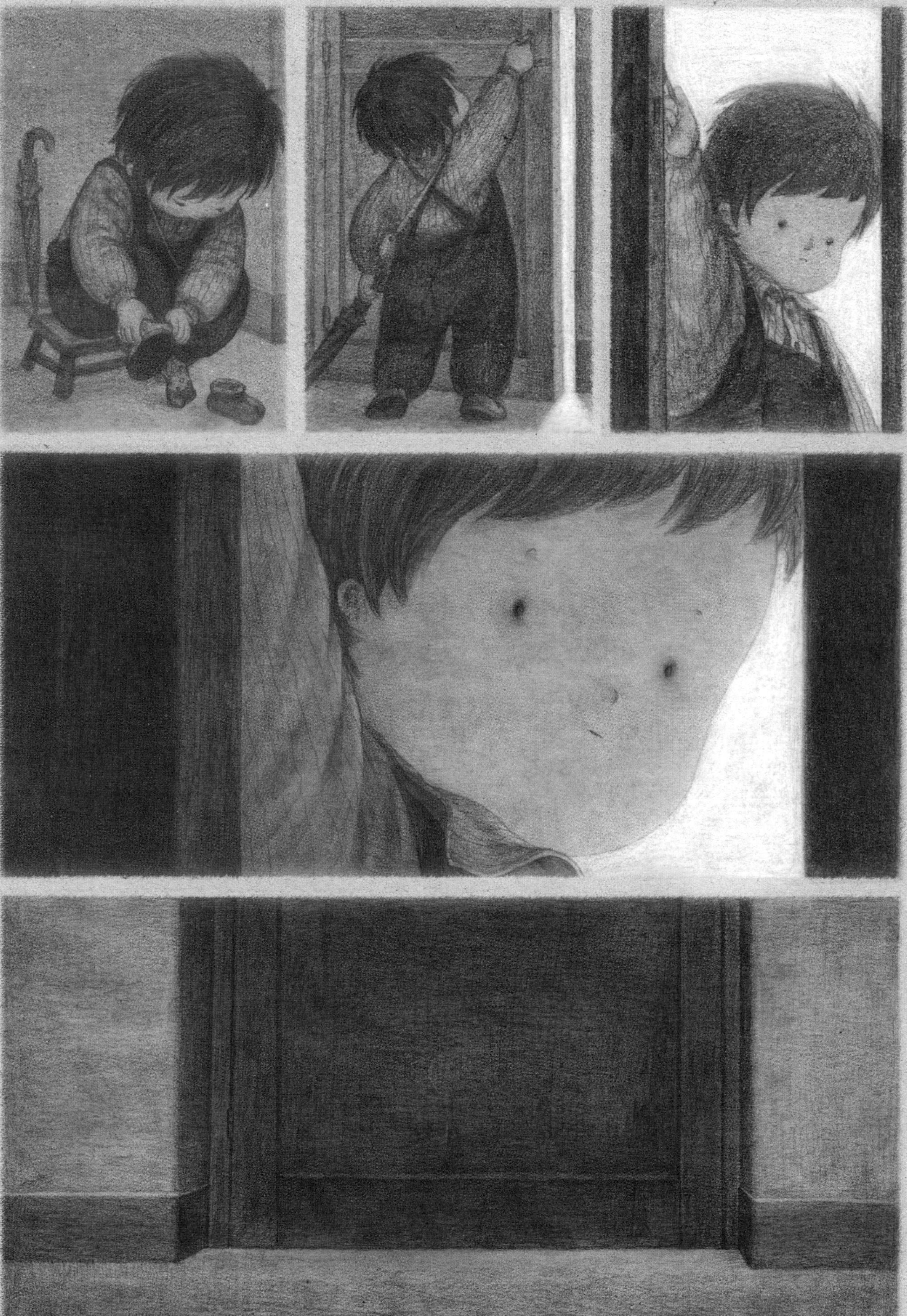

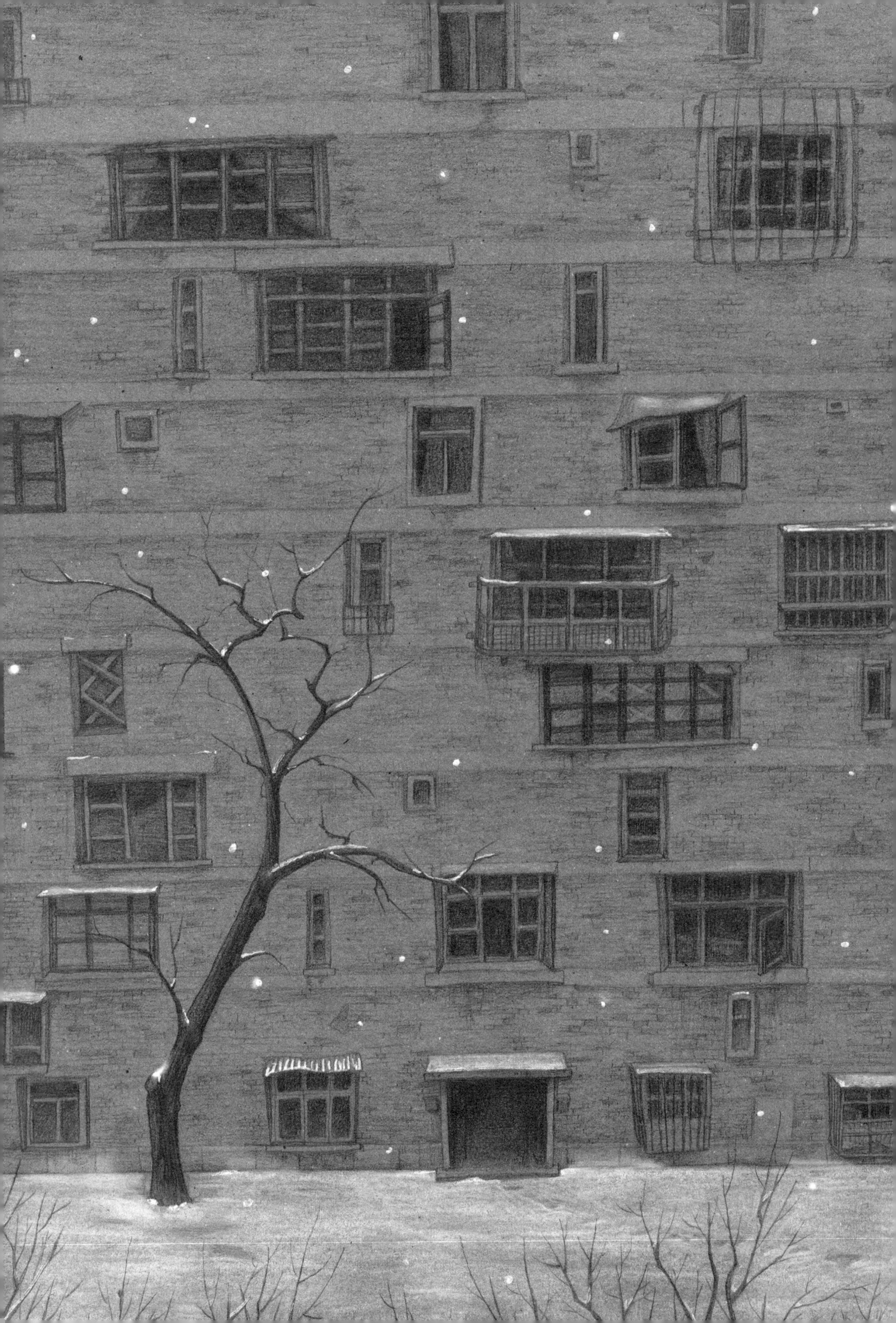

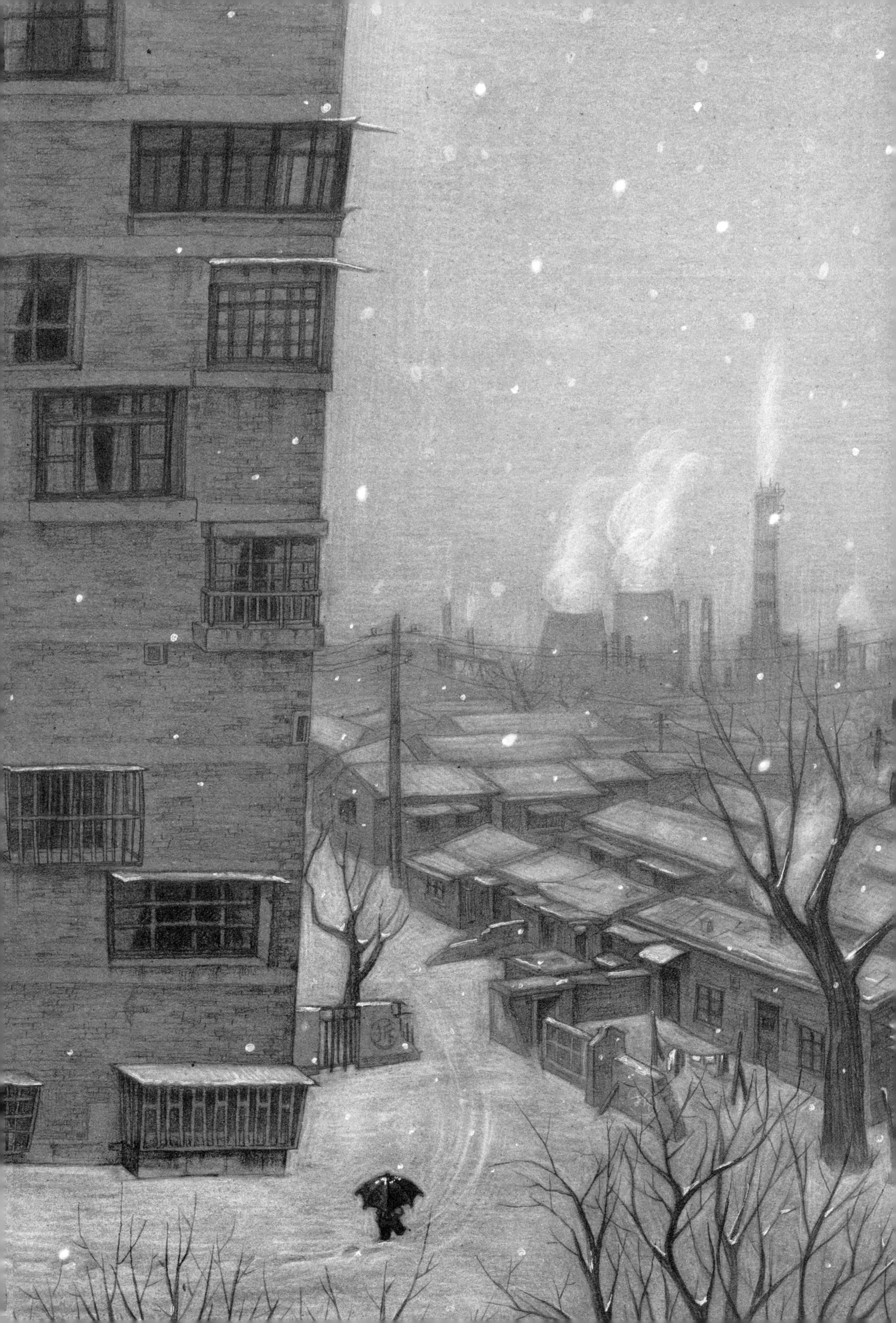

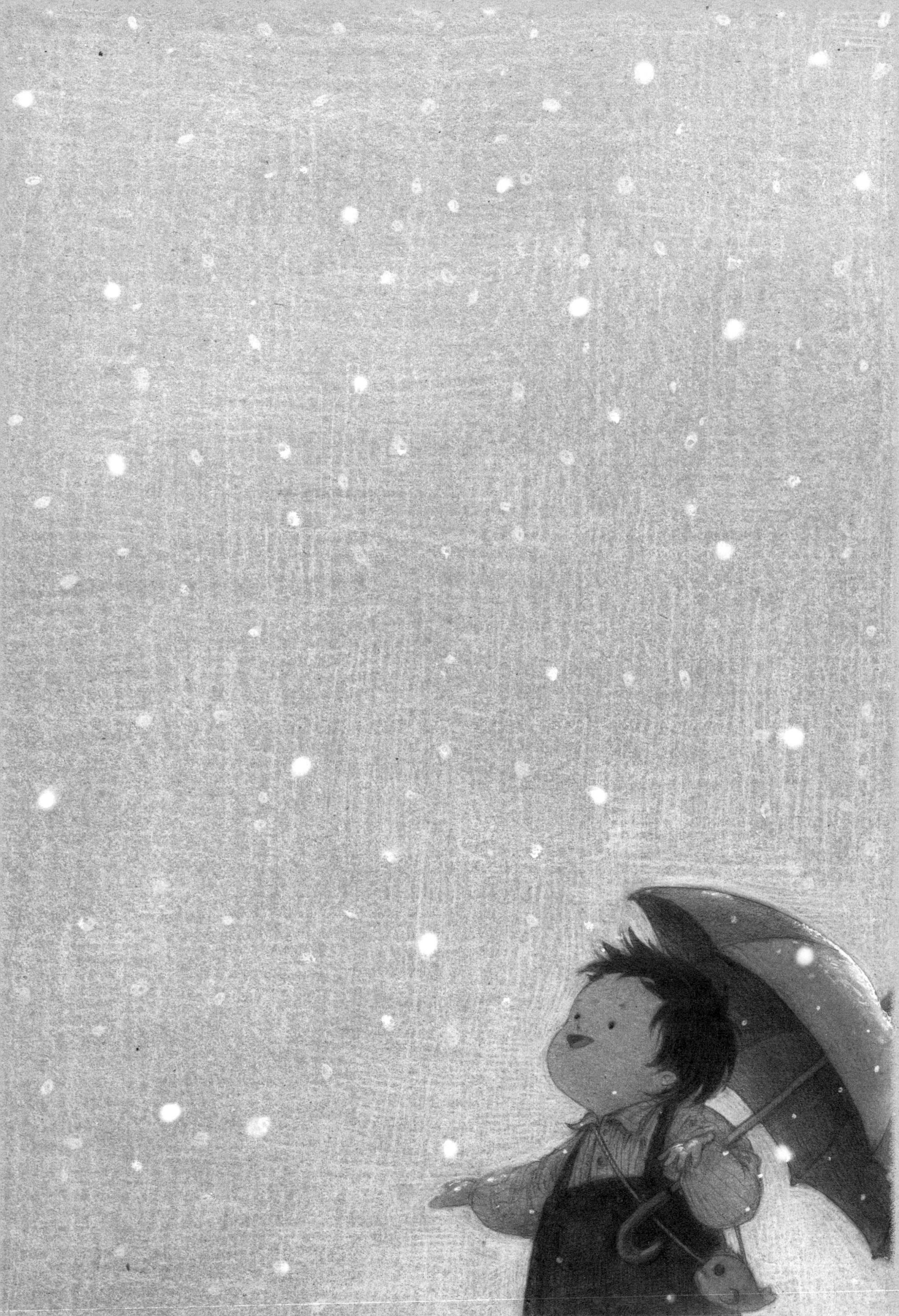

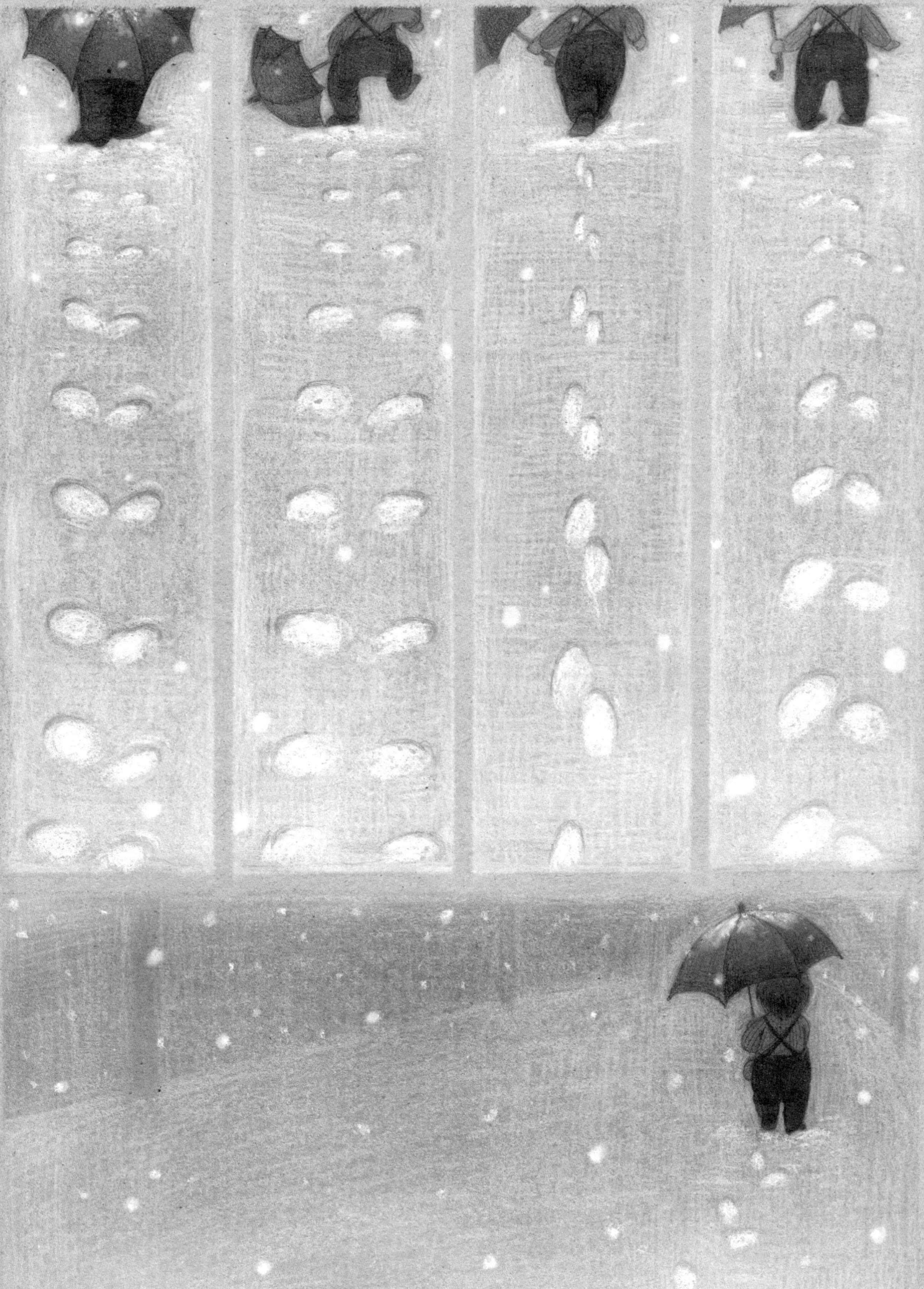

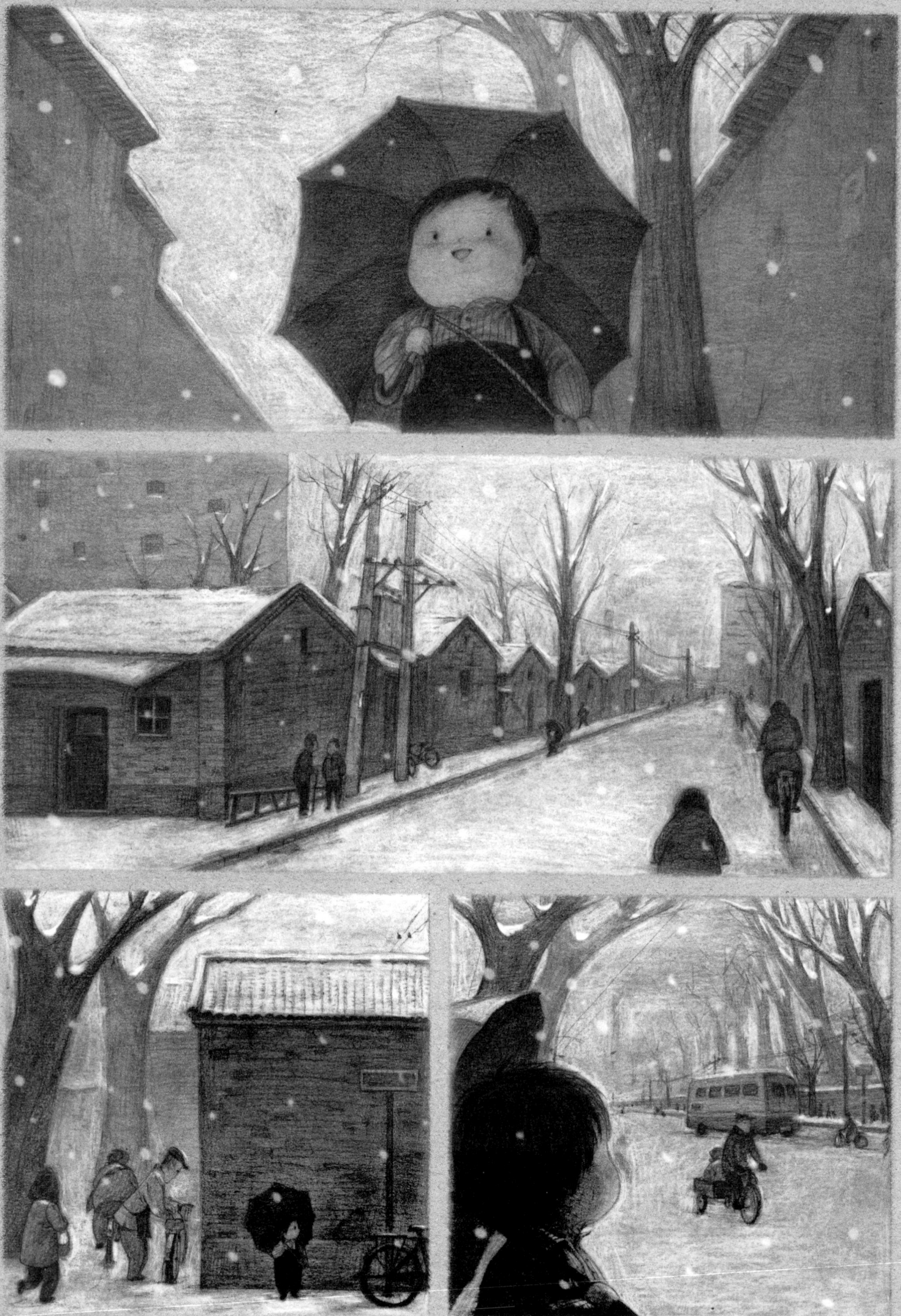

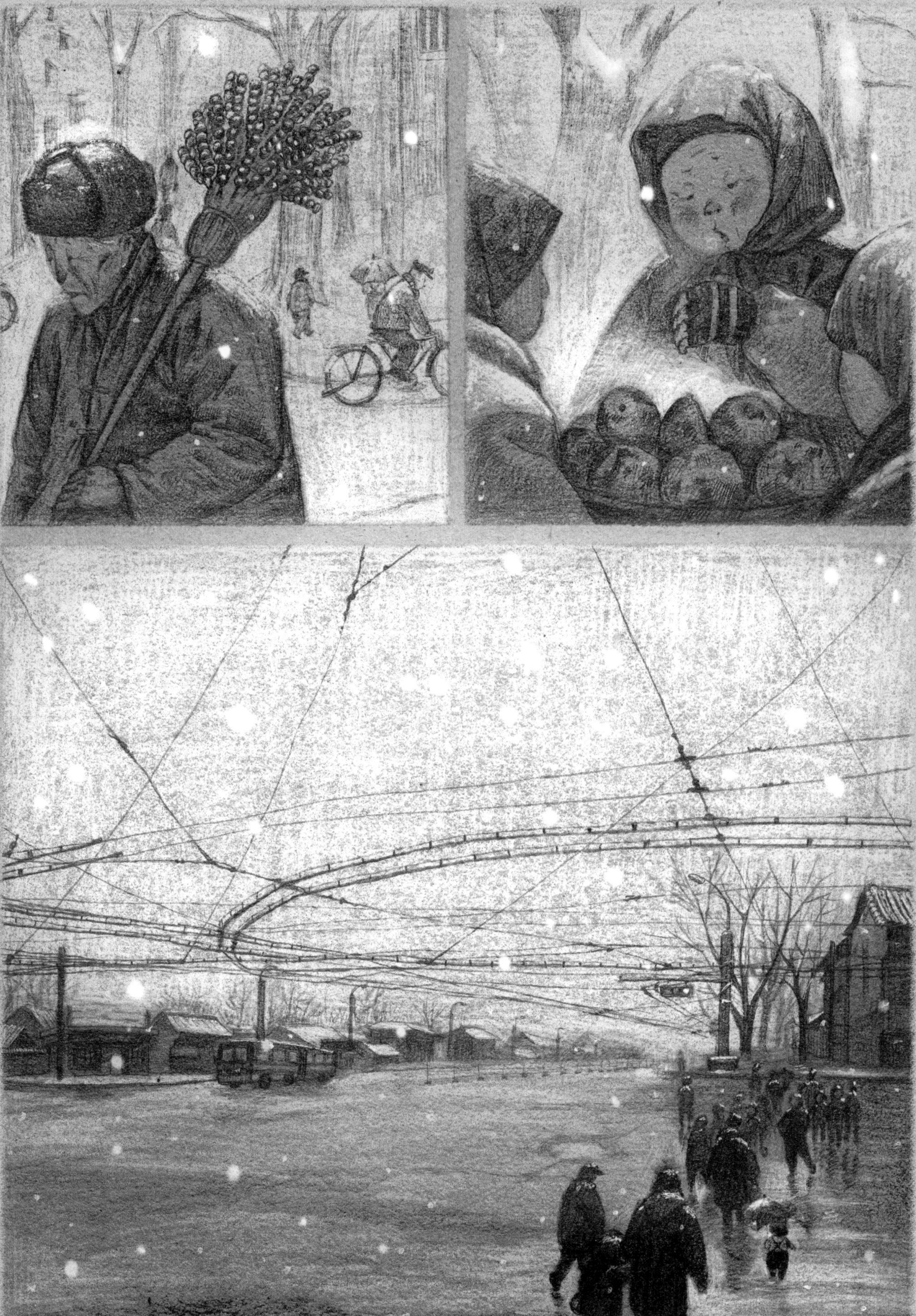

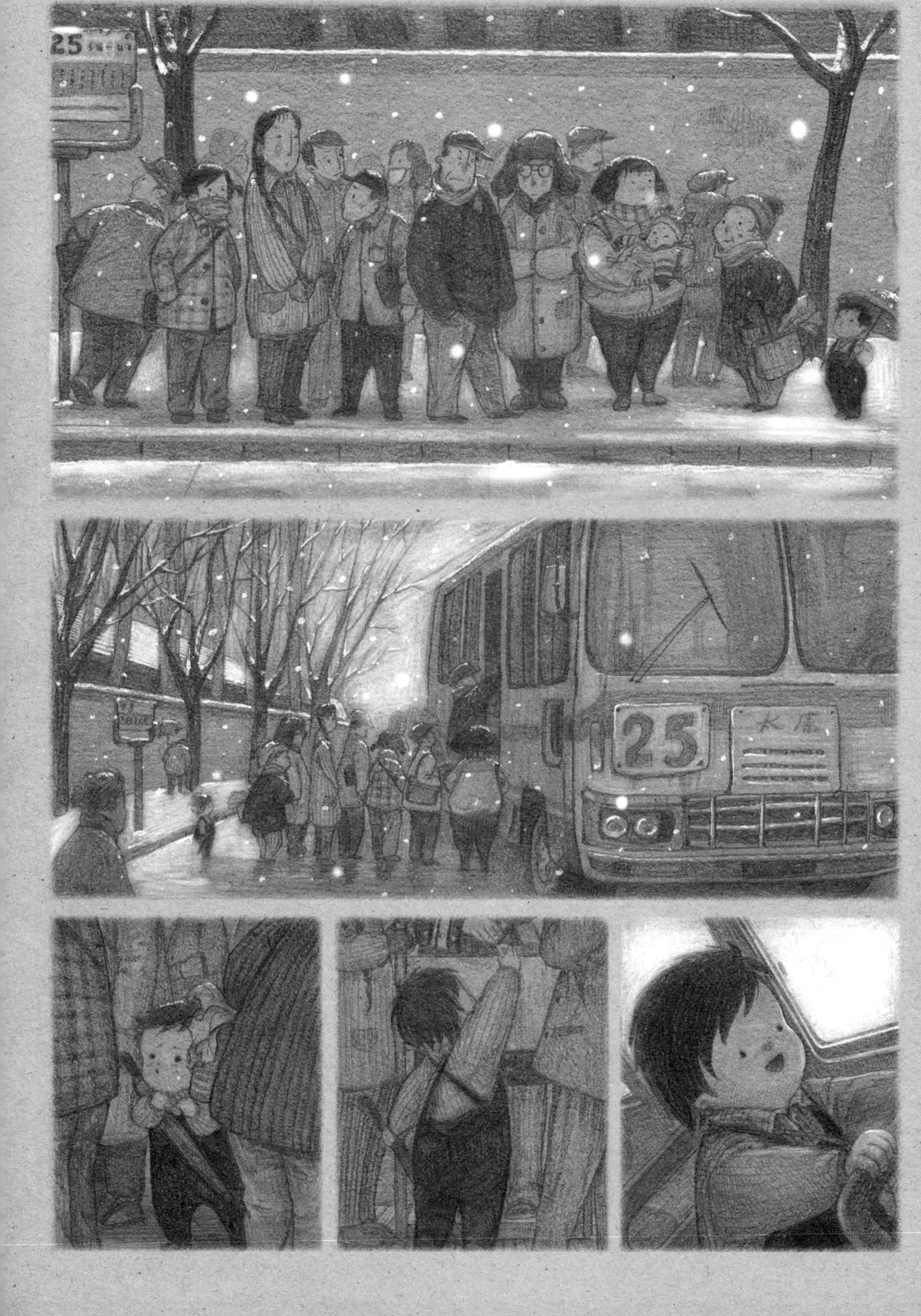
25
25

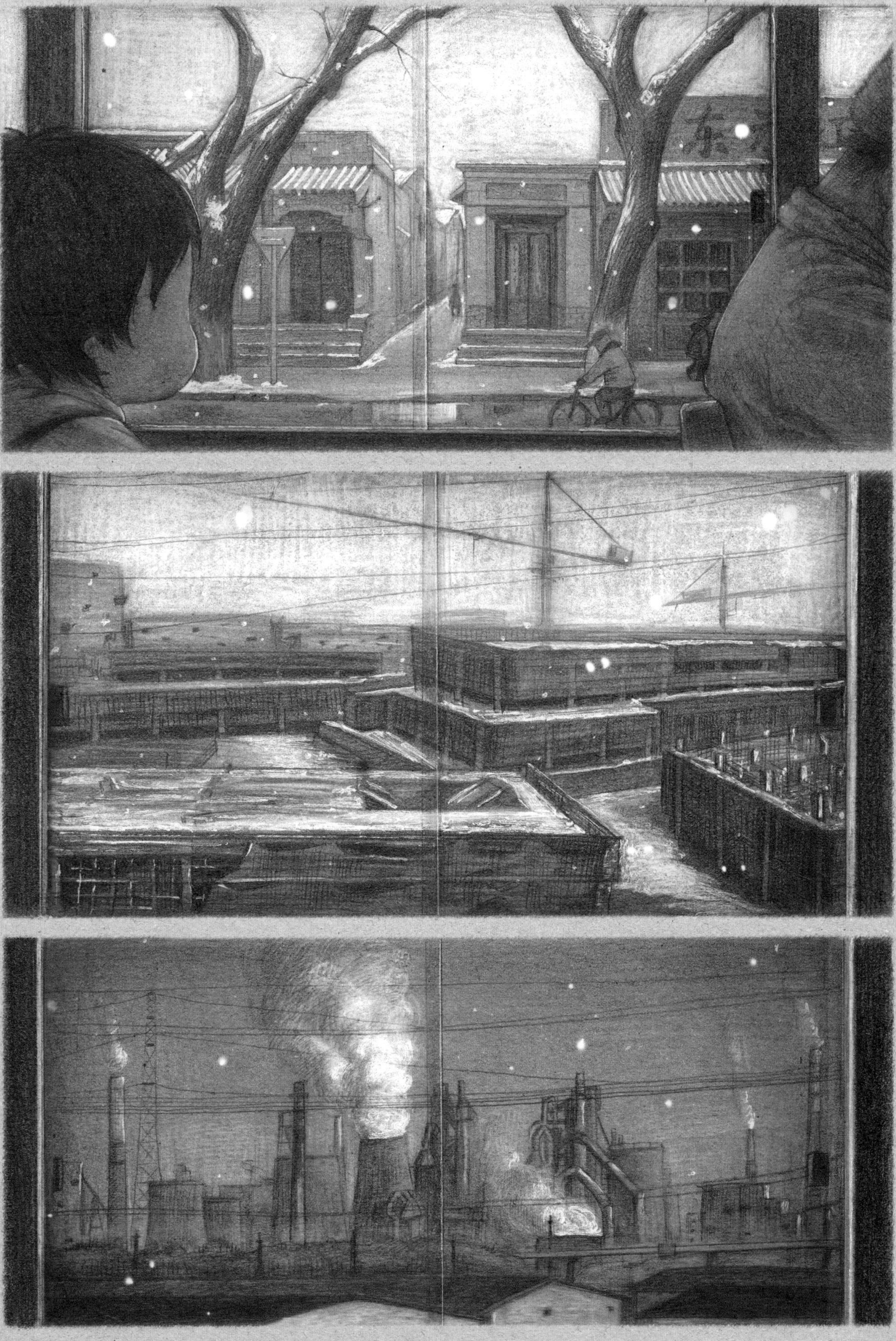

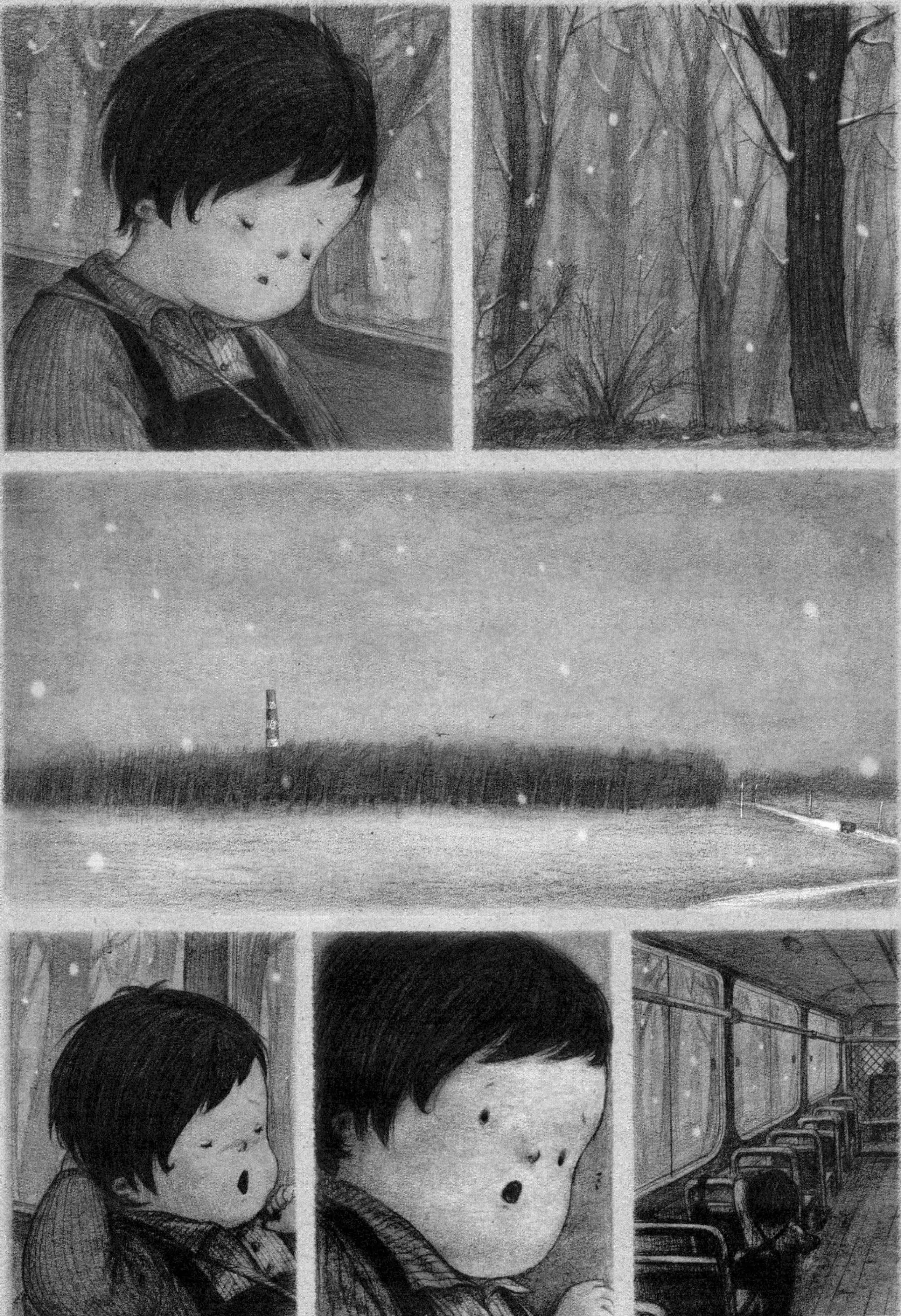

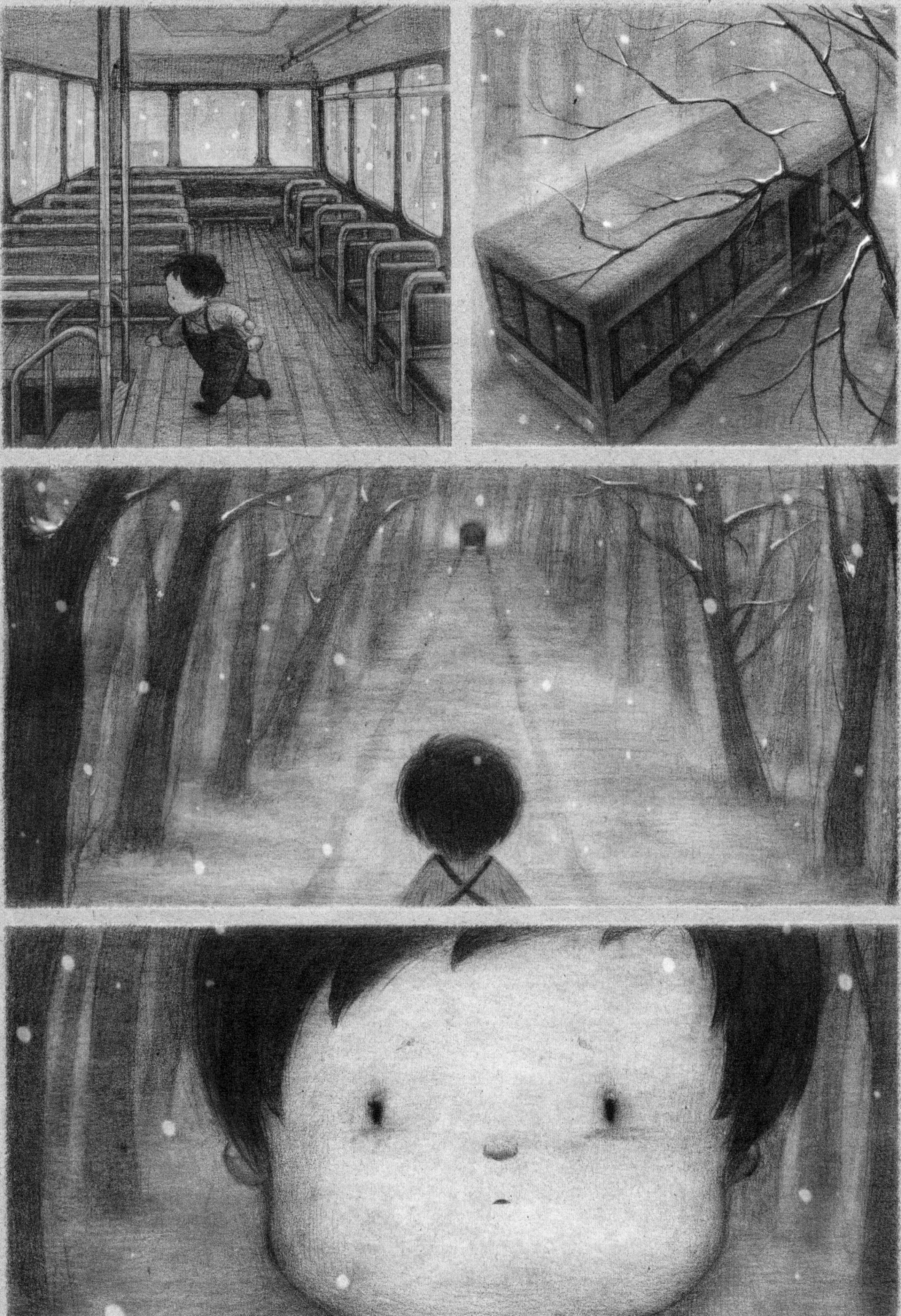

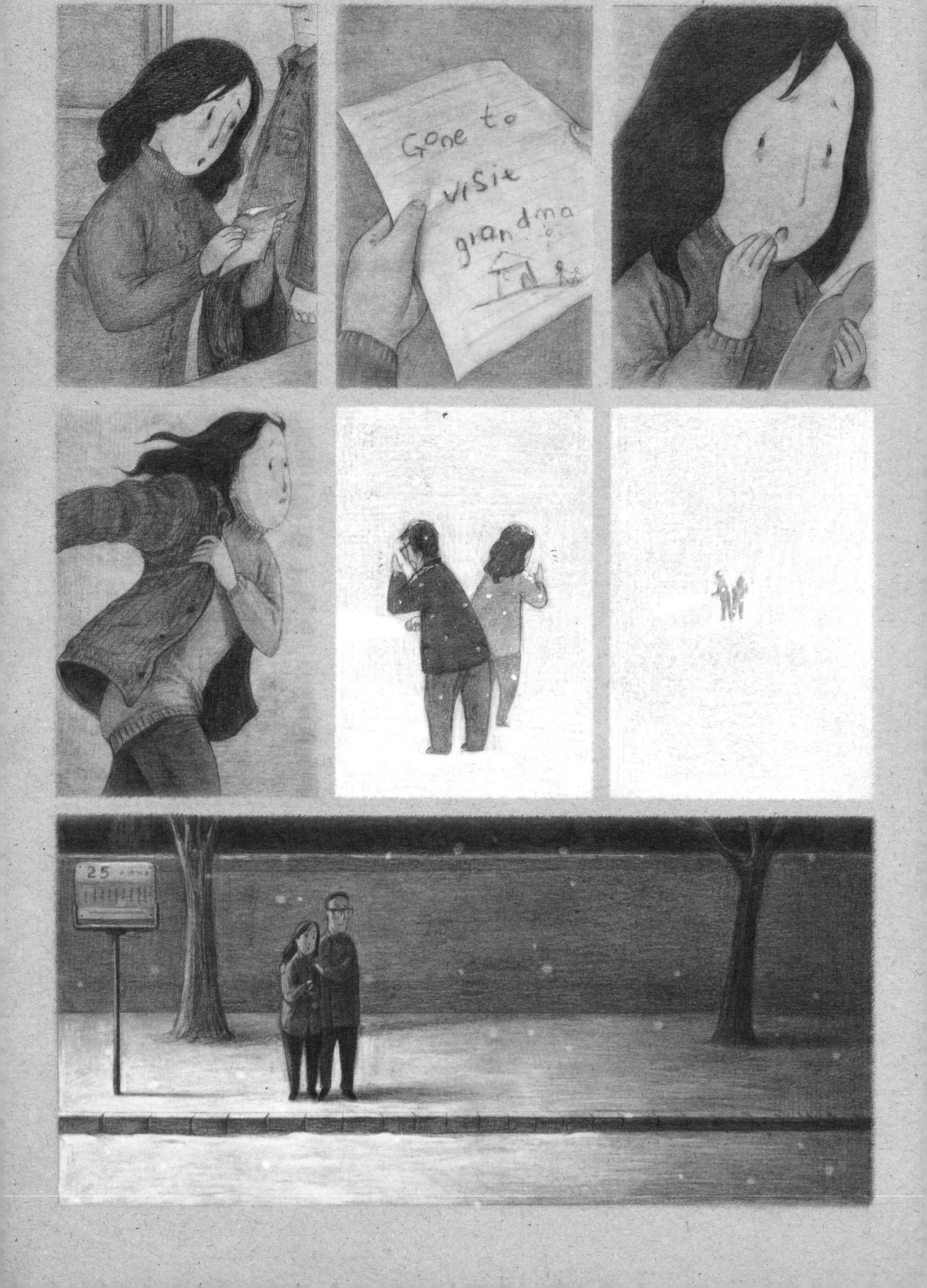
Gone to visit grandma
25

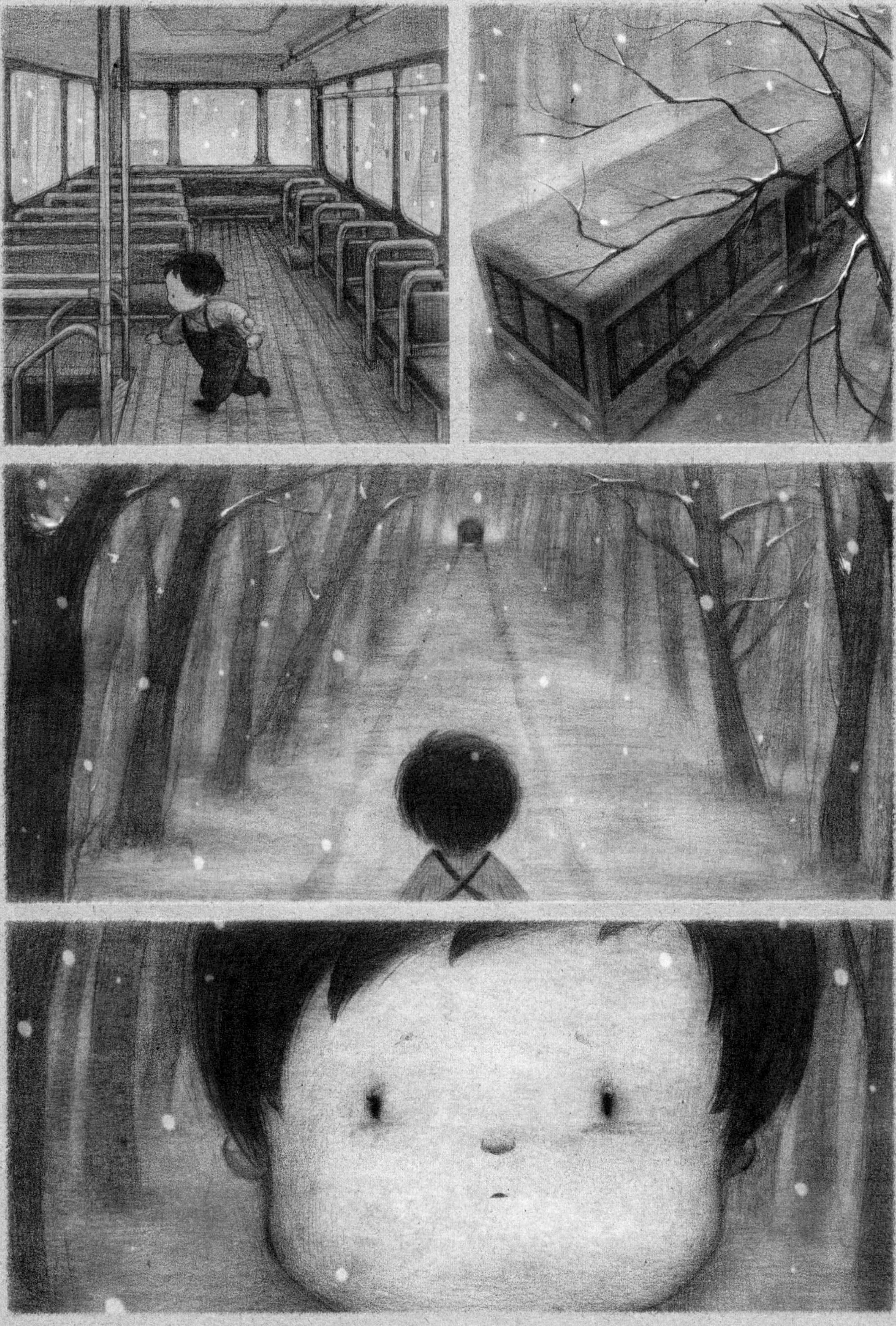

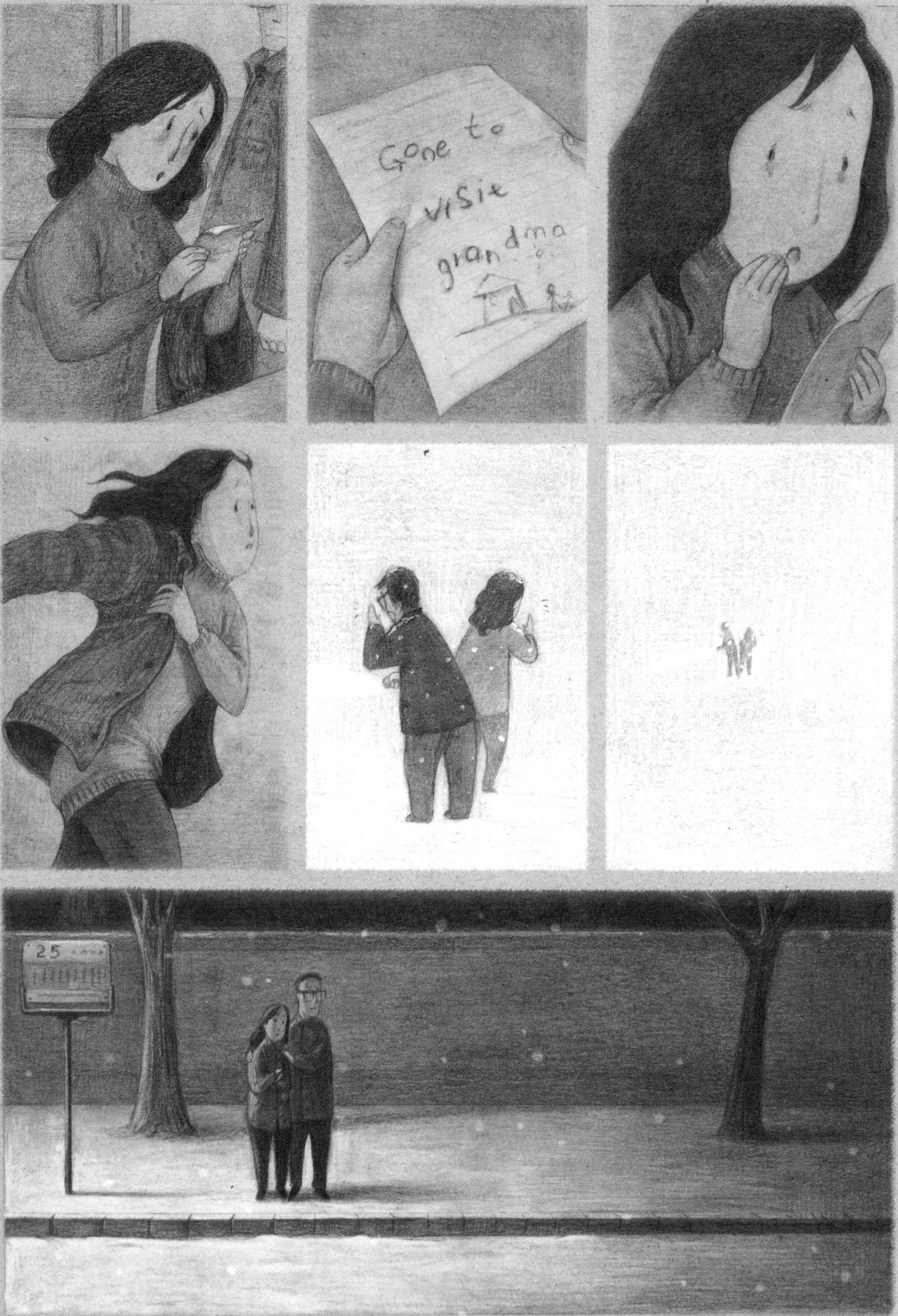
Gone to
visit
grandma
25

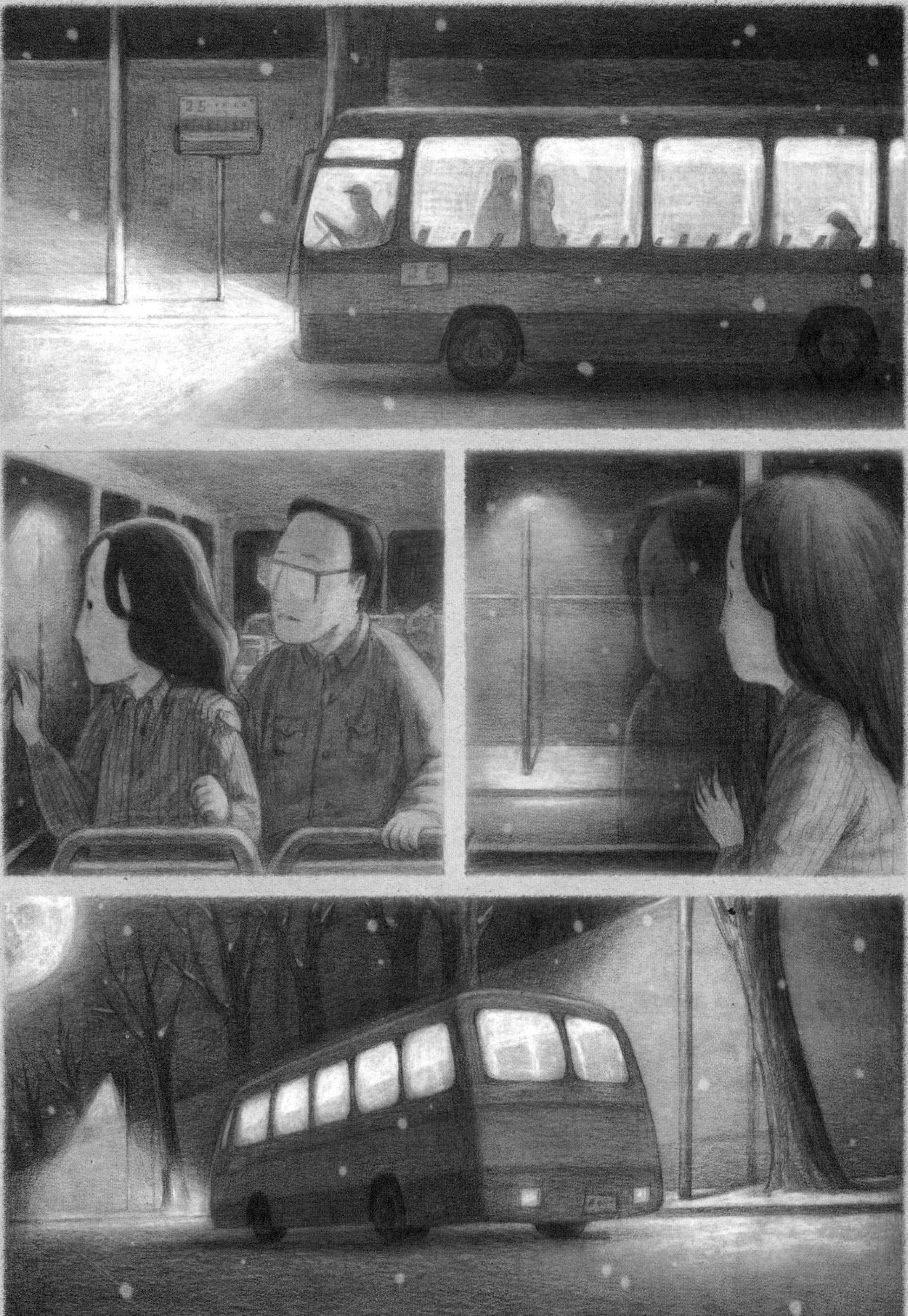

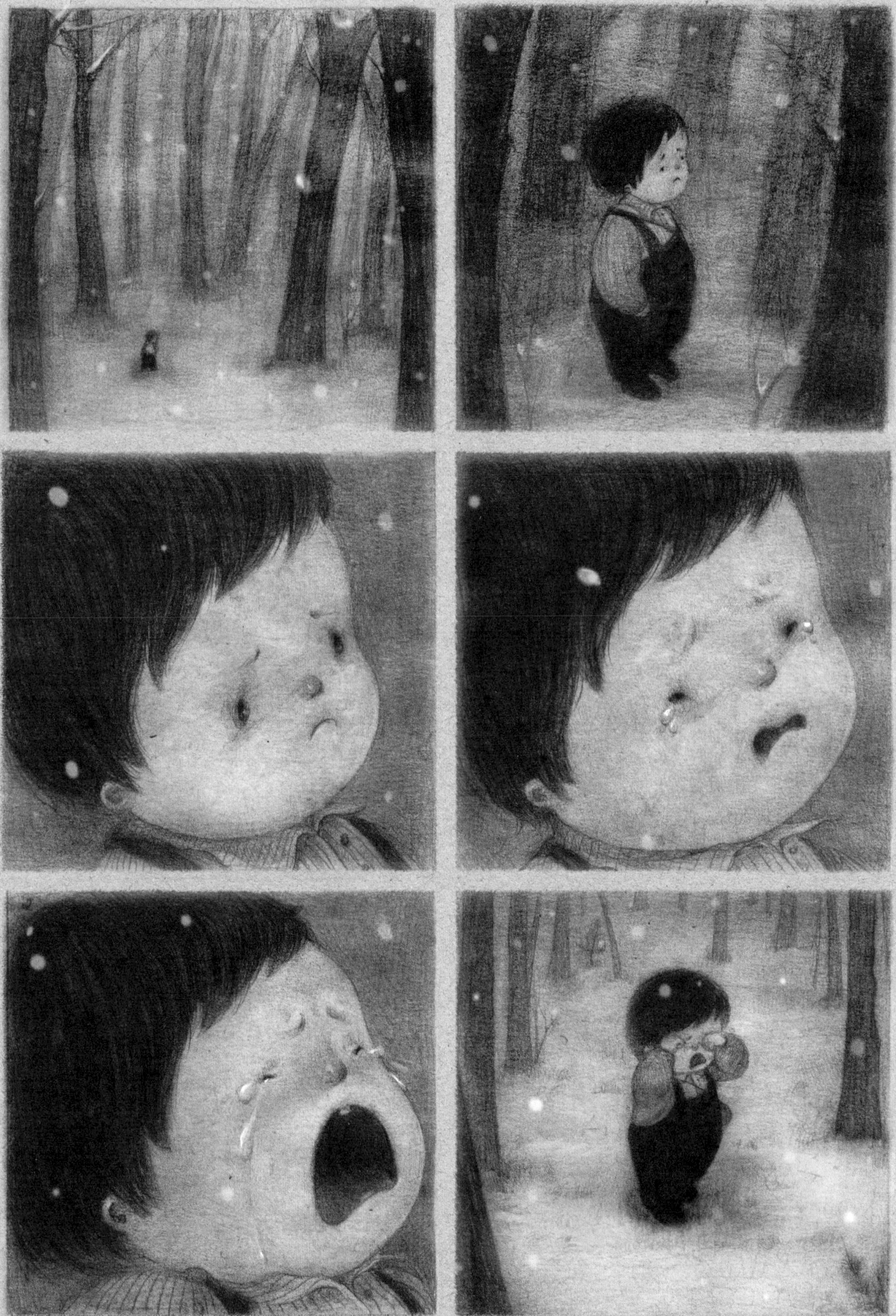

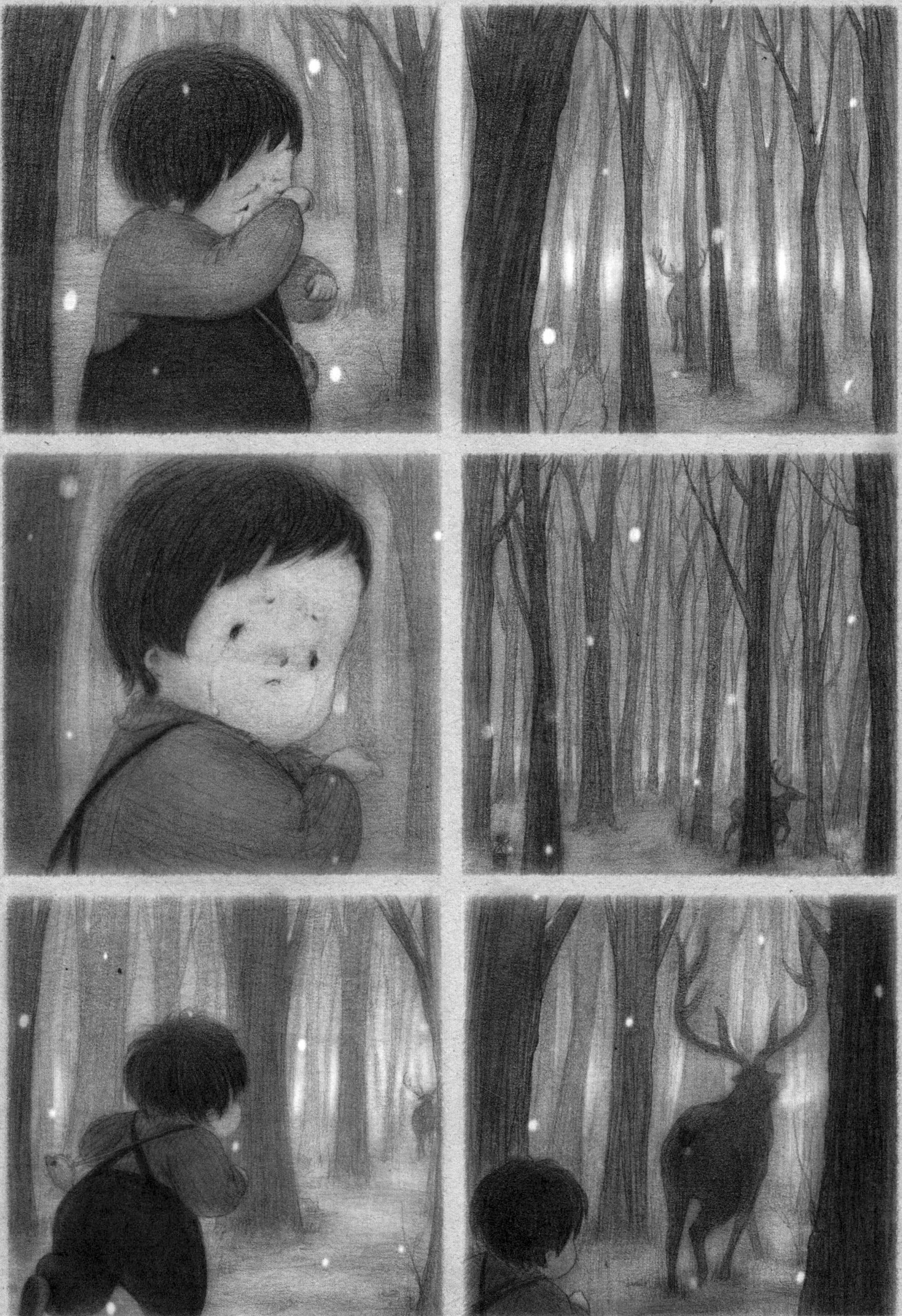

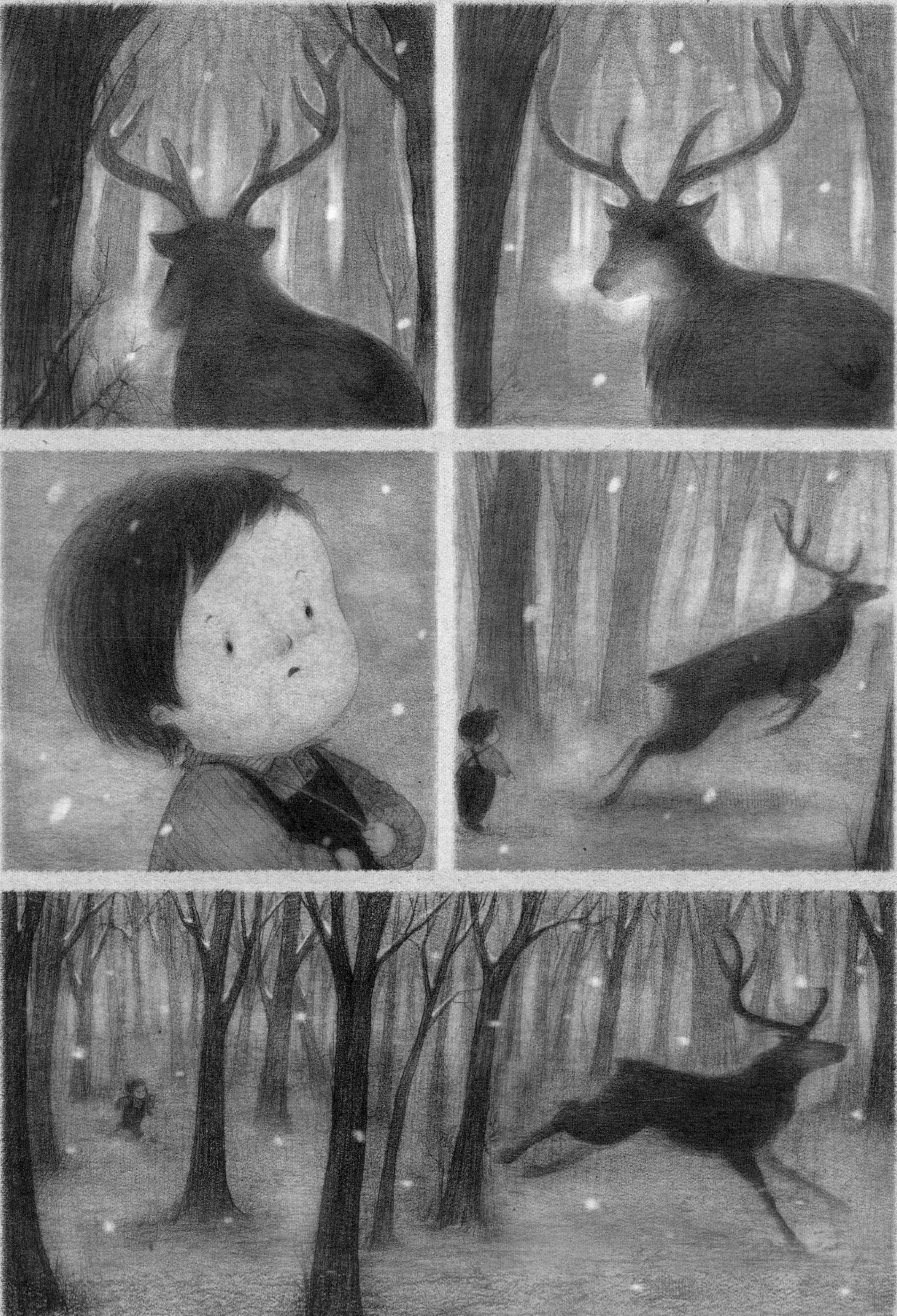

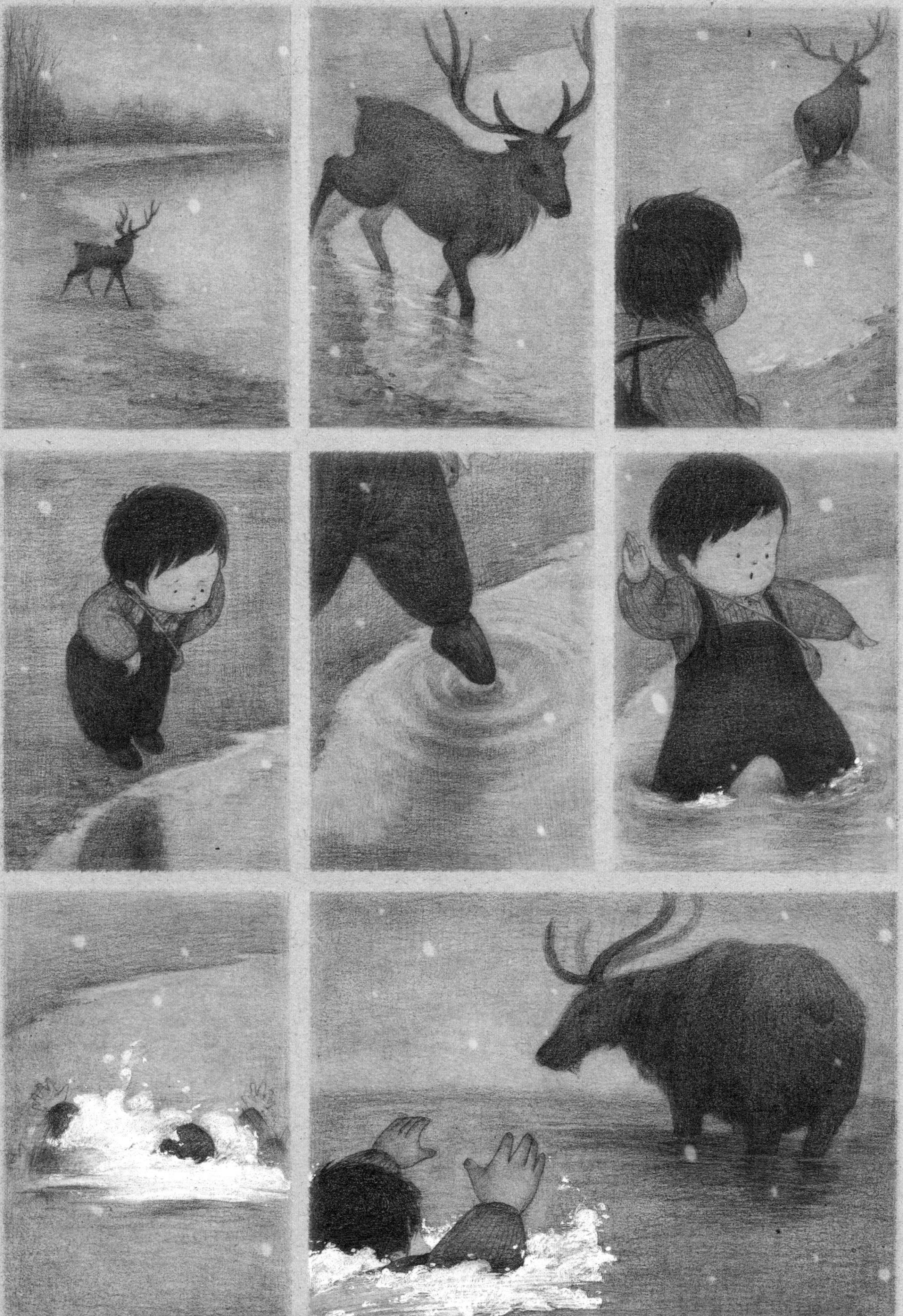

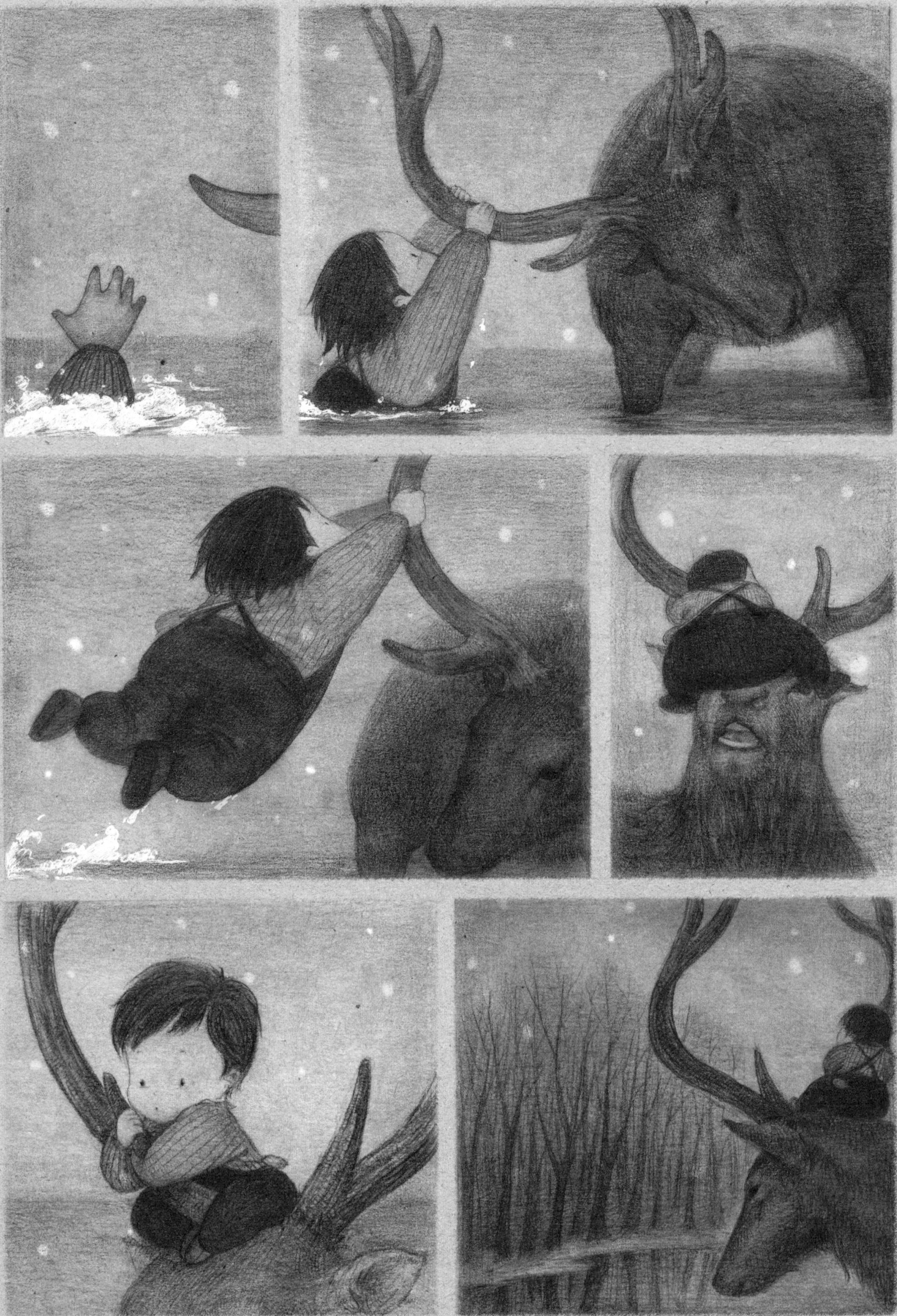

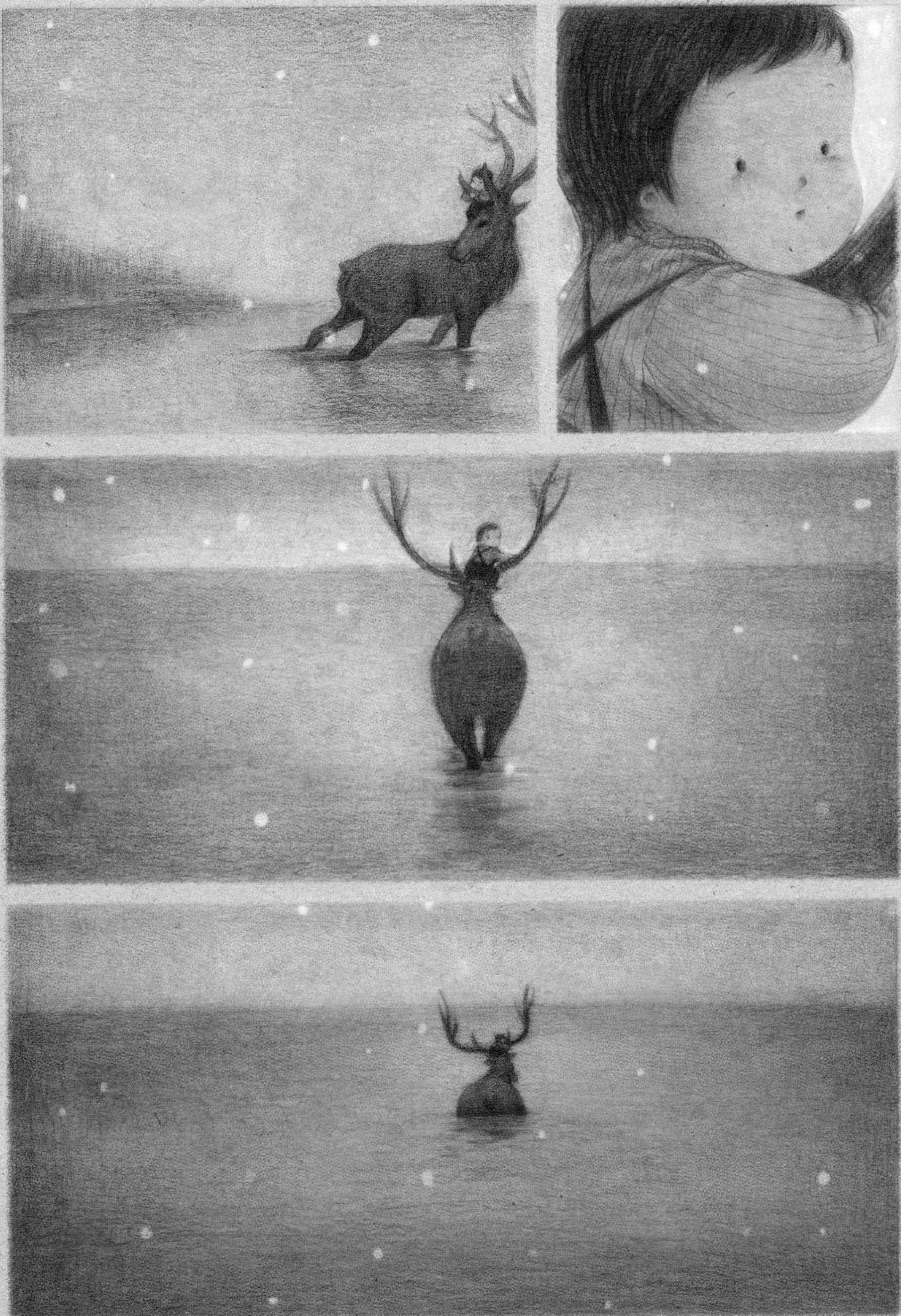

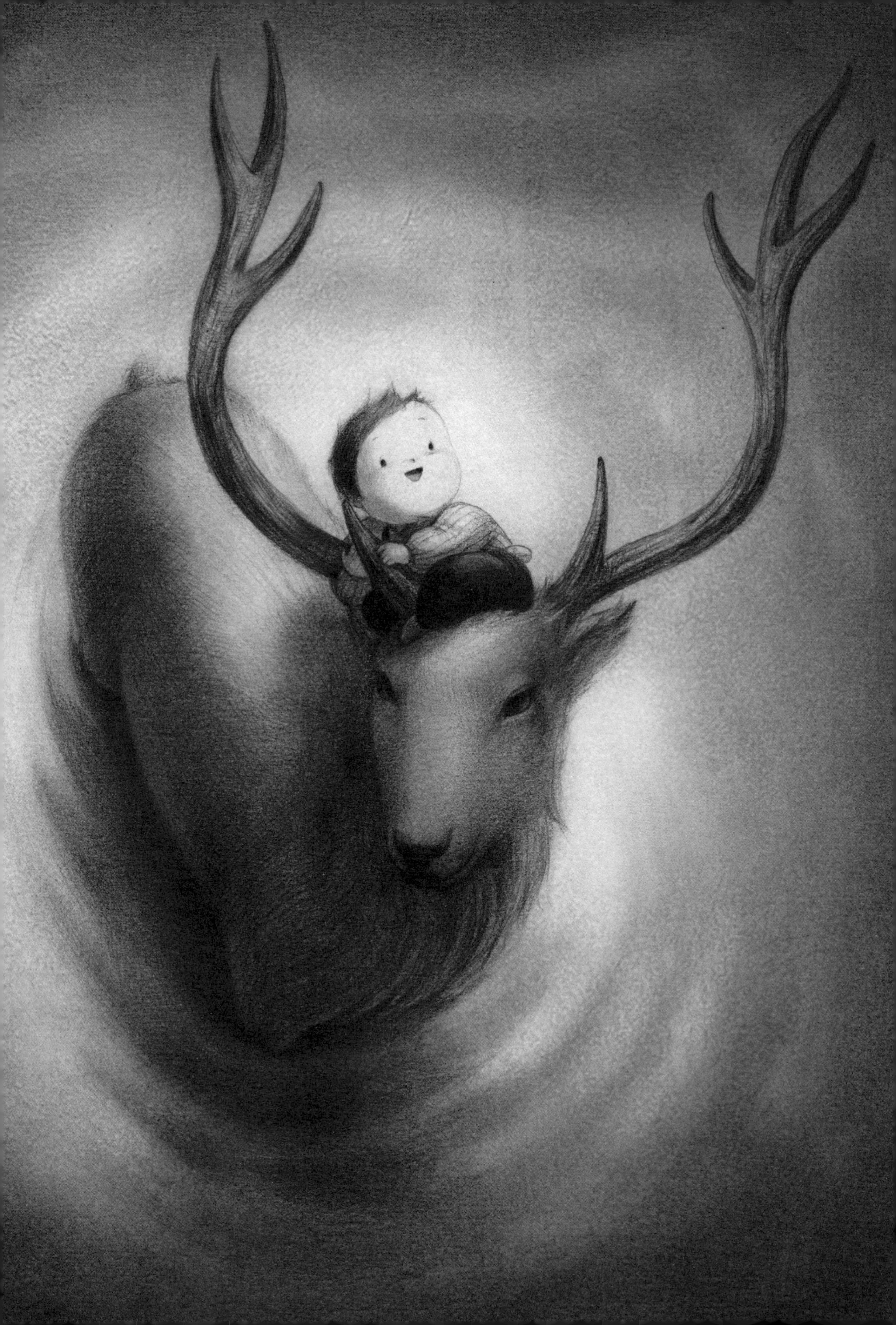

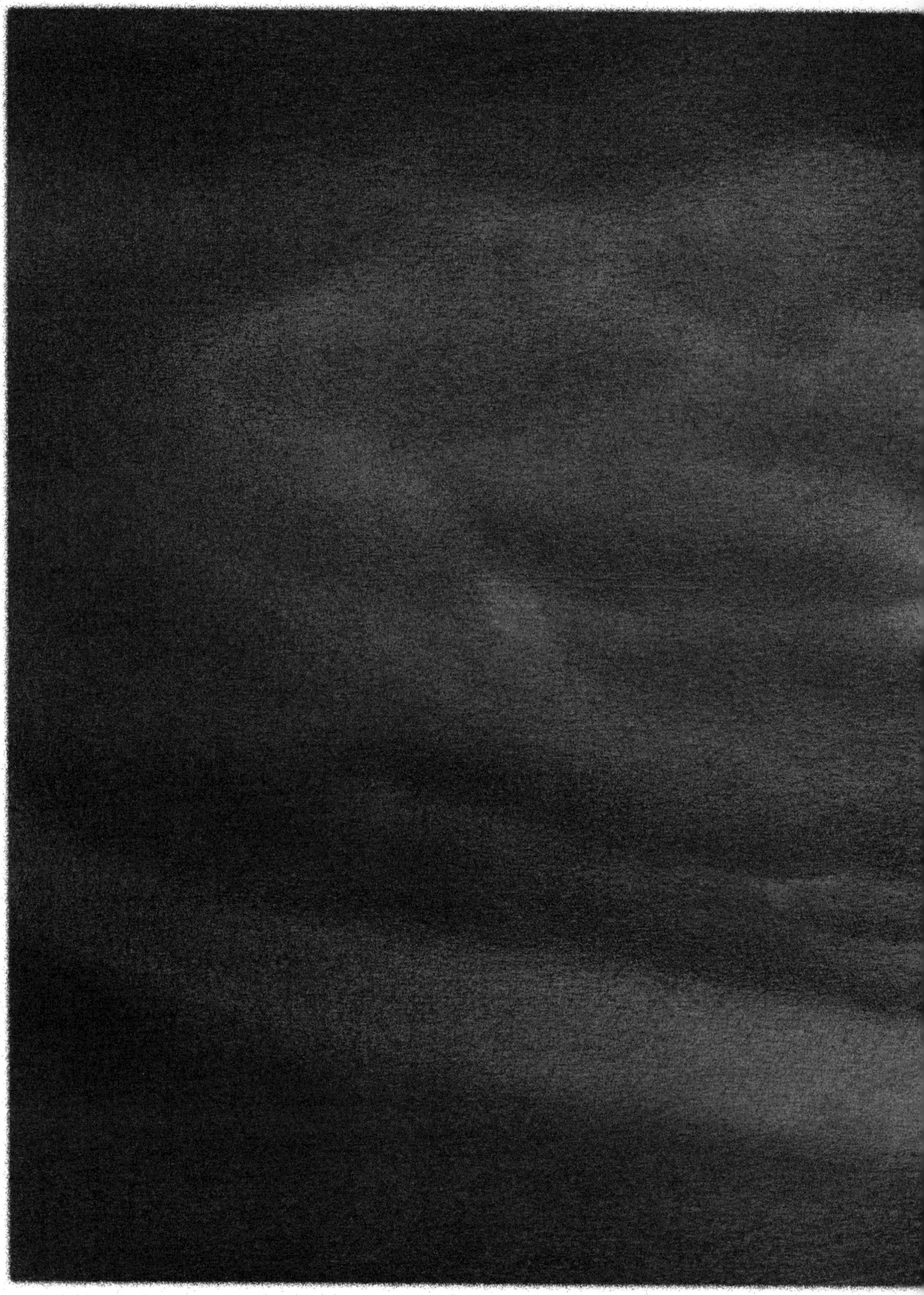

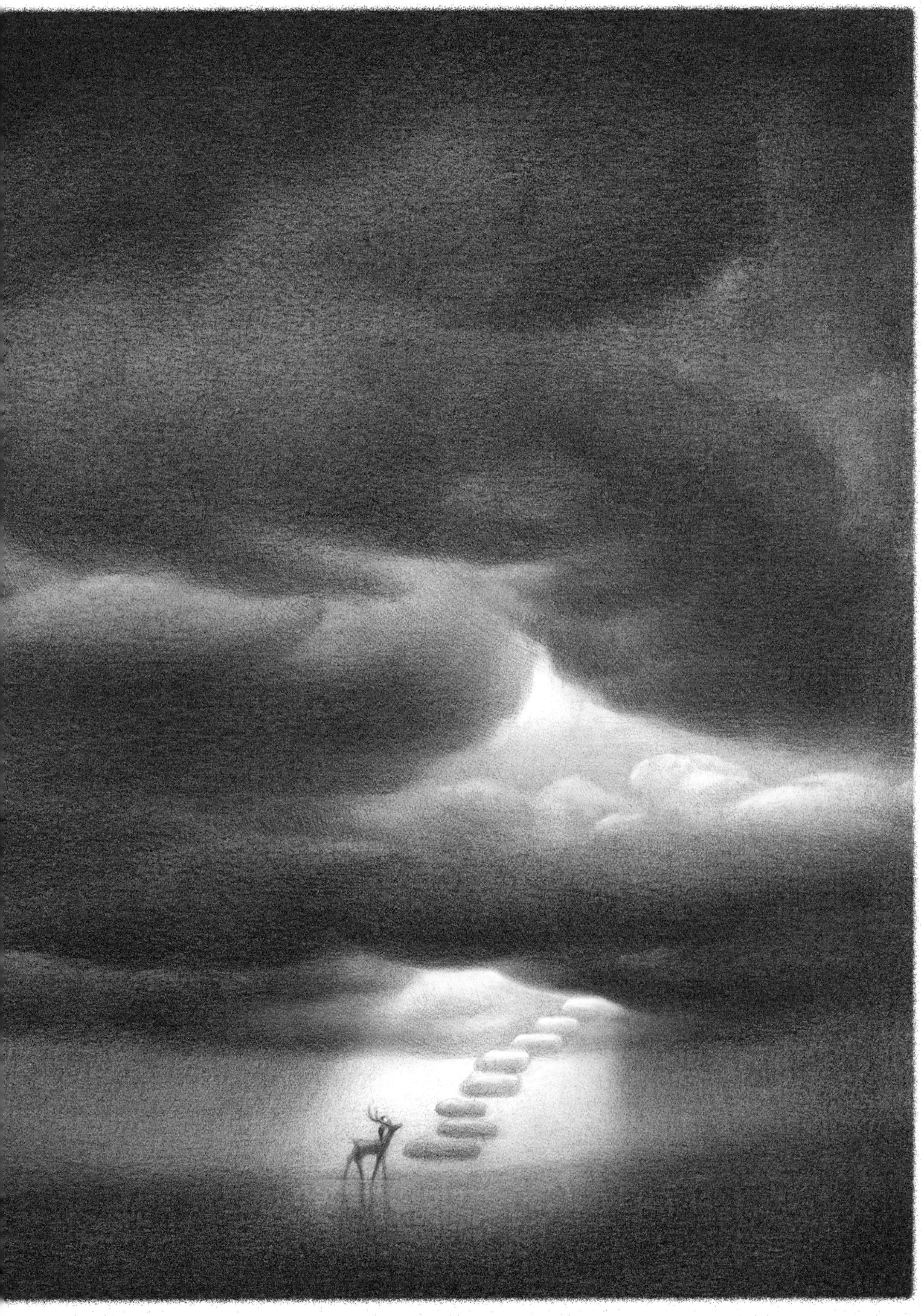

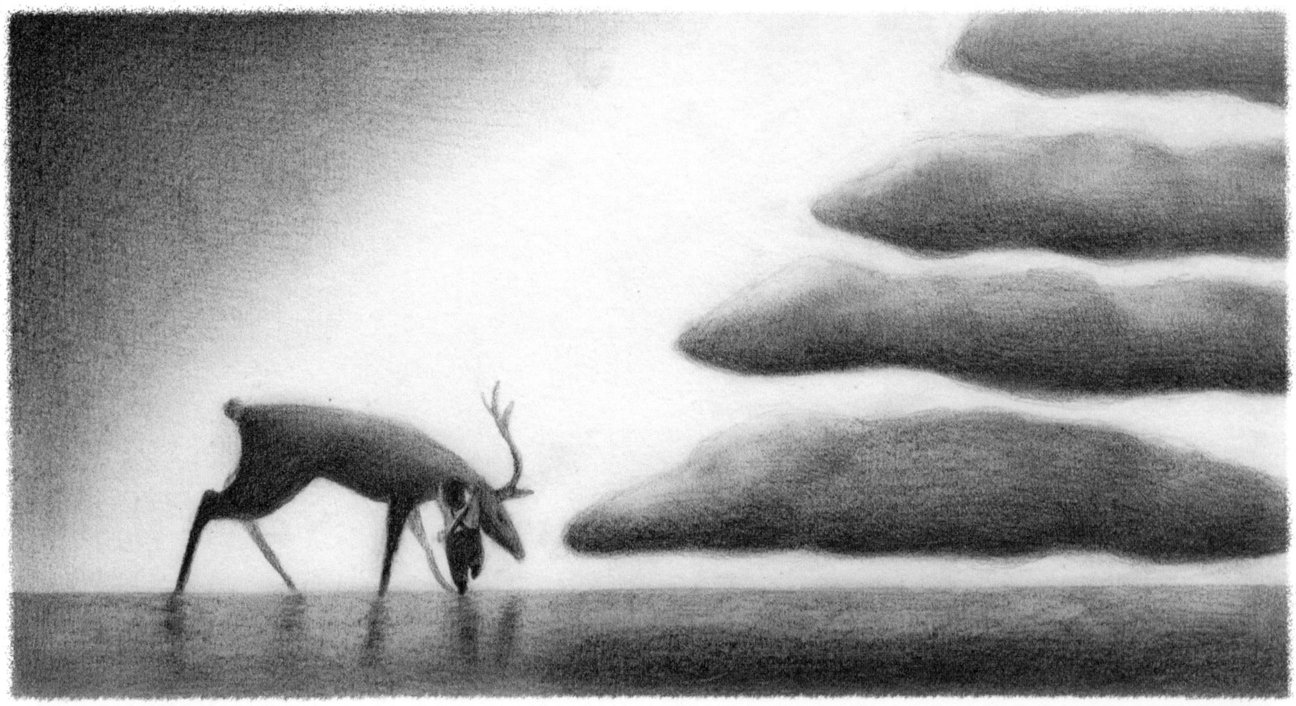

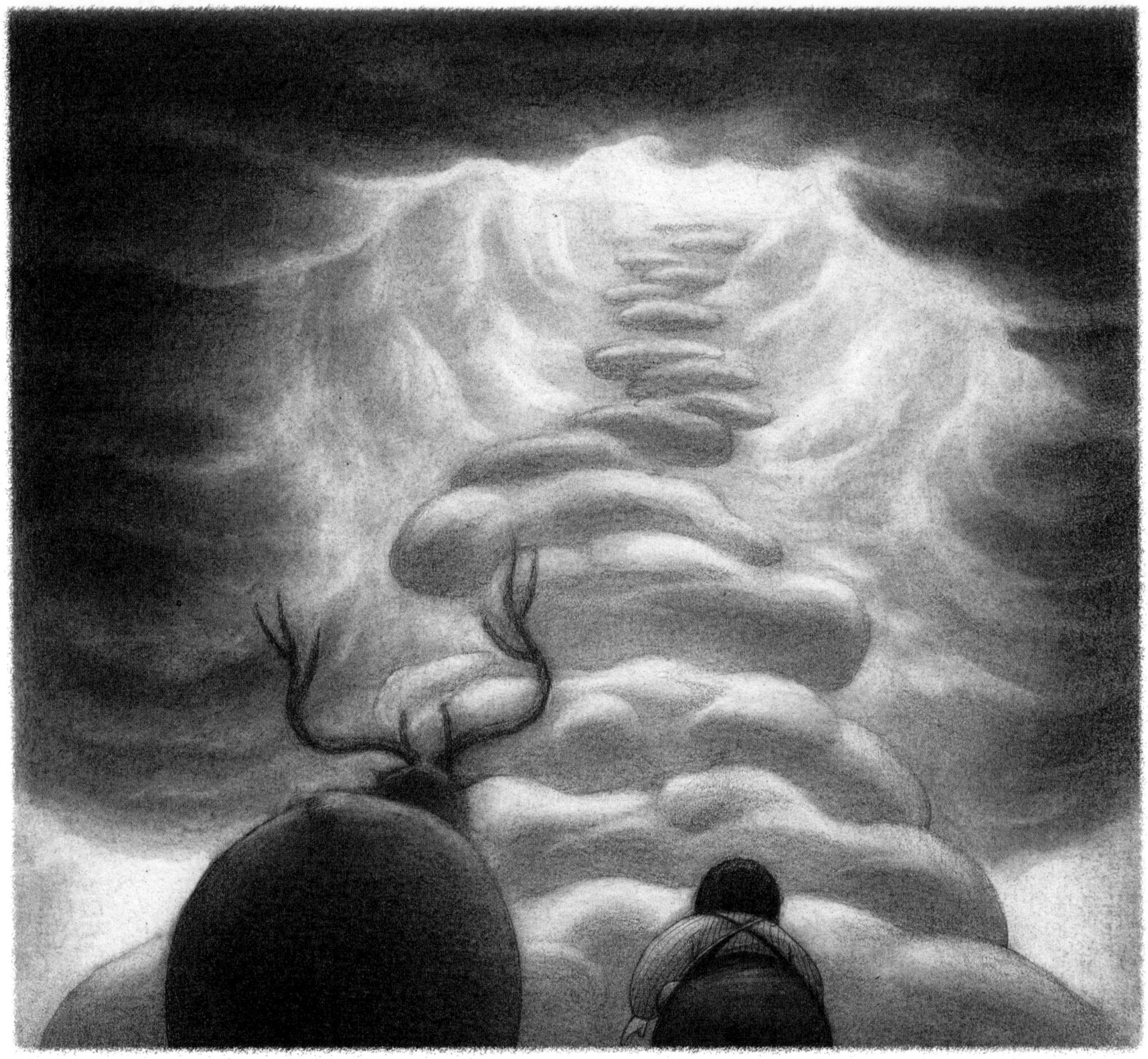

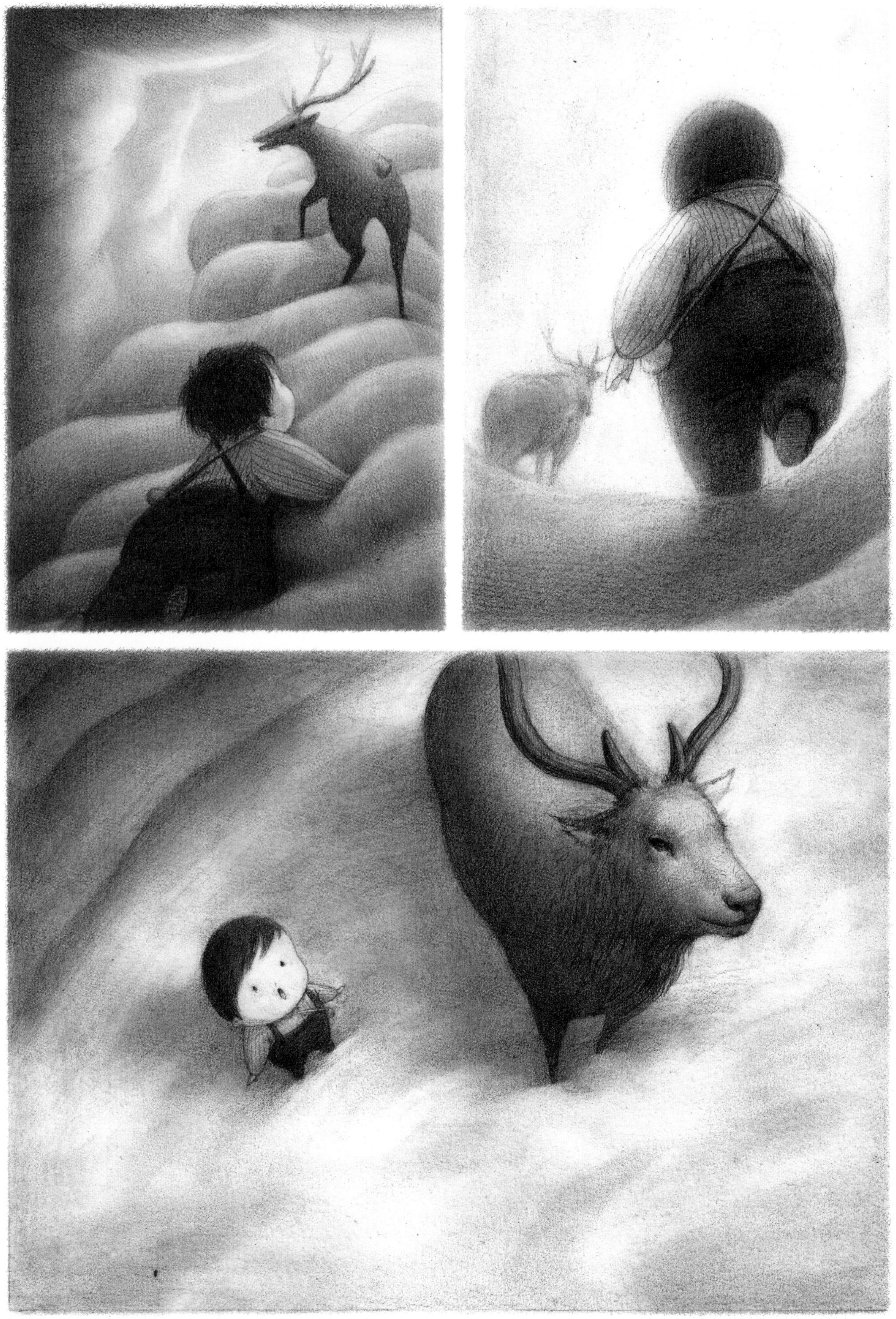

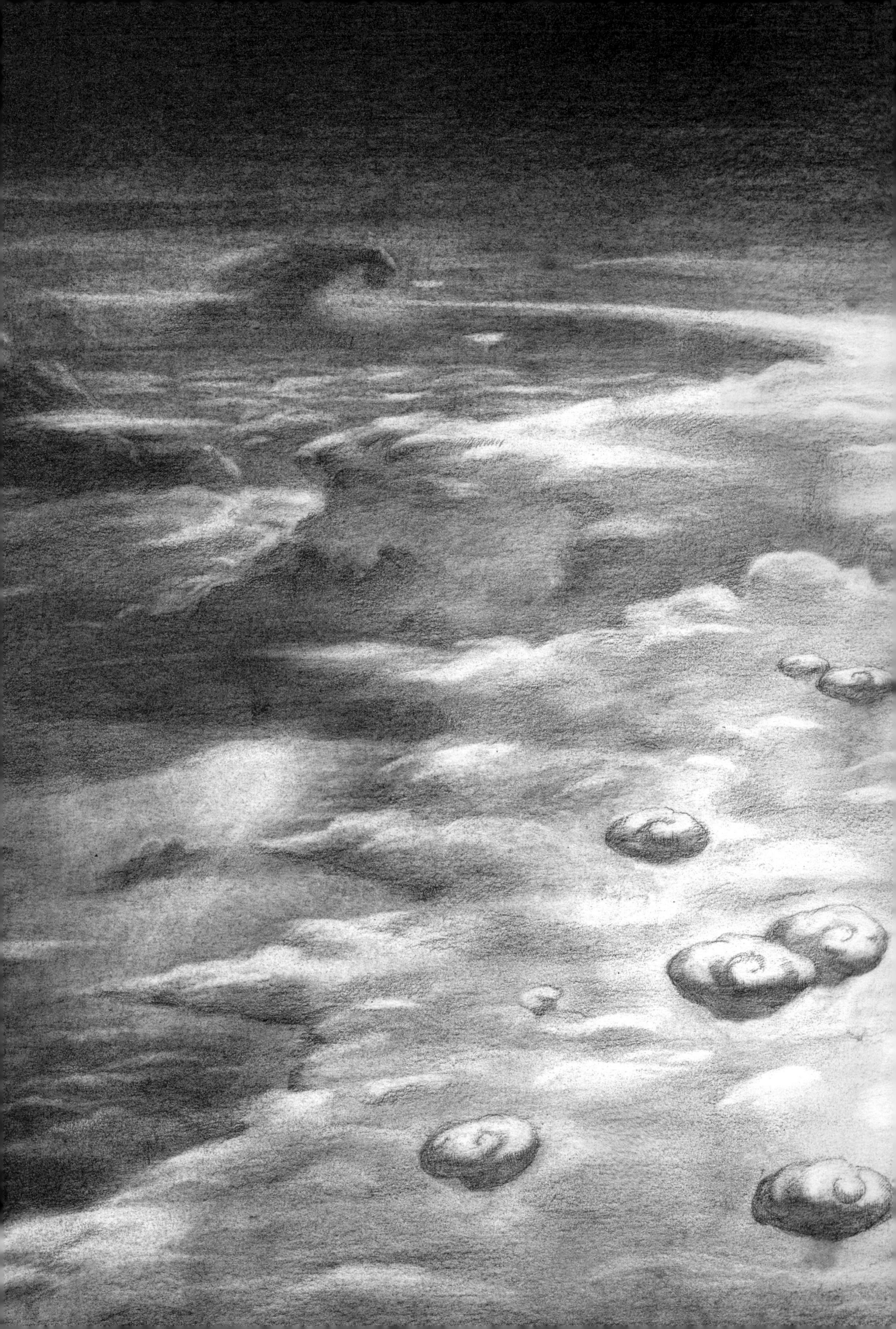

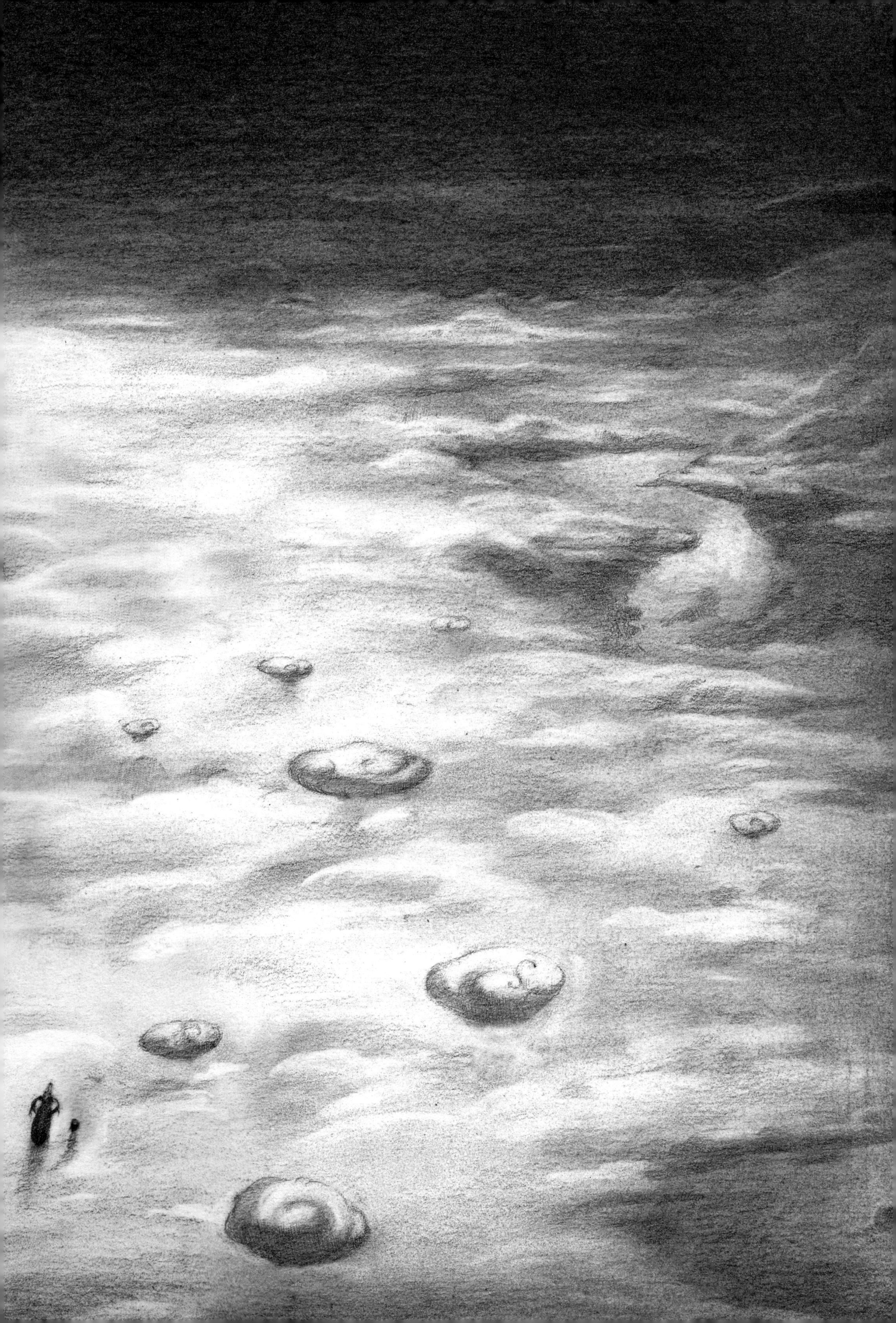

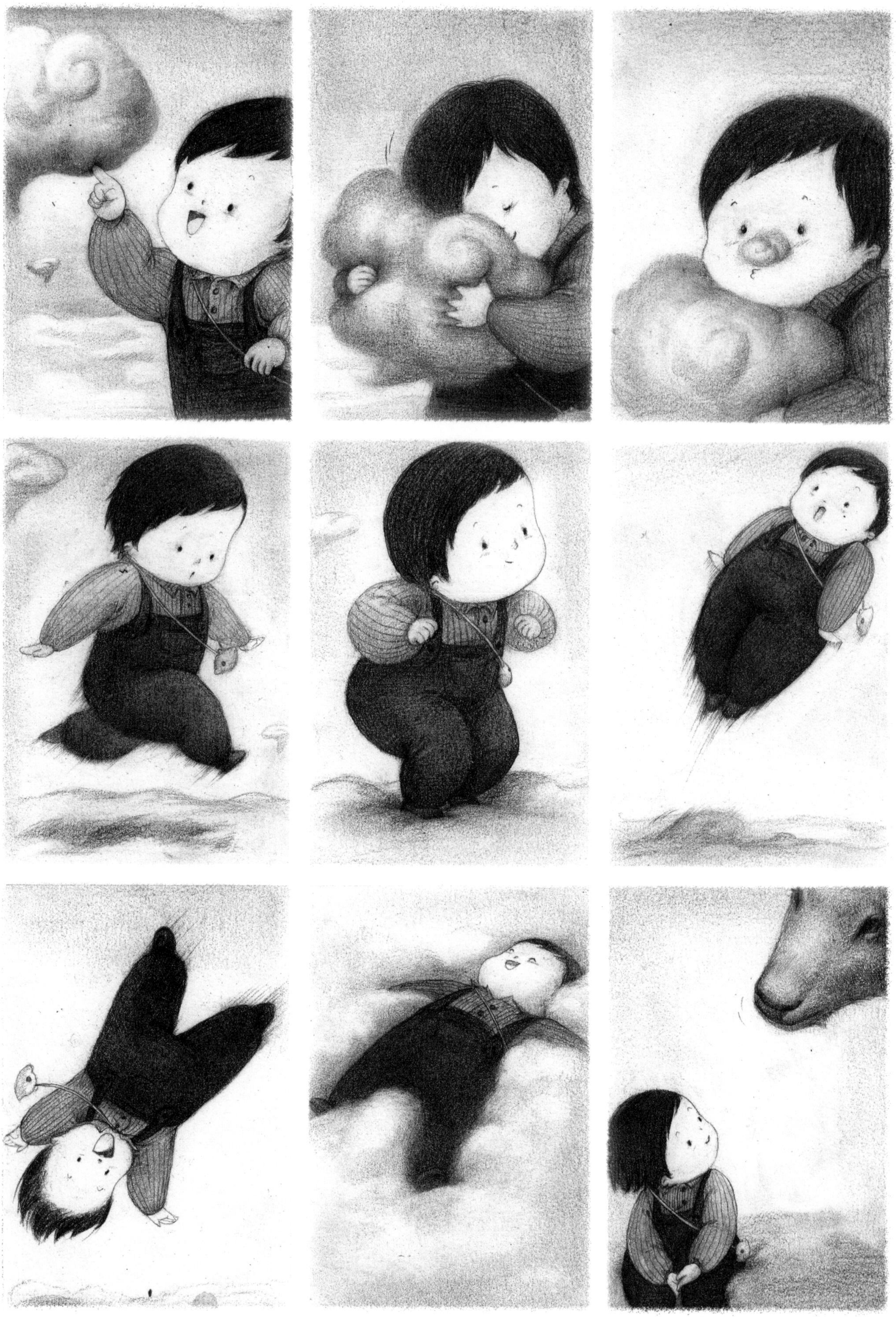

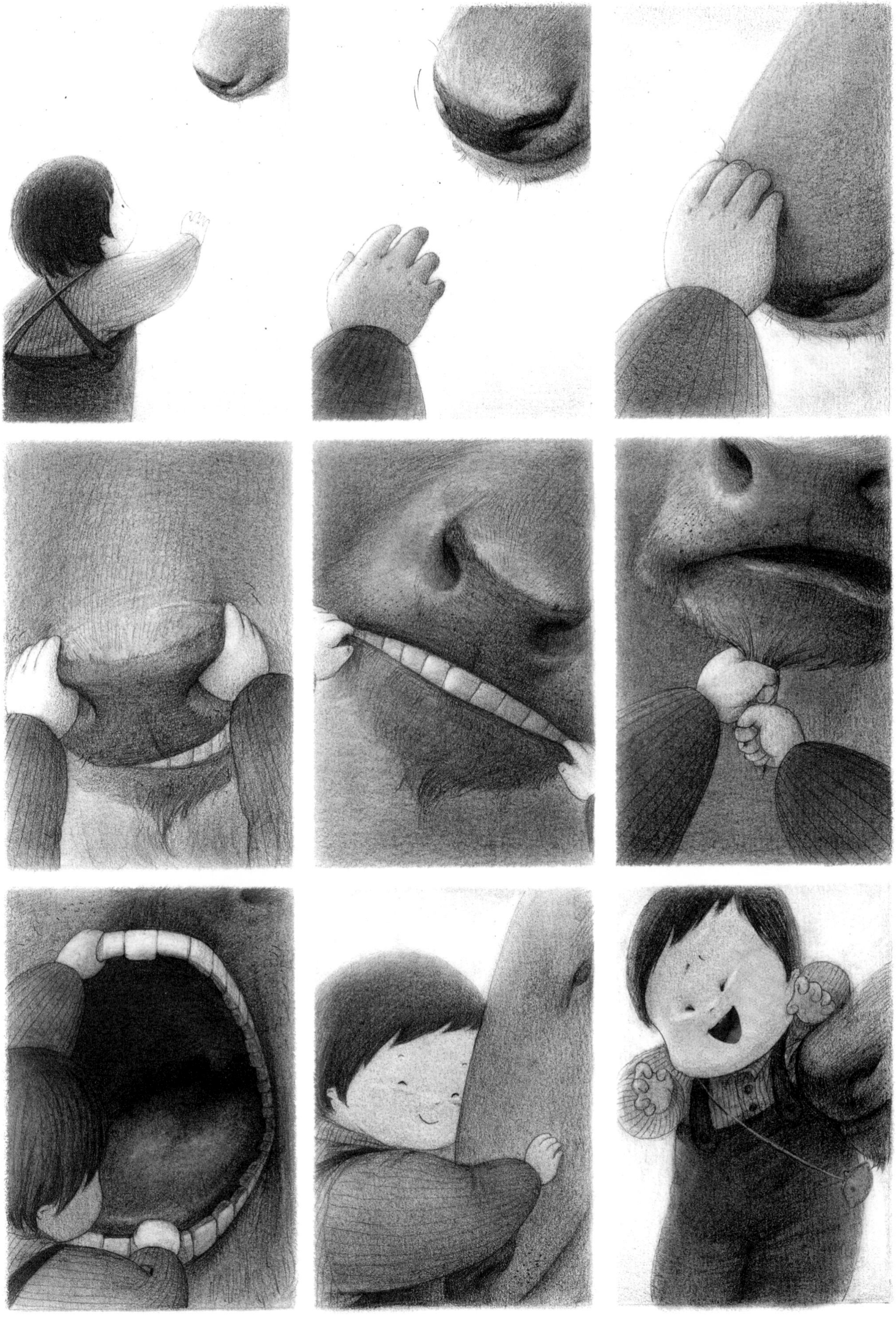

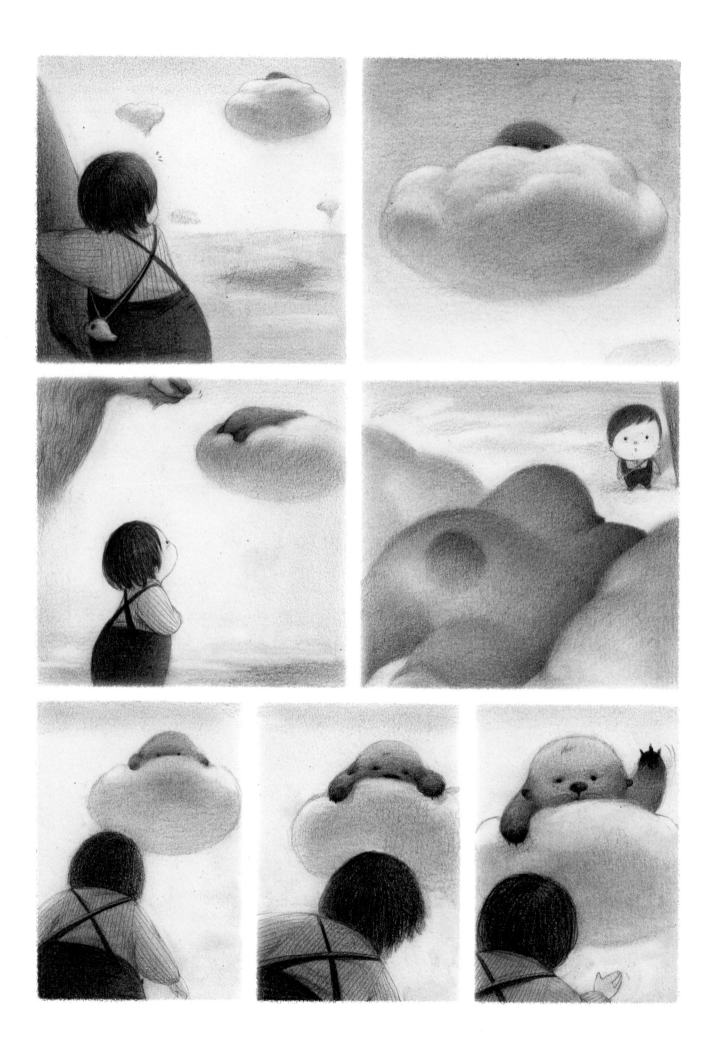

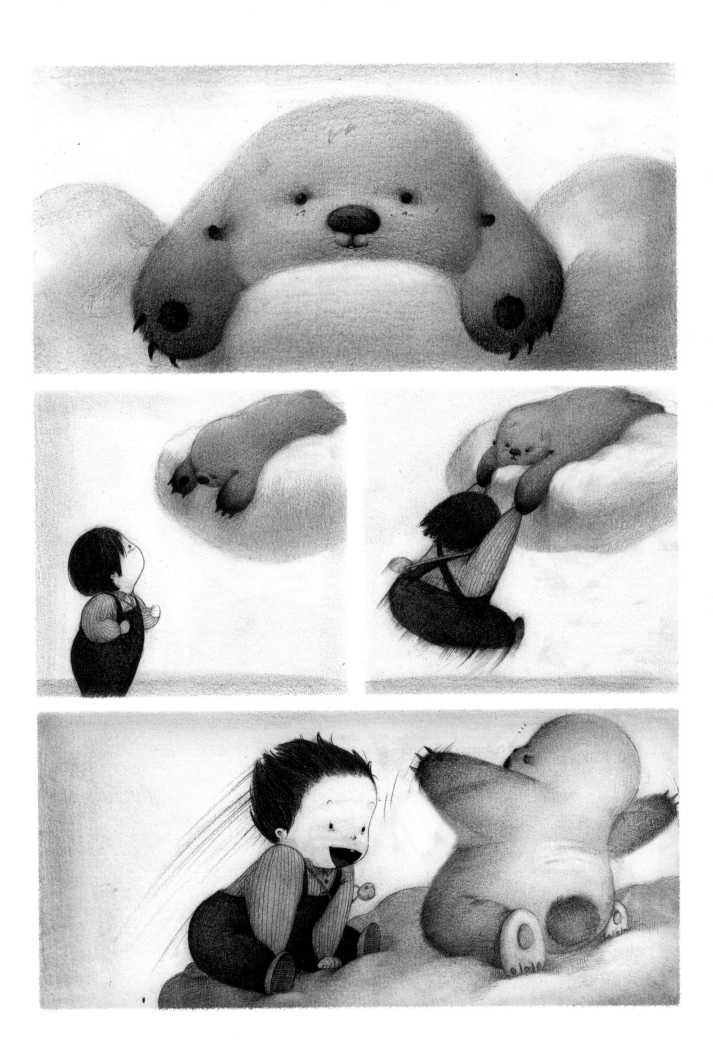

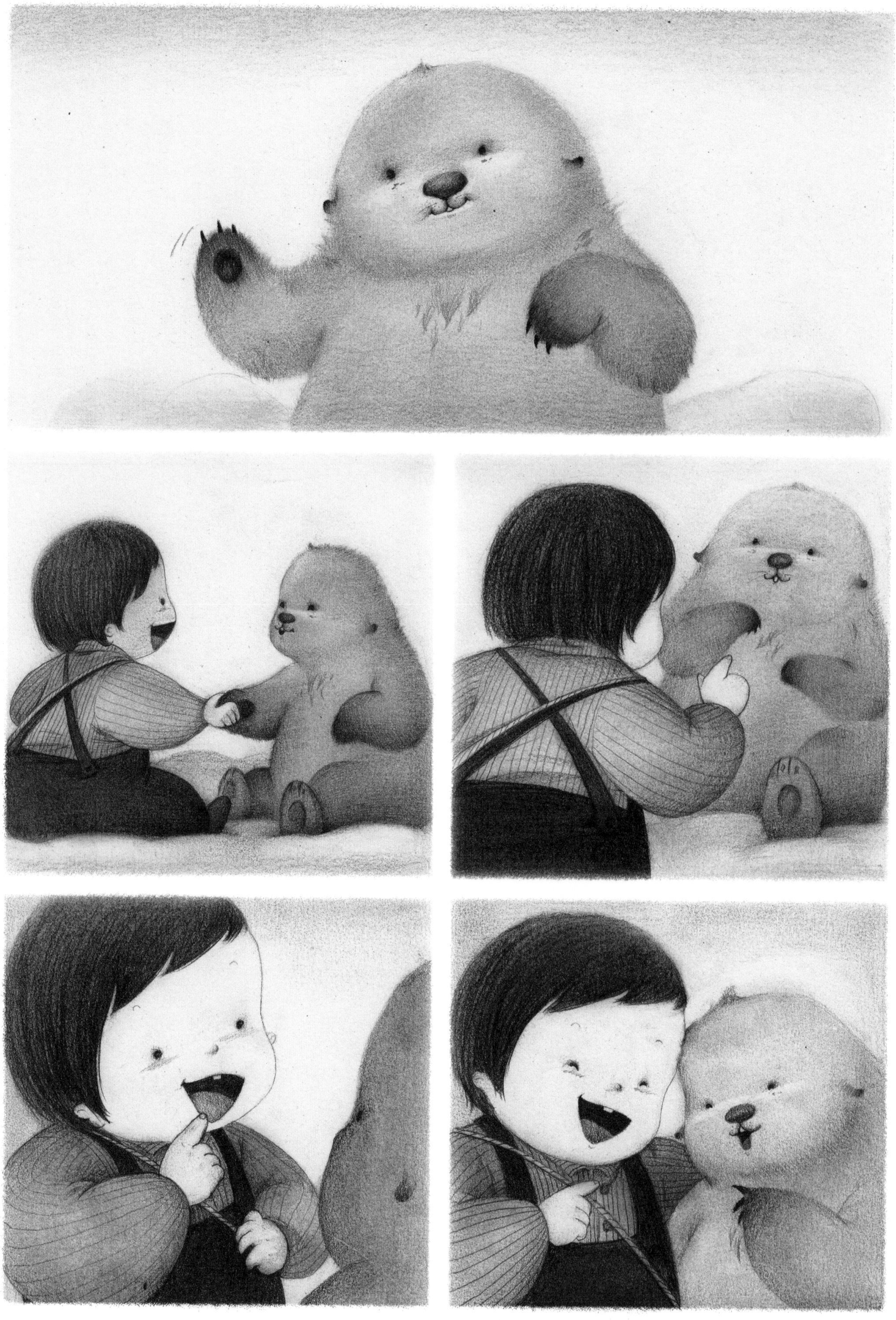

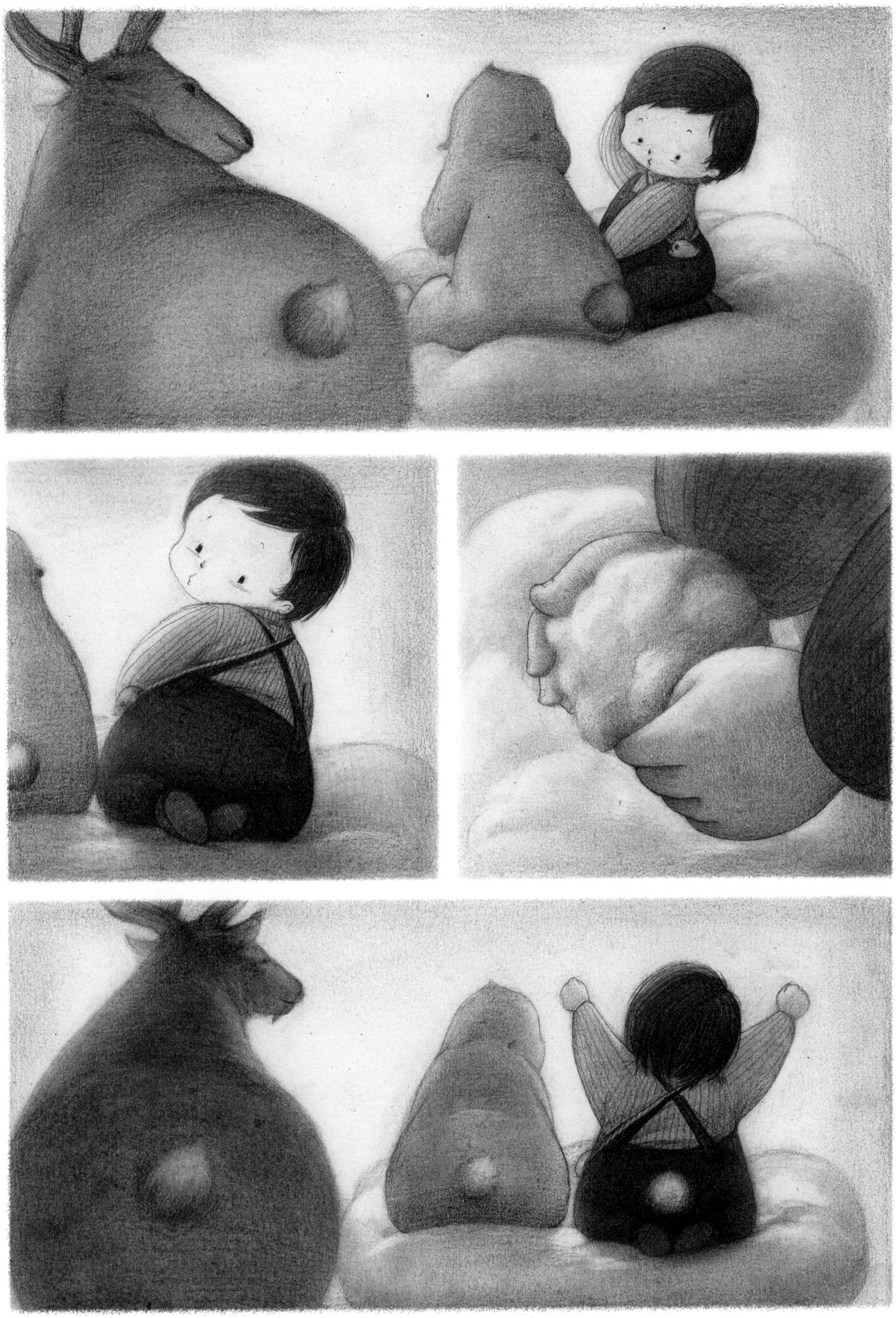

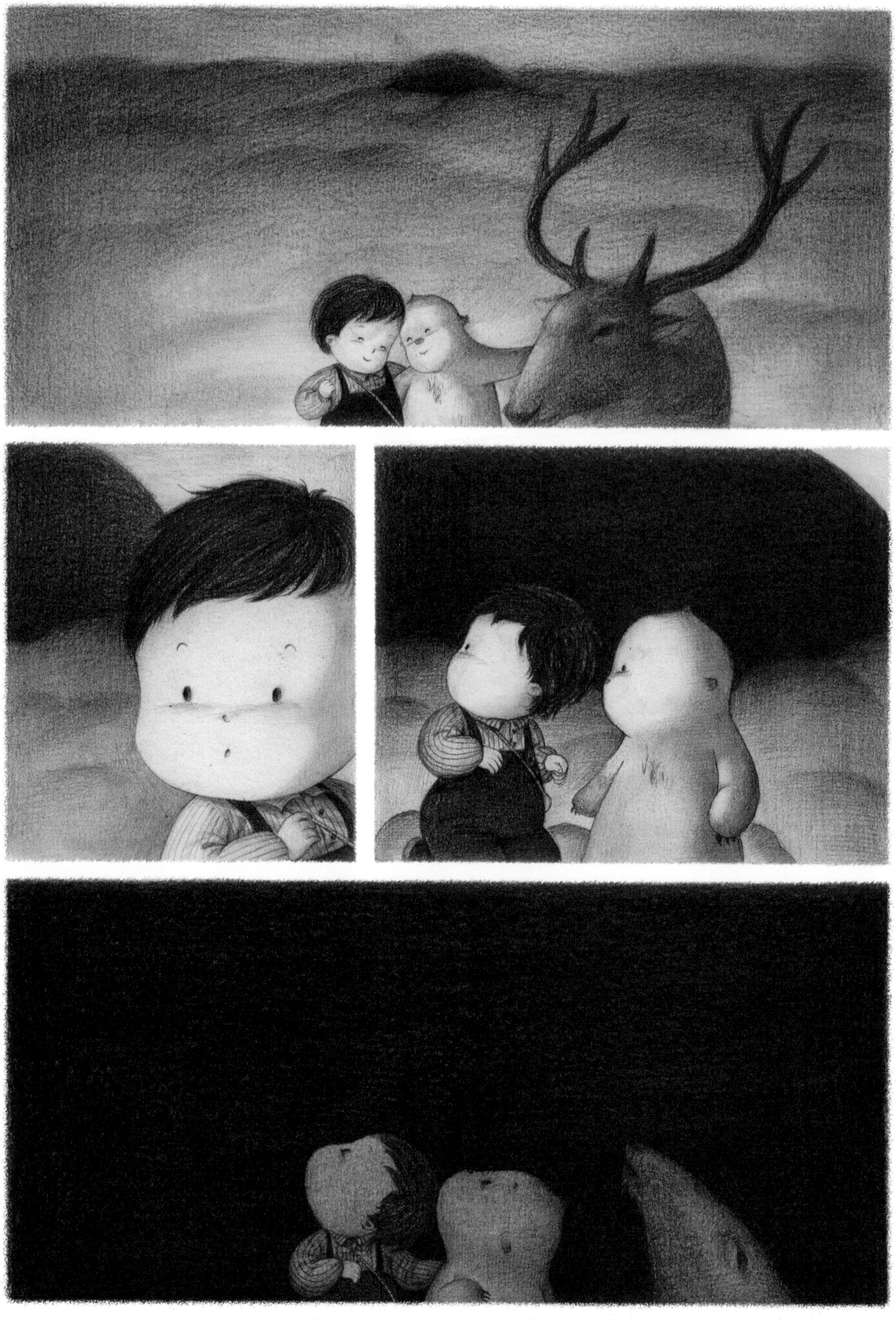

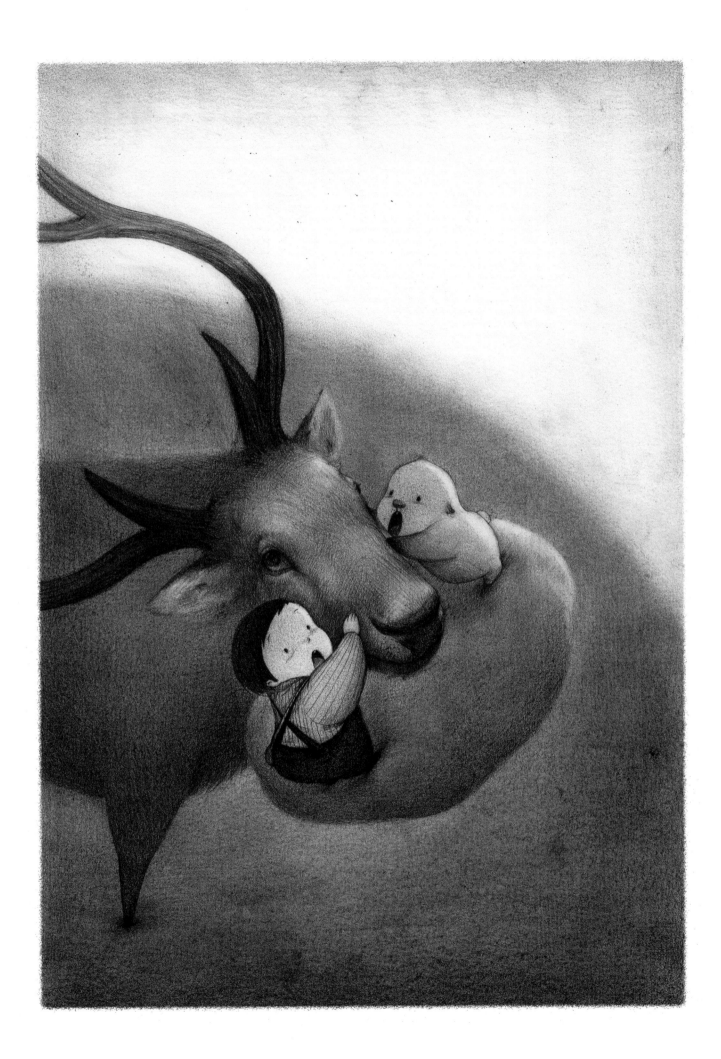

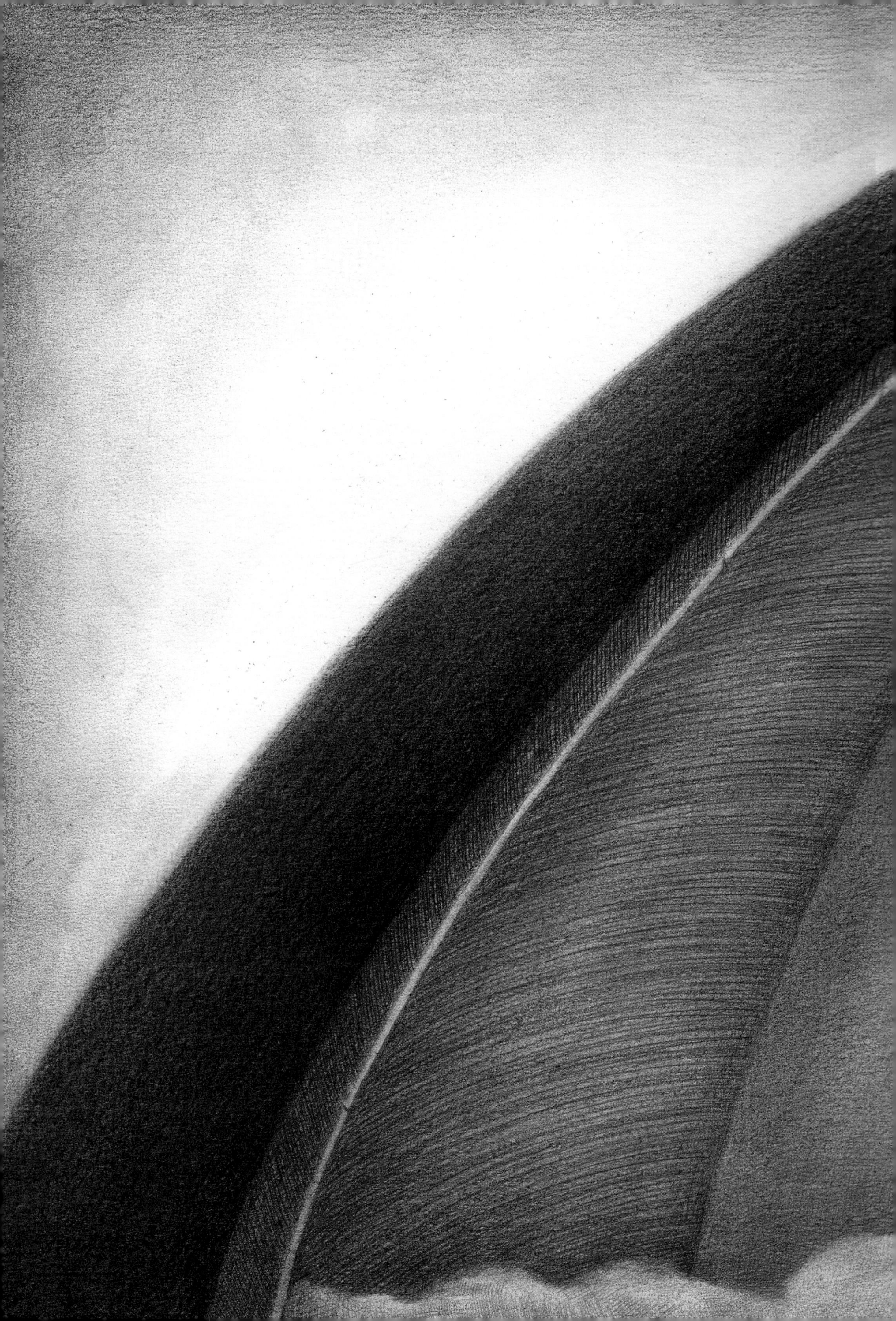

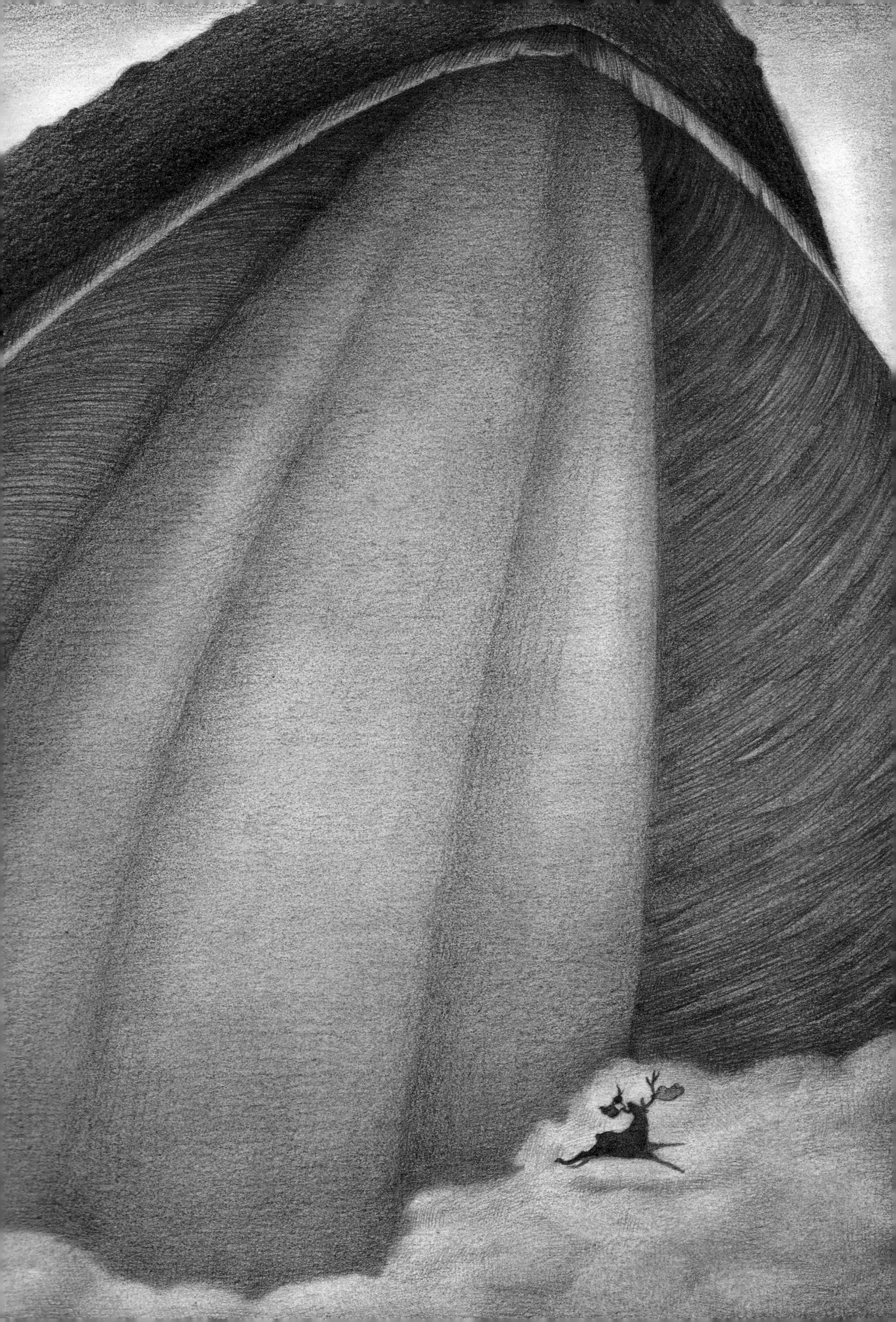

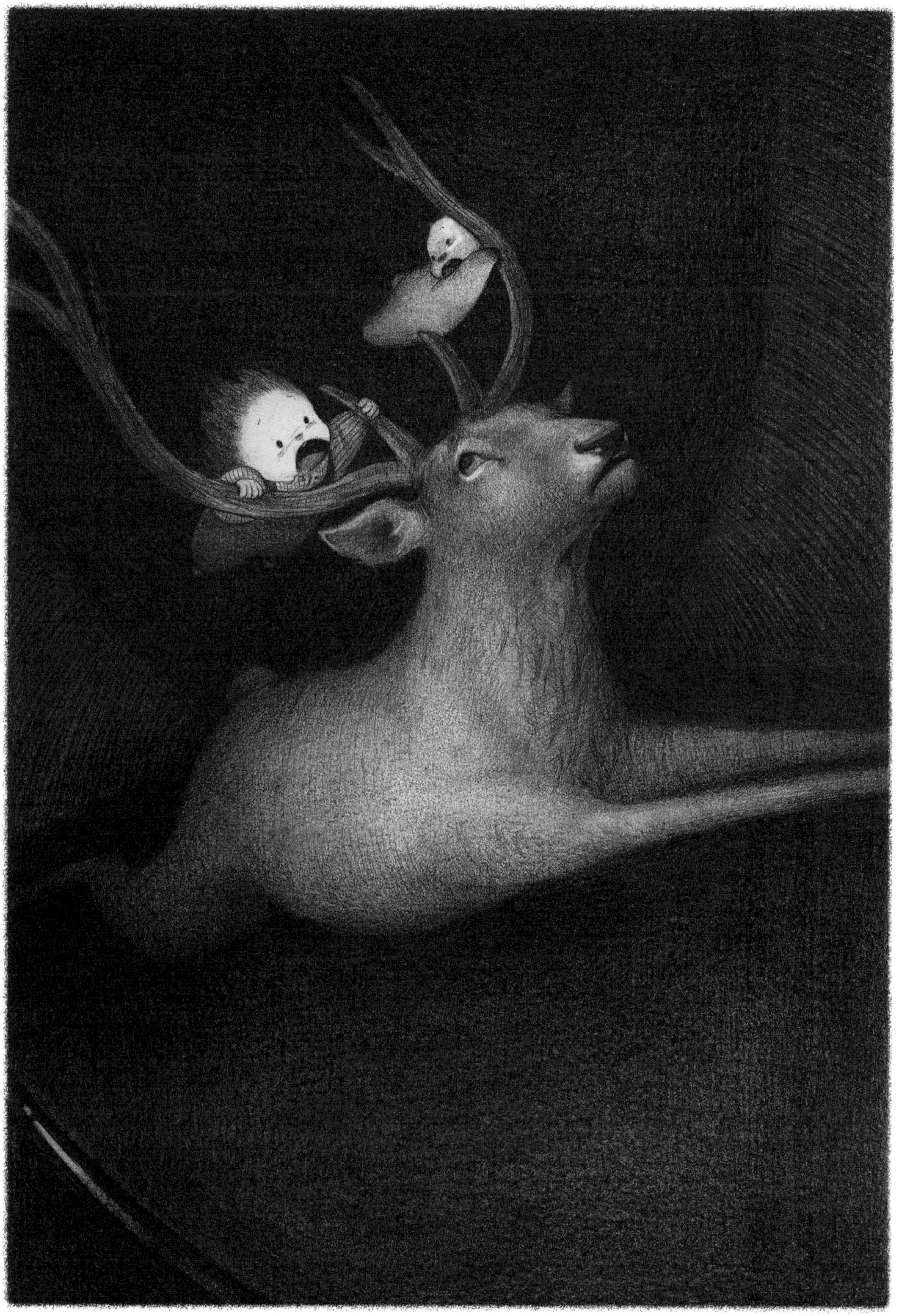

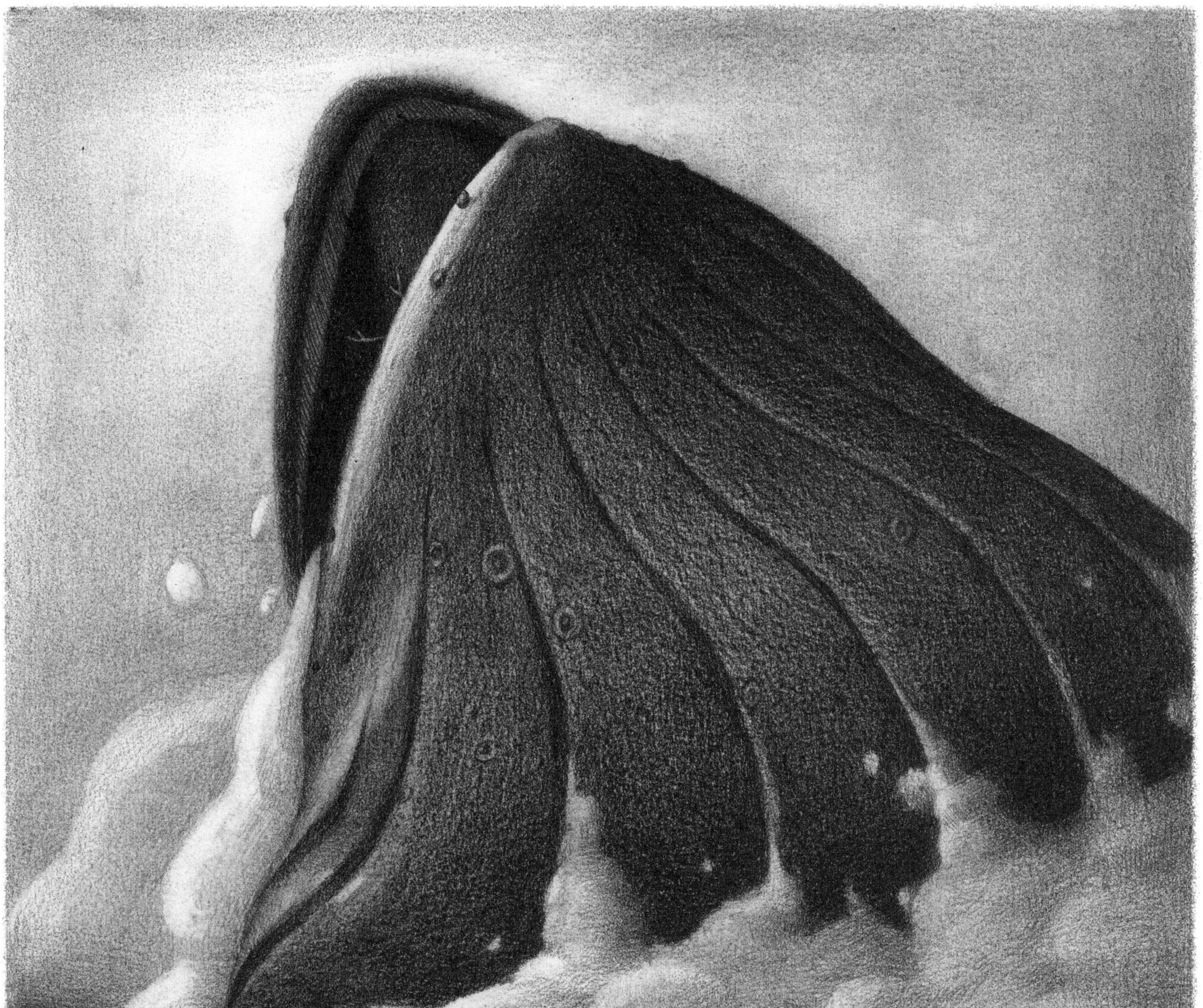
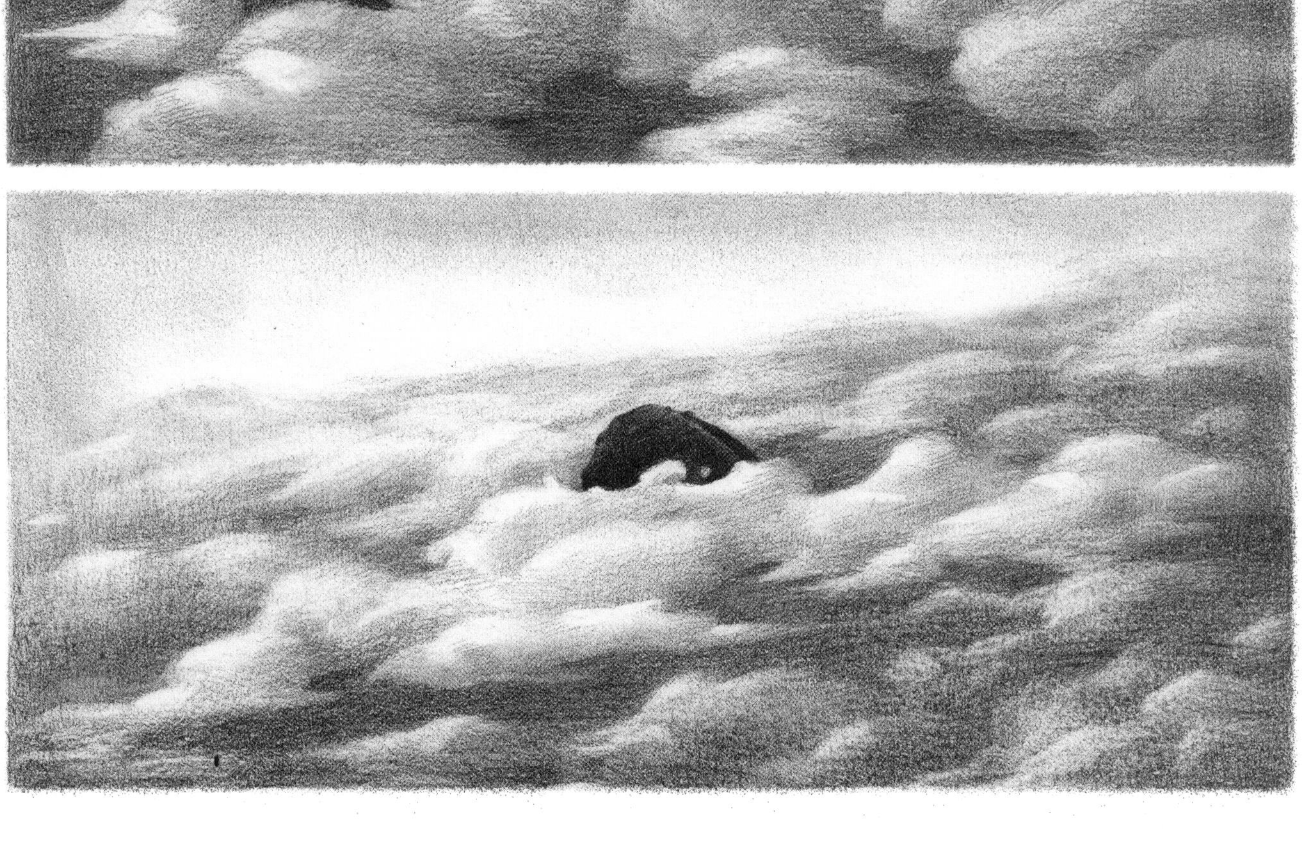

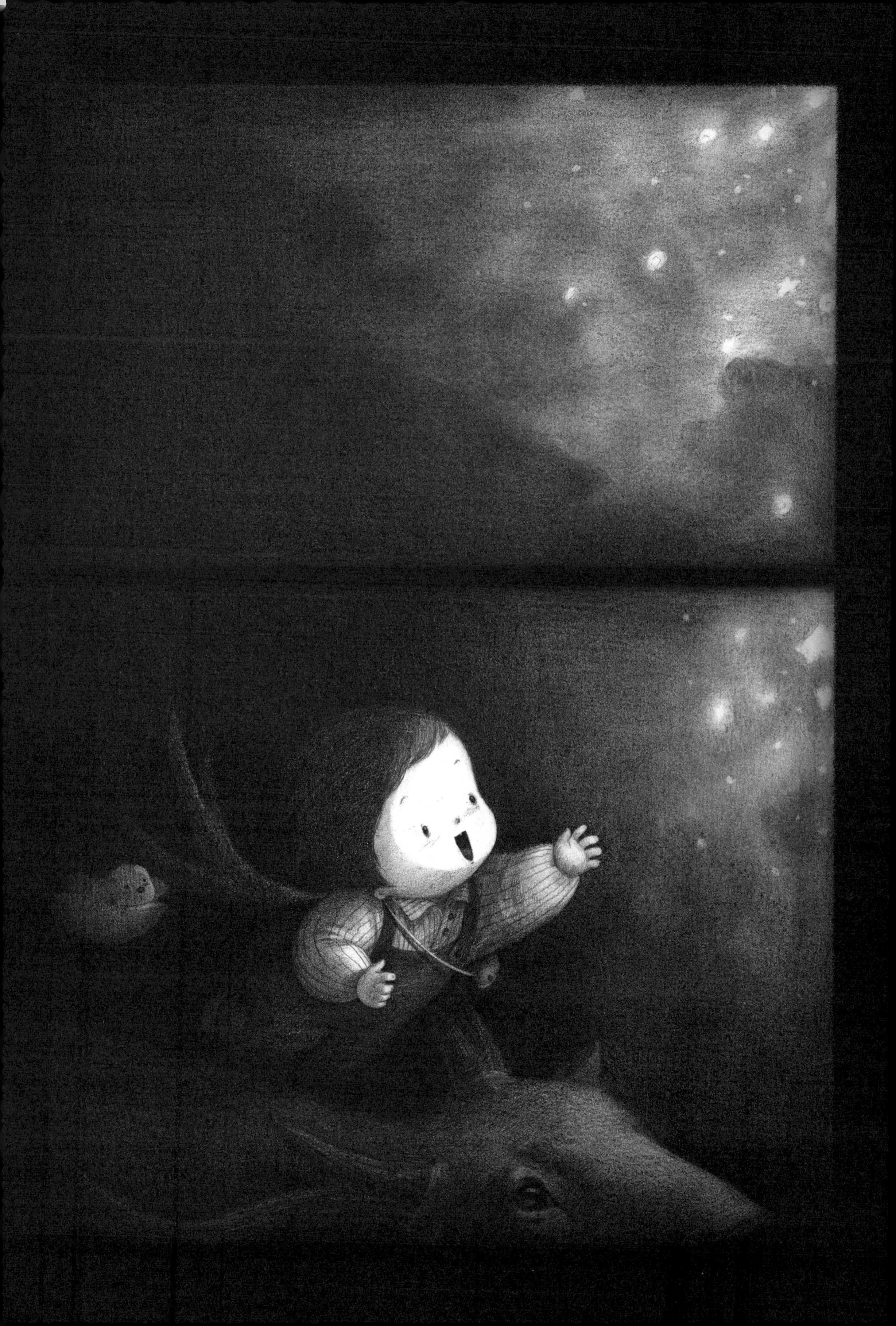

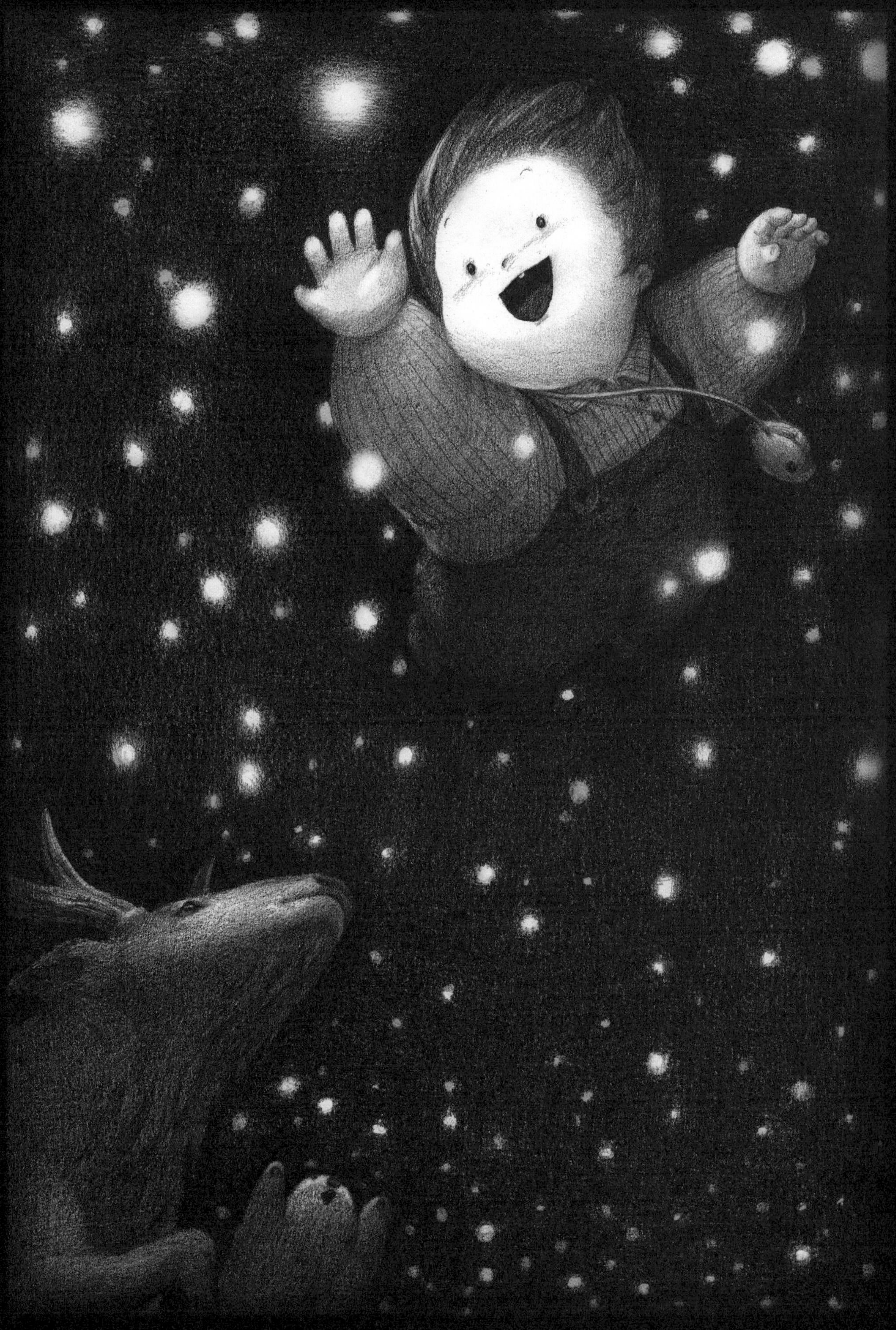

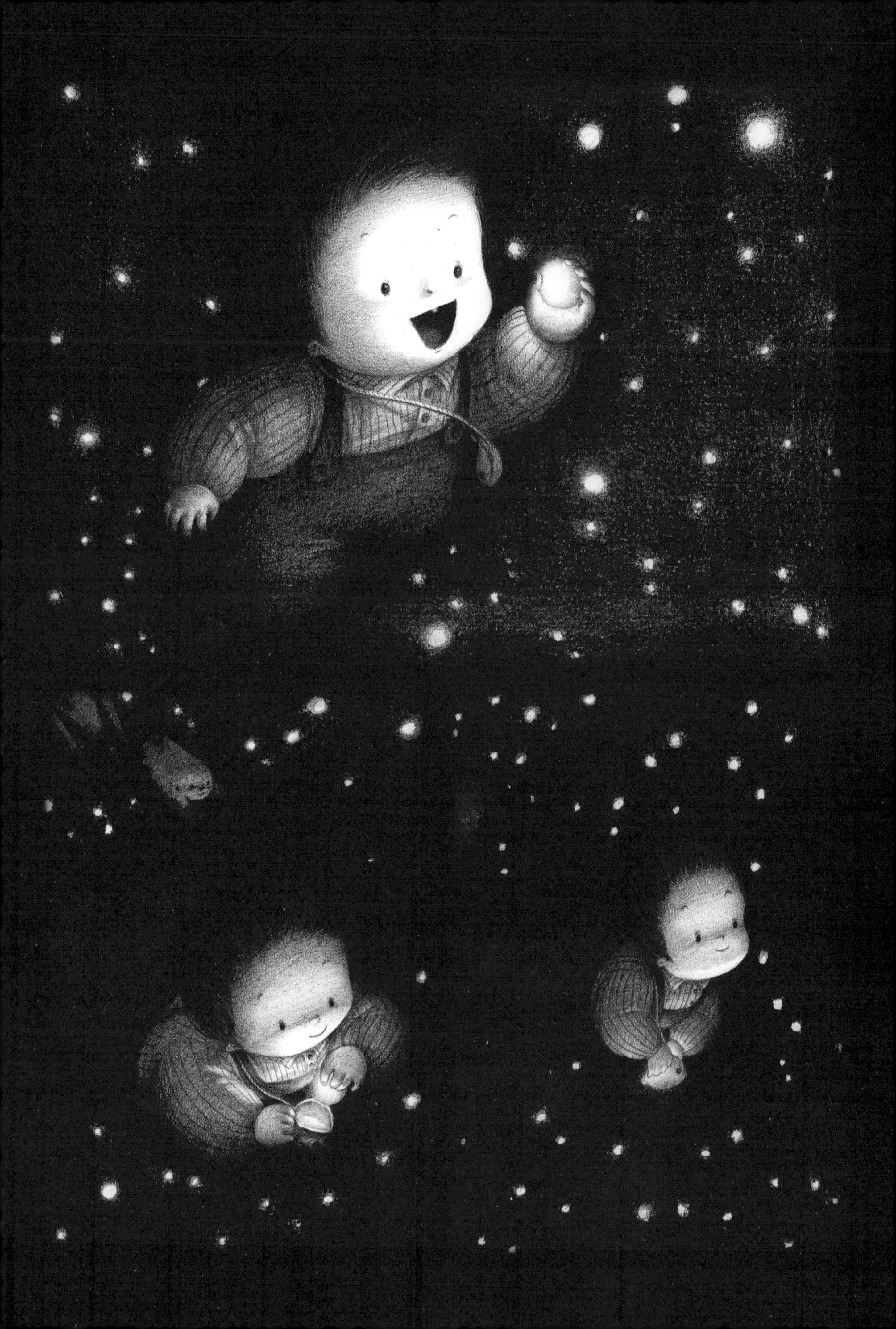

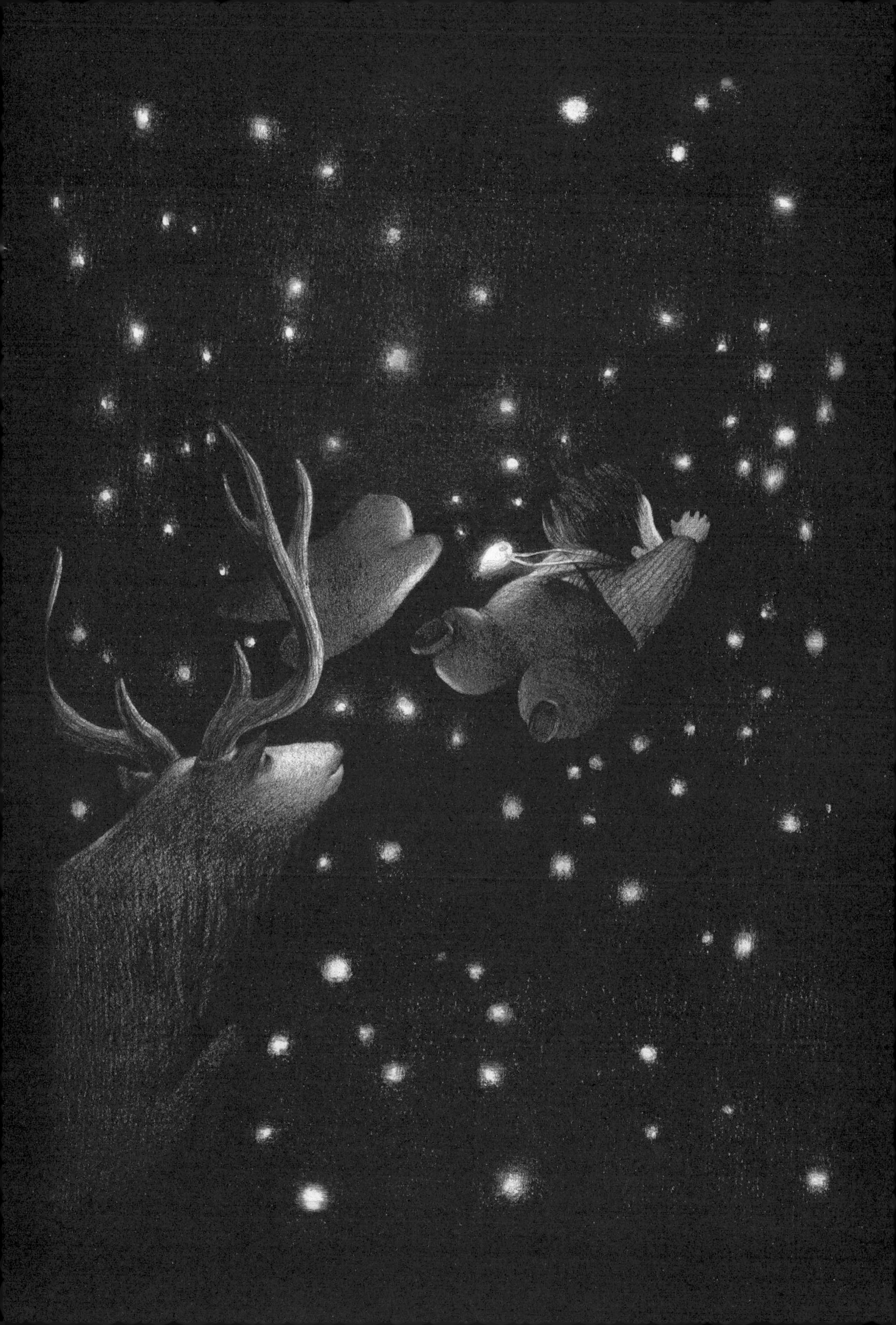

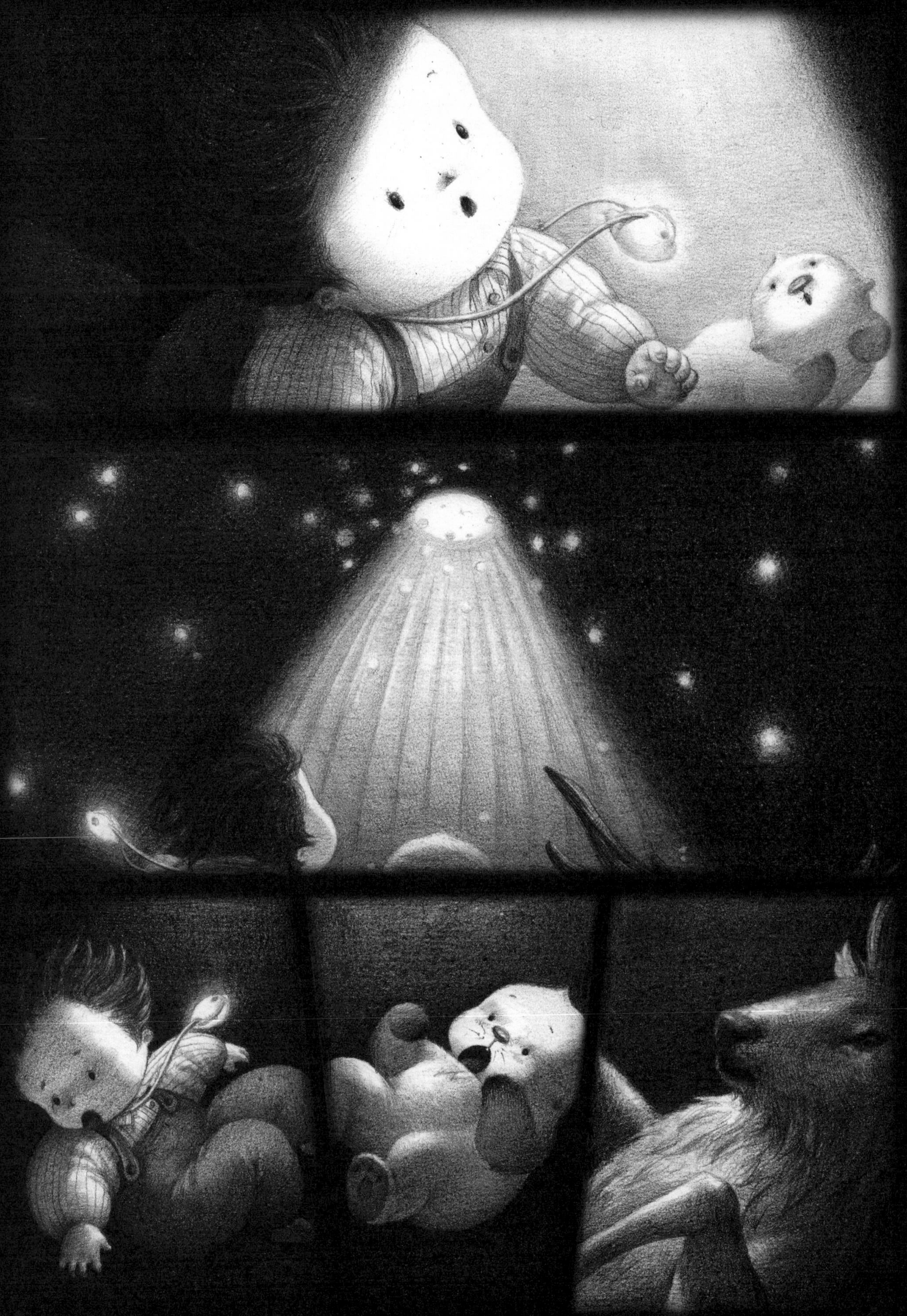

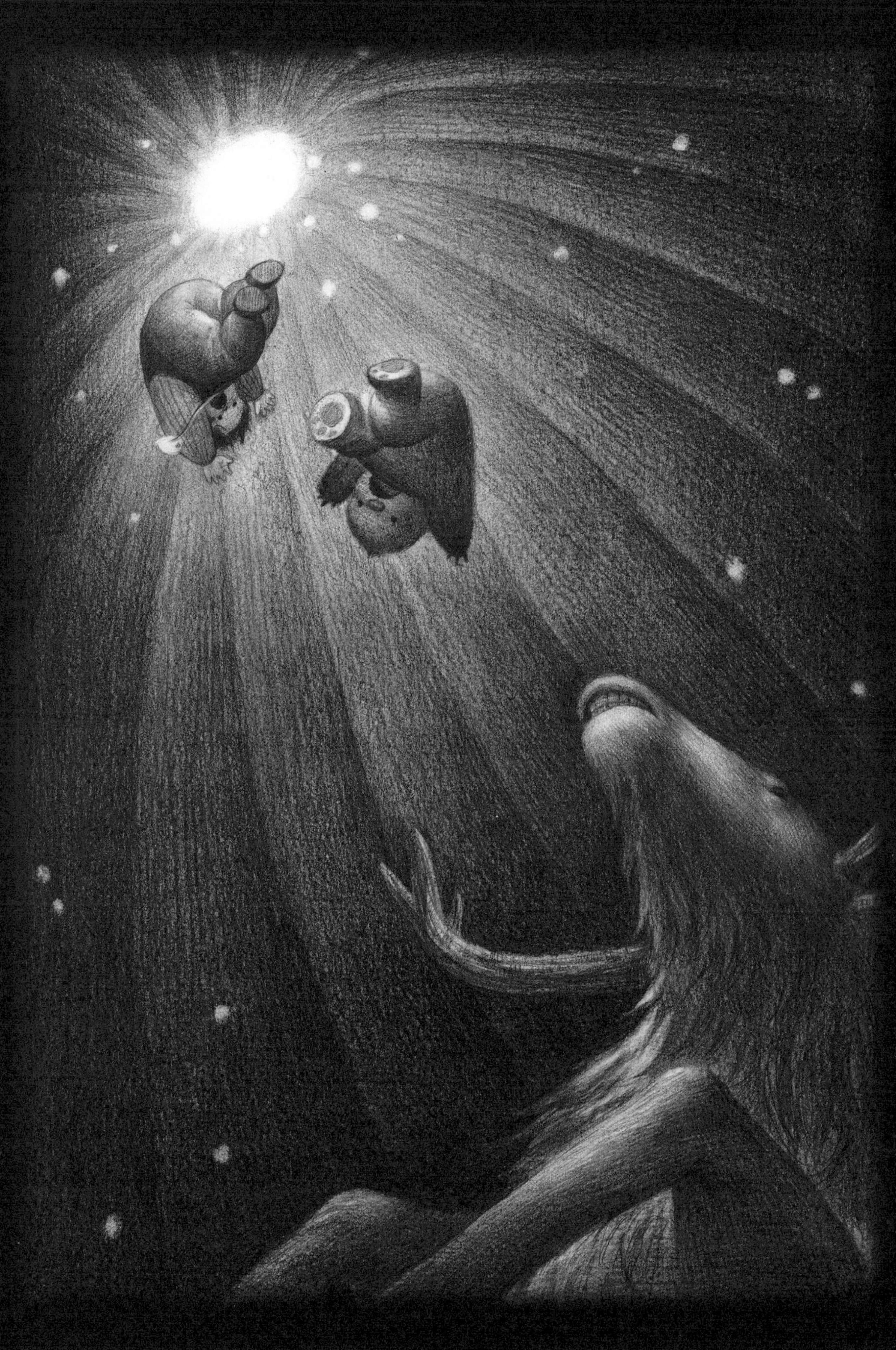

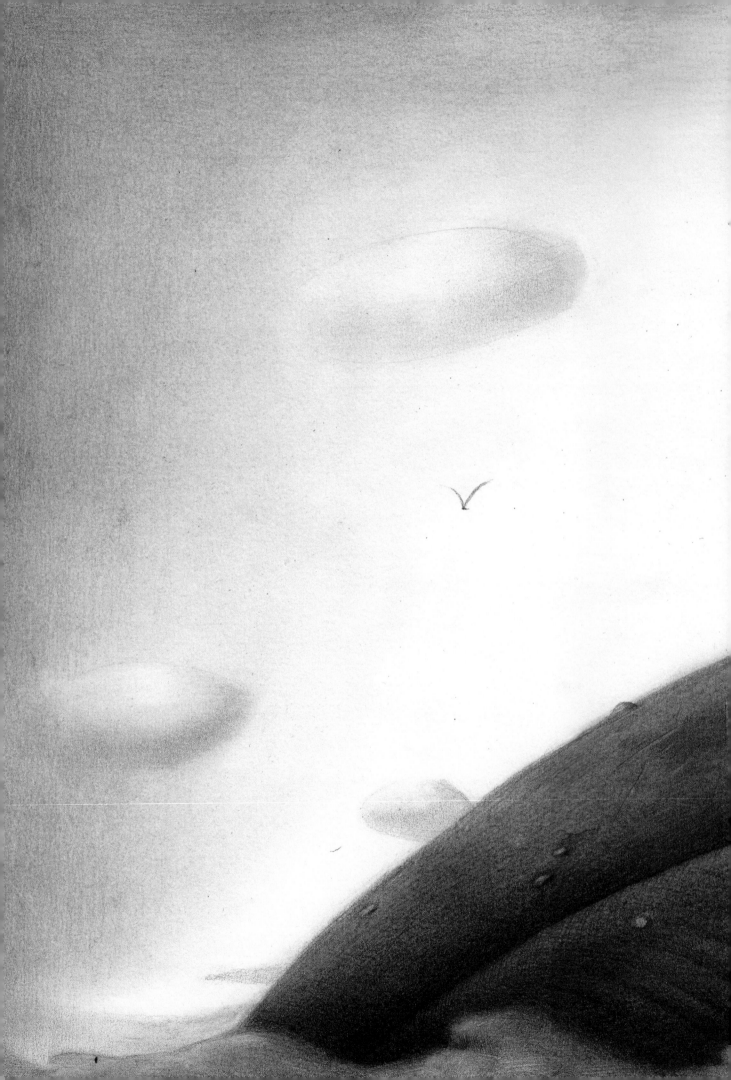

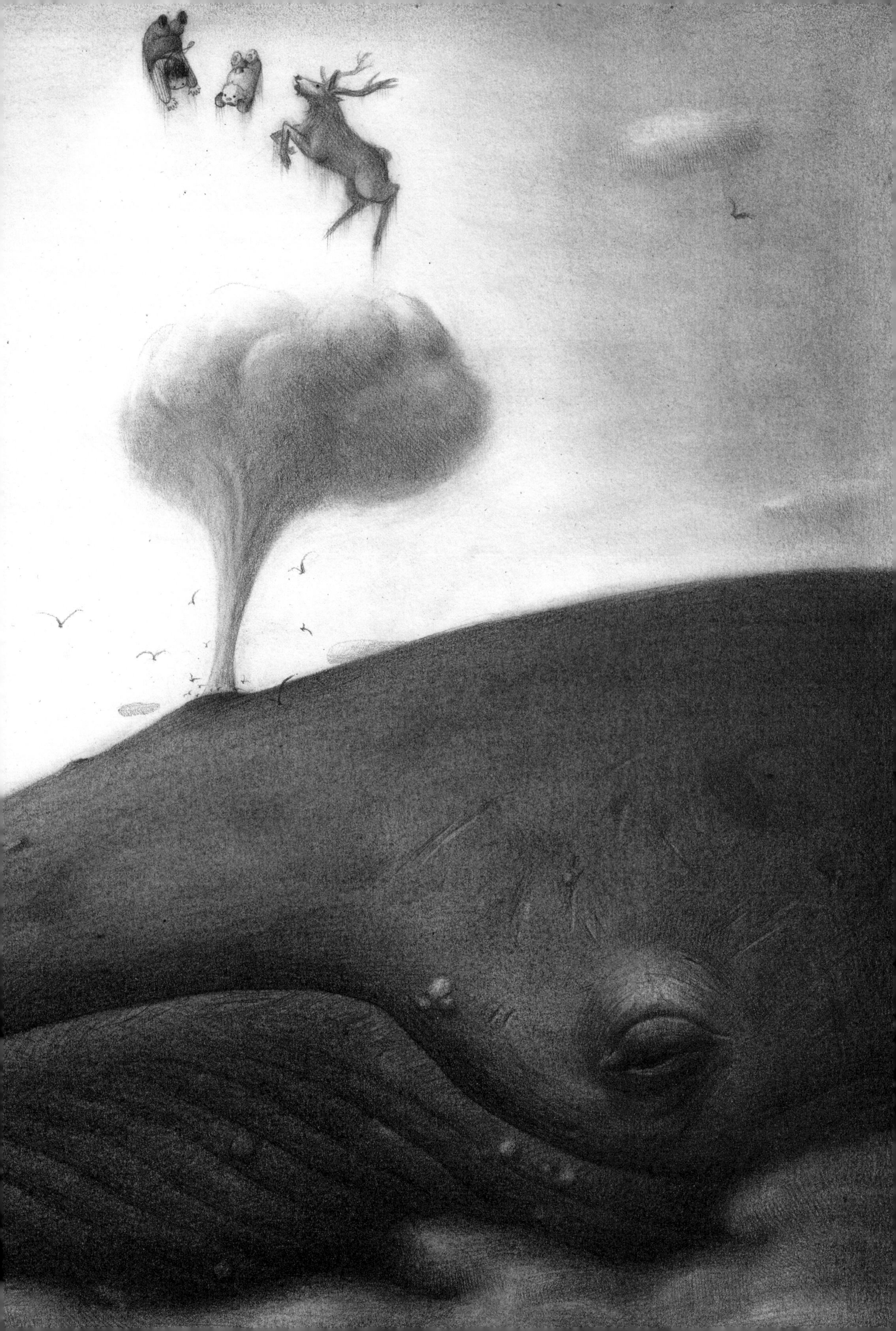

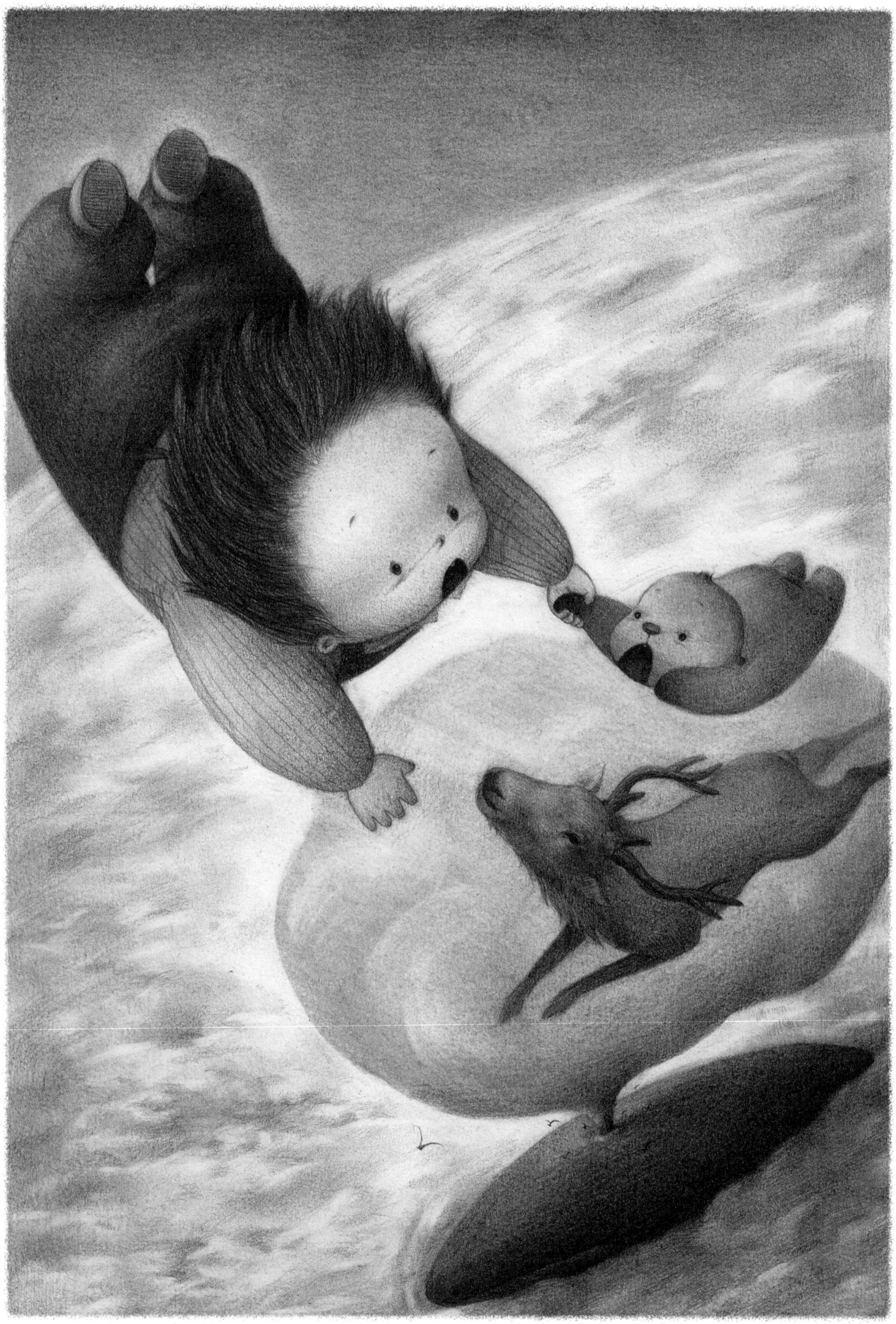

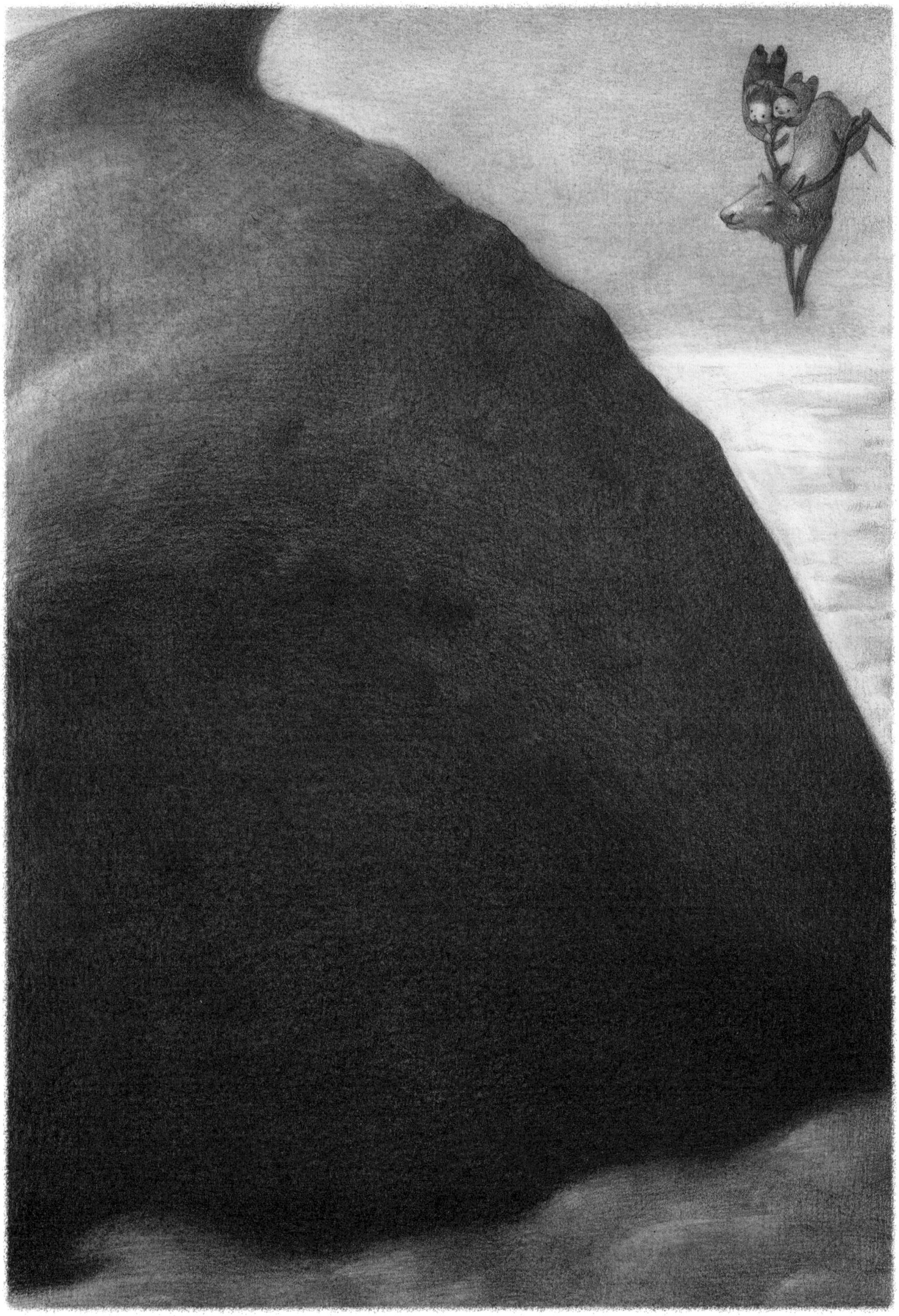

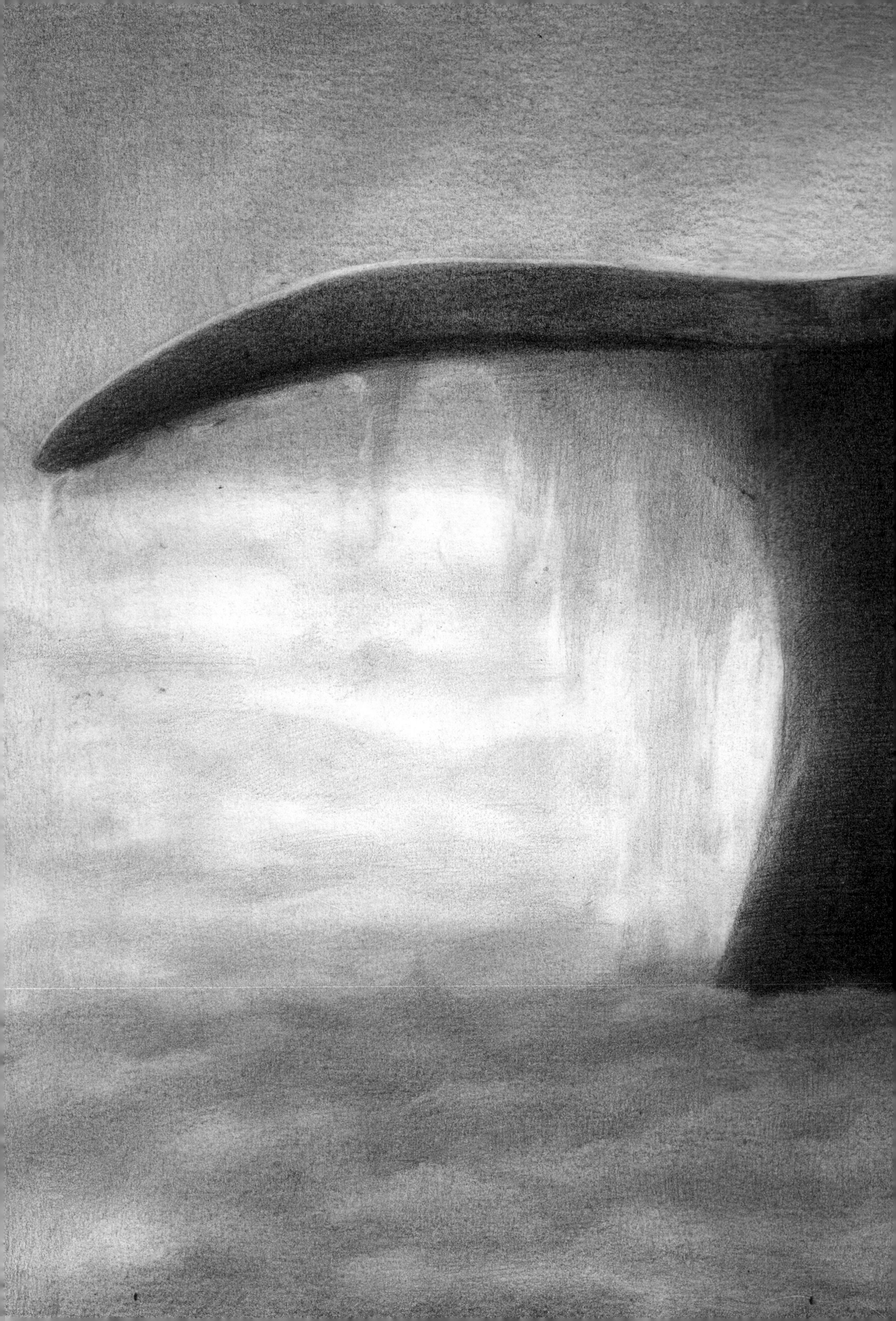

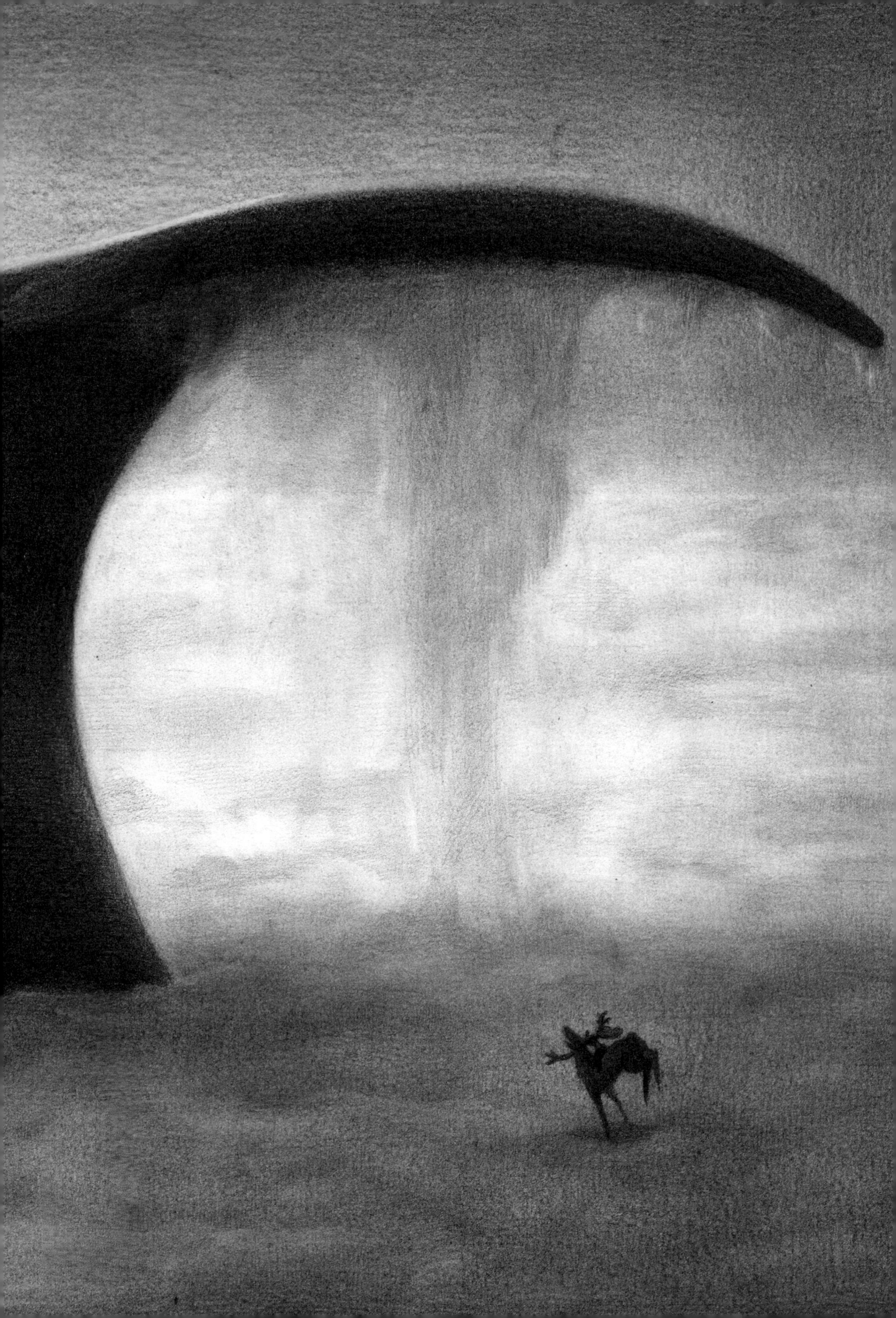

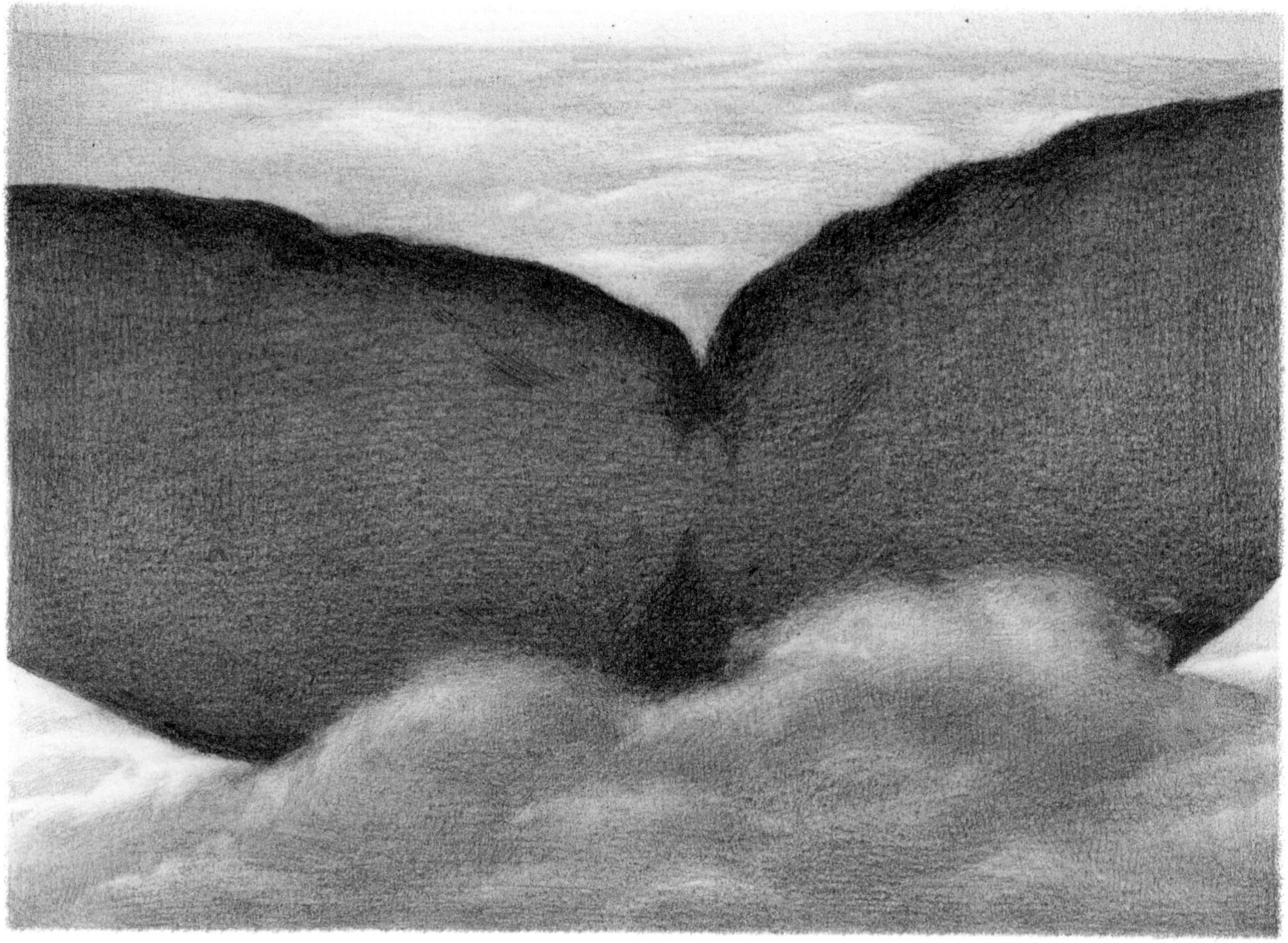

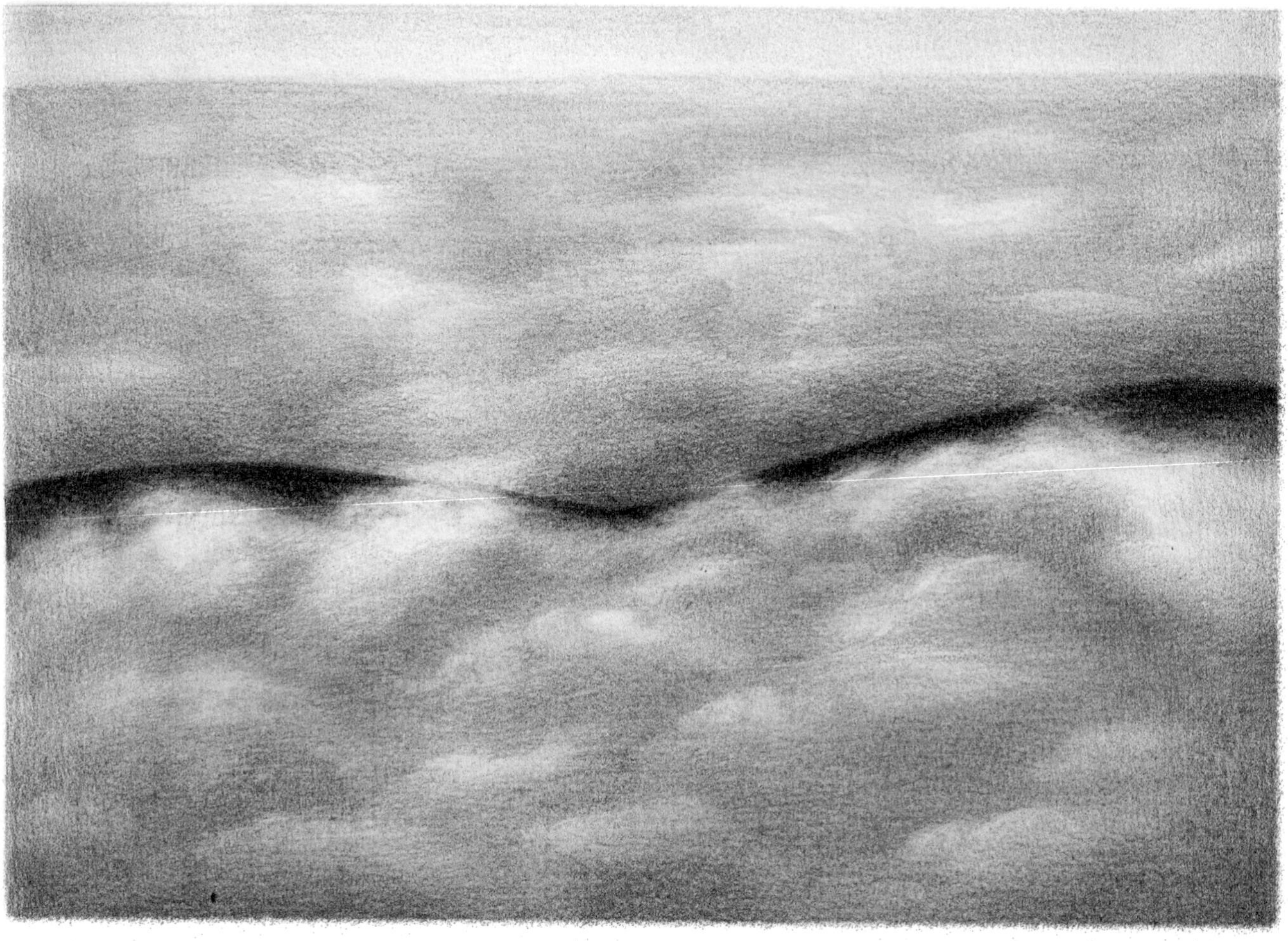

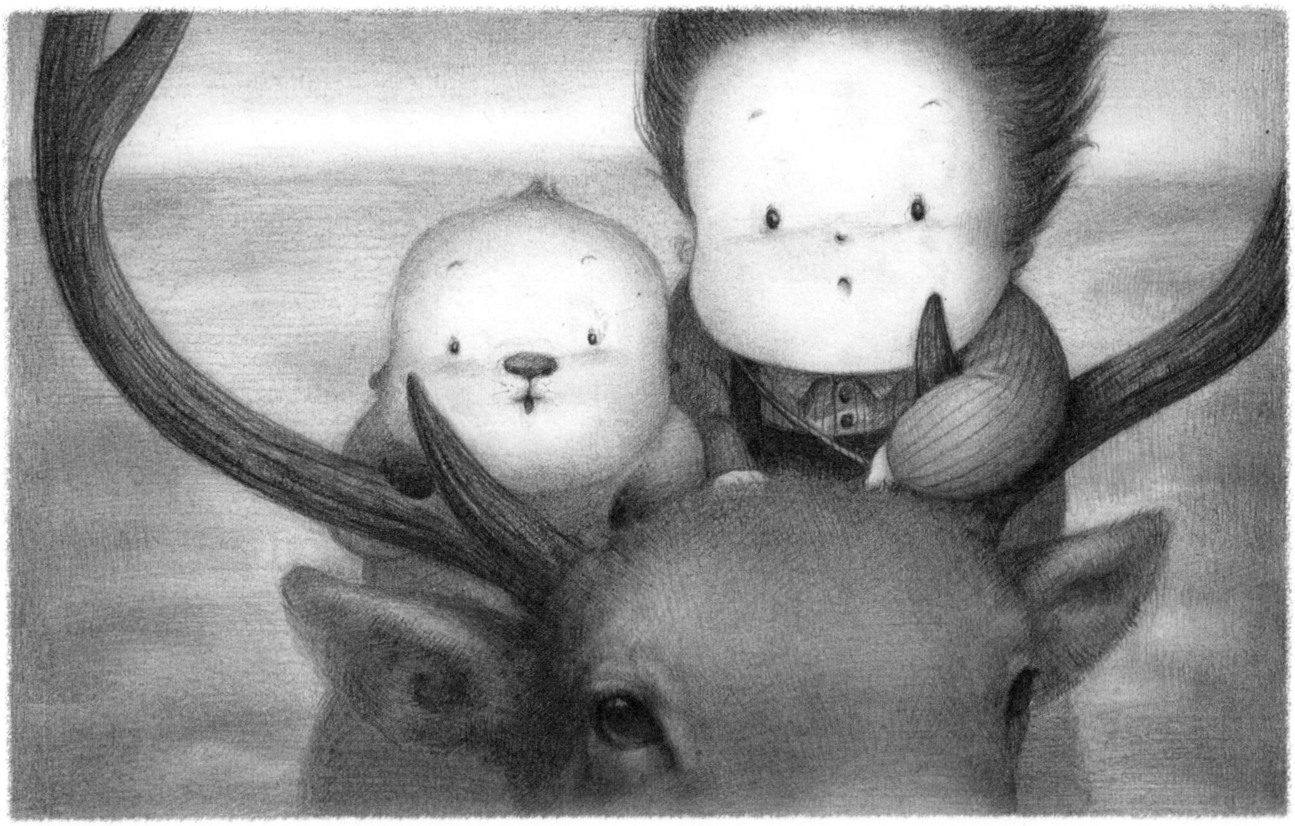

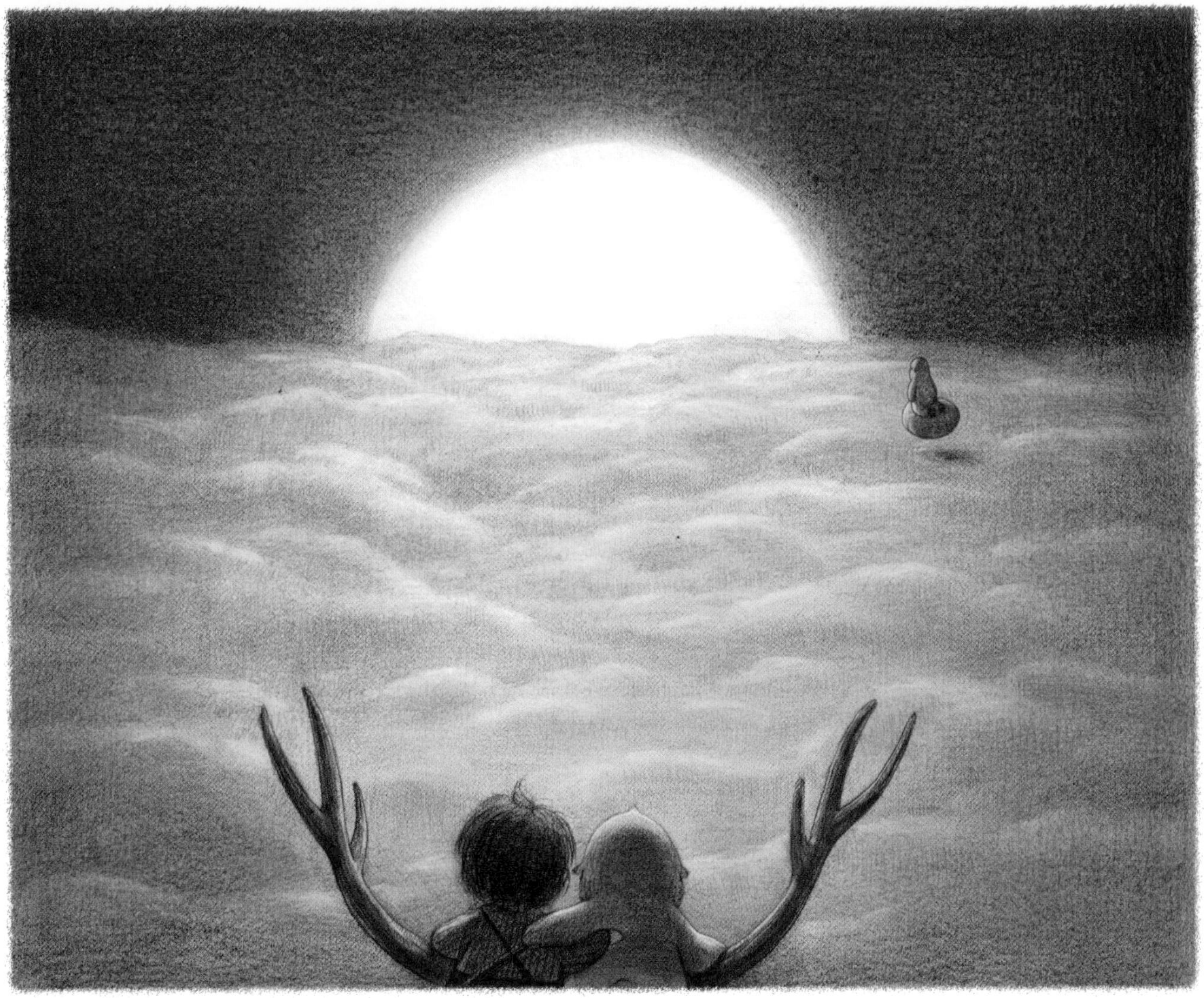

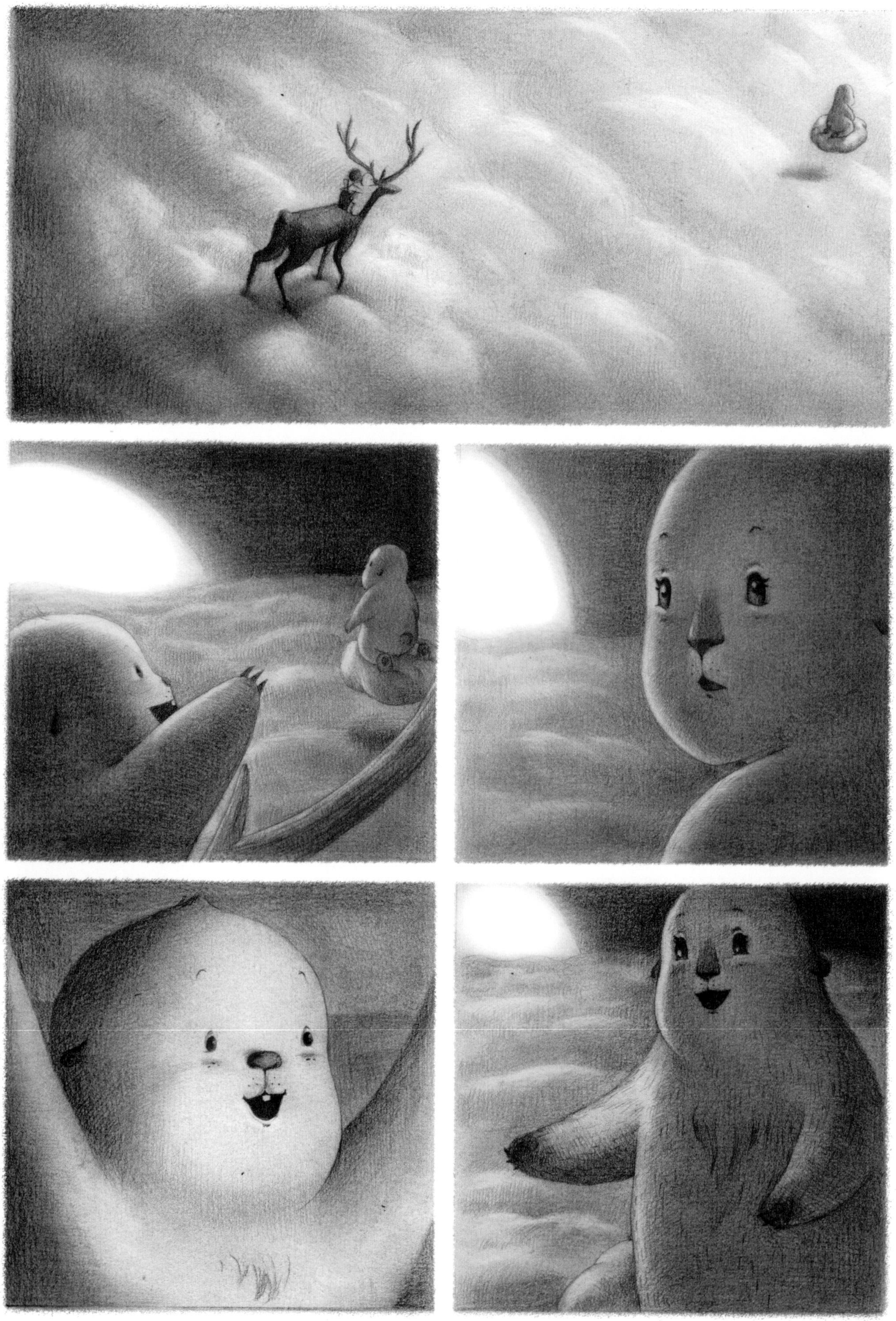

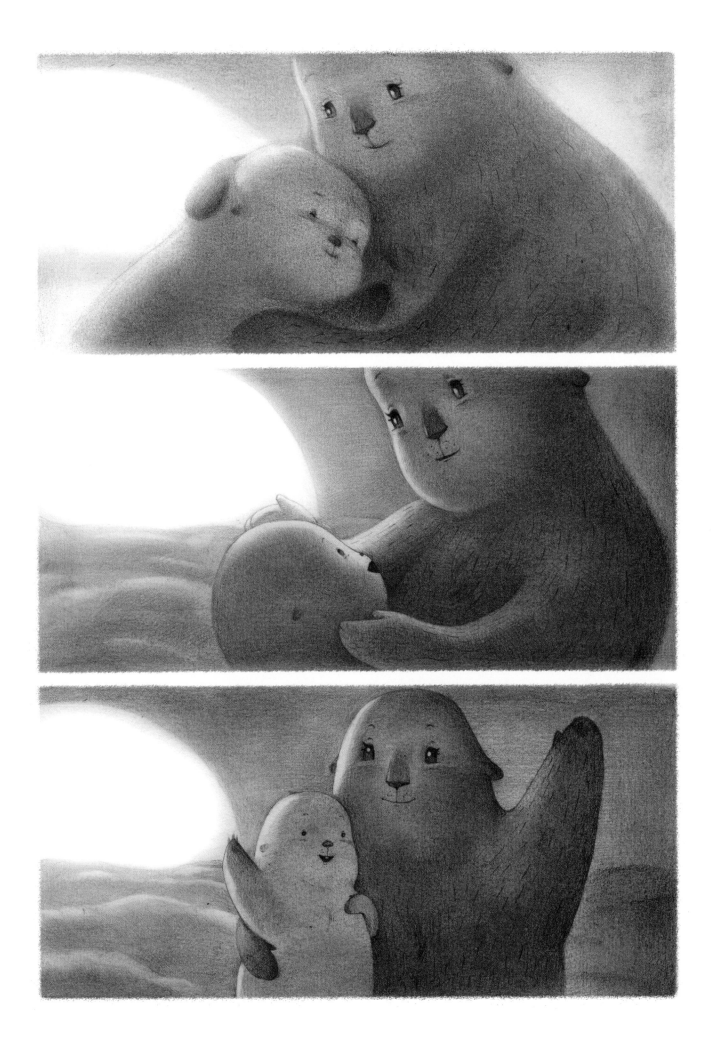

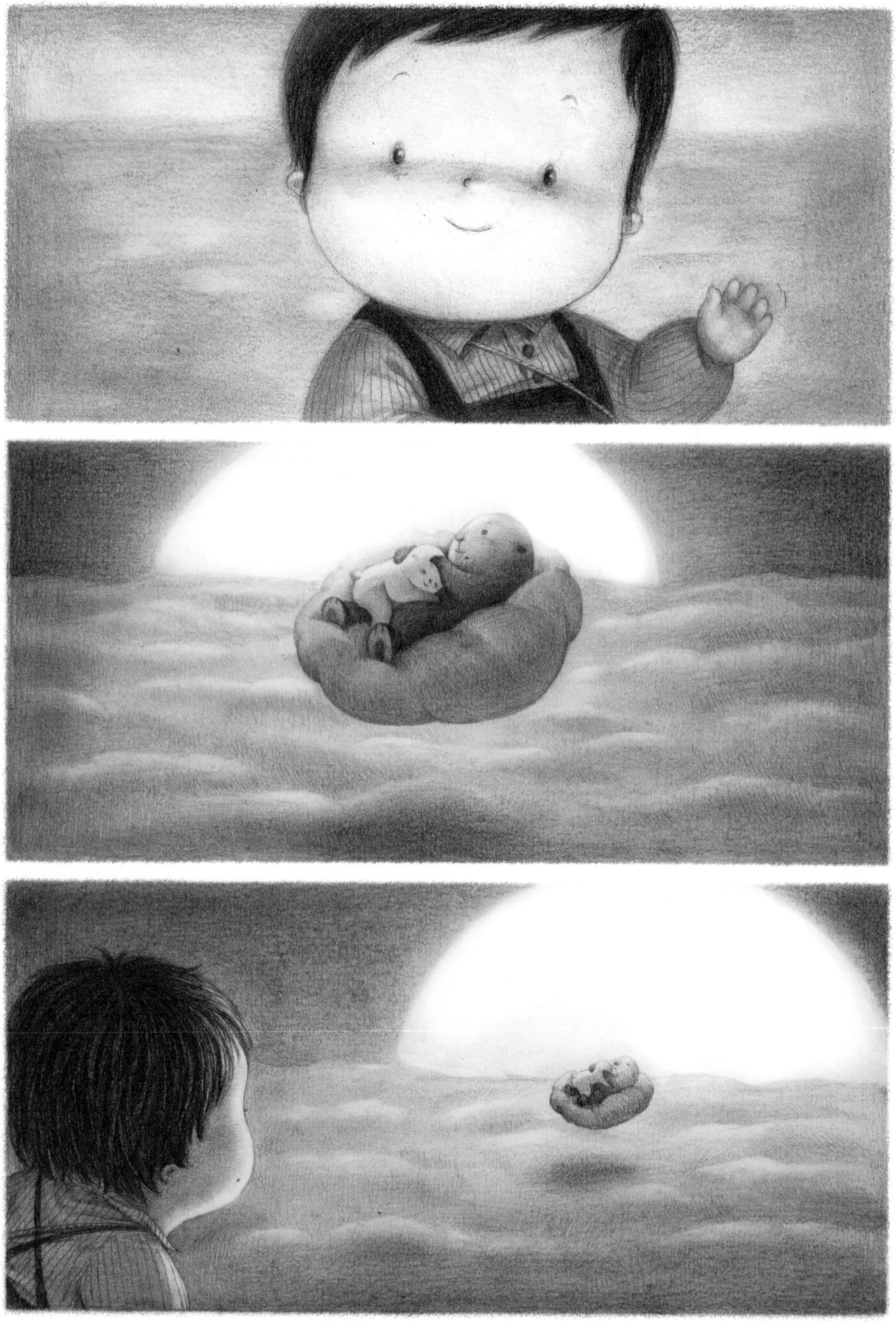

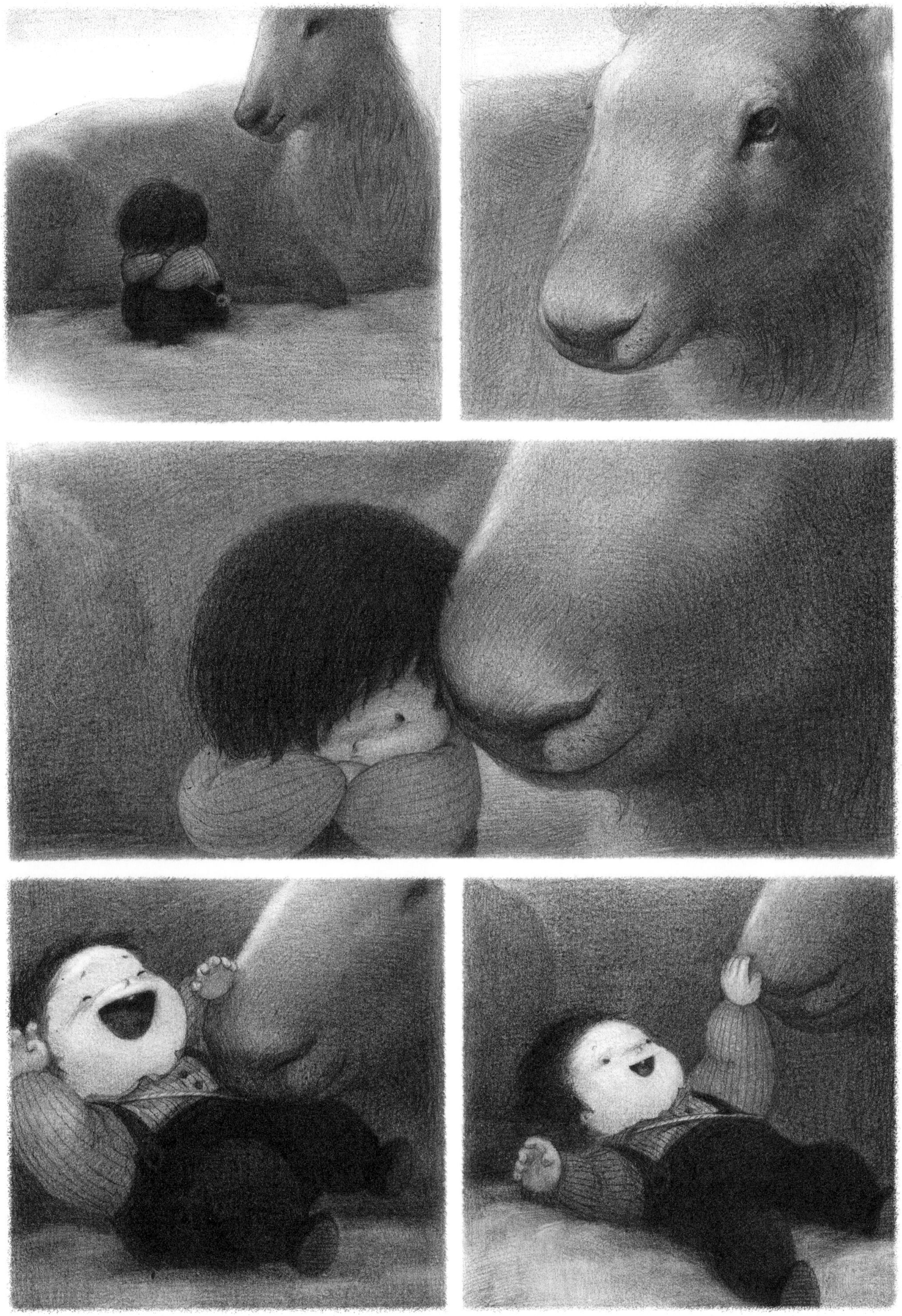

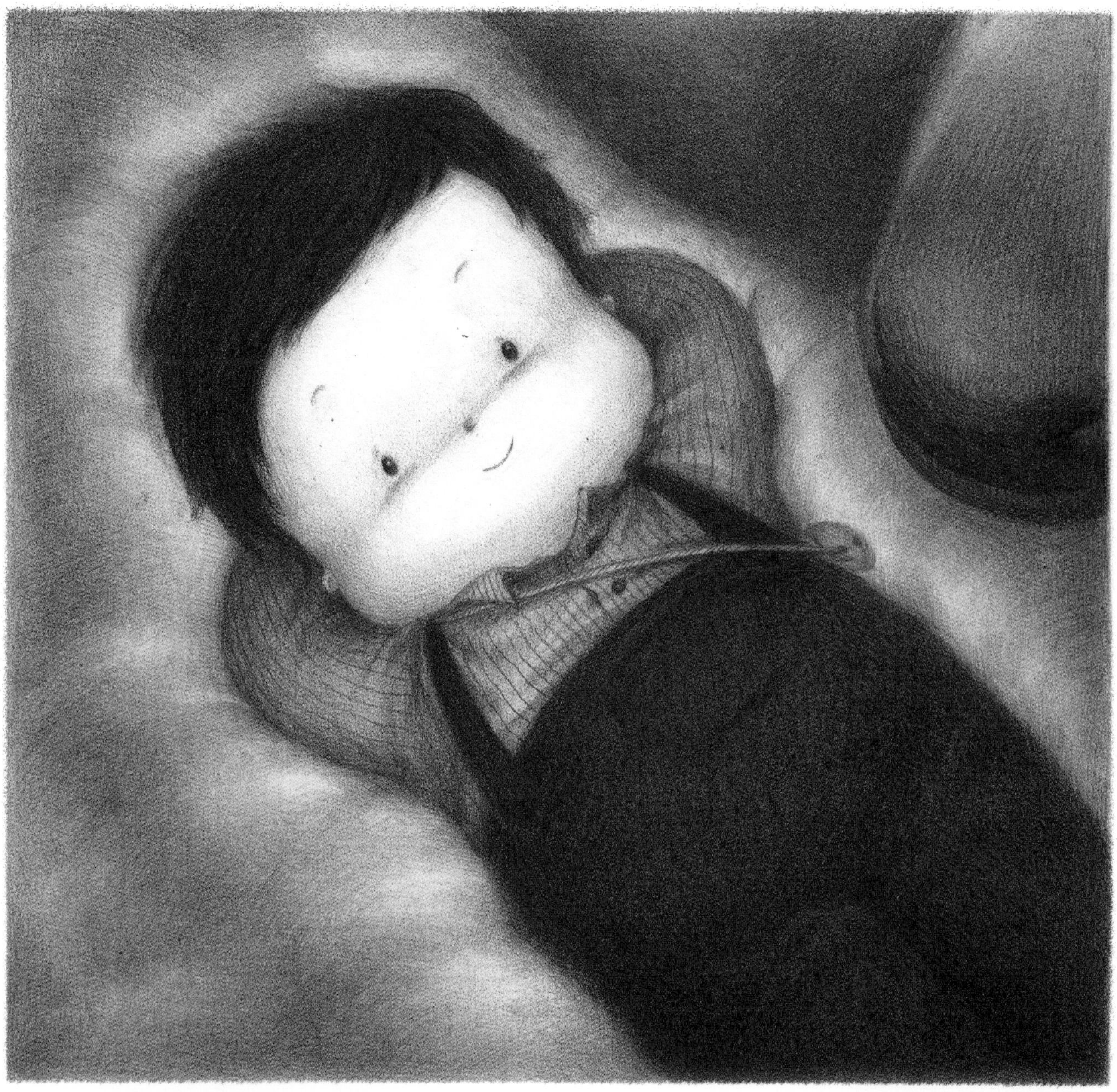

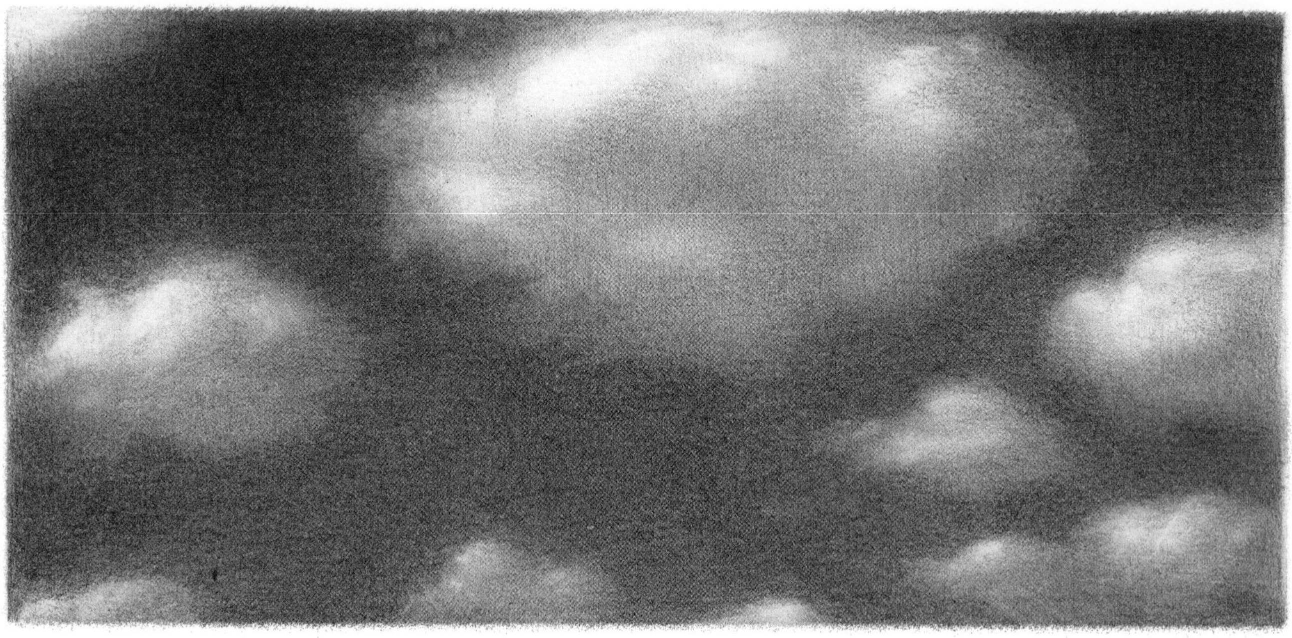

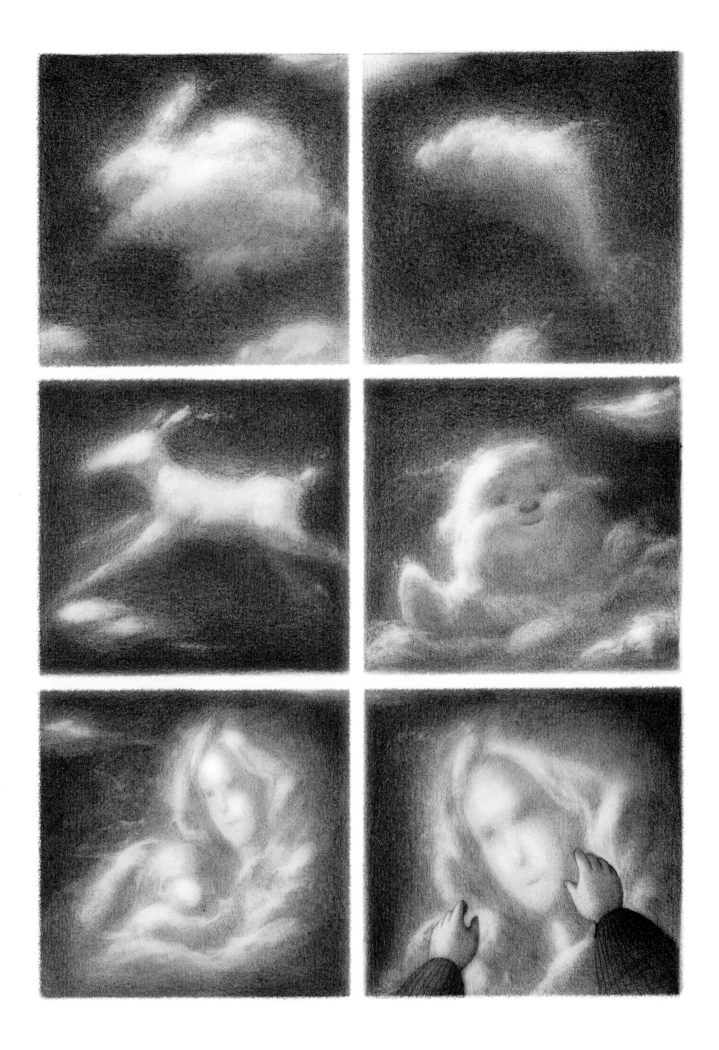

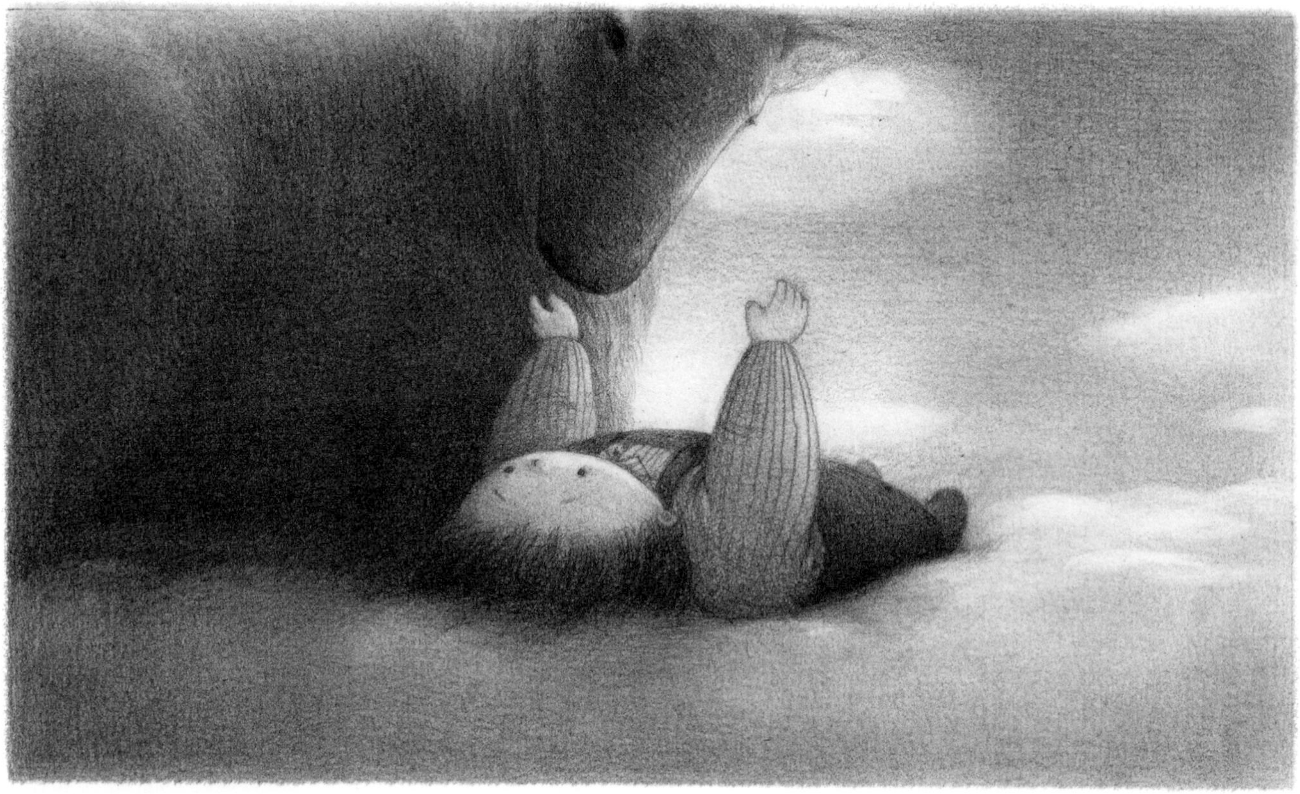
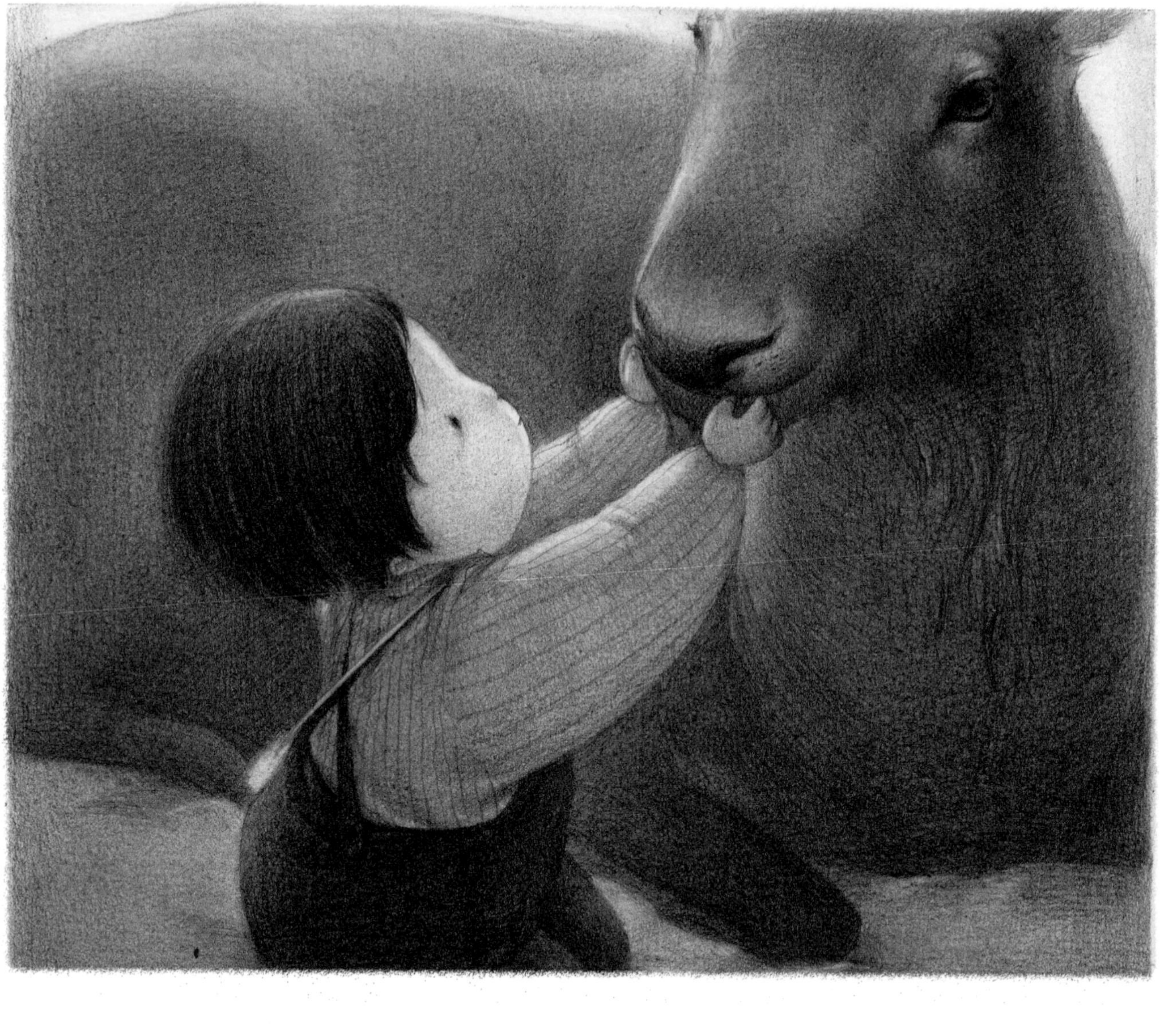

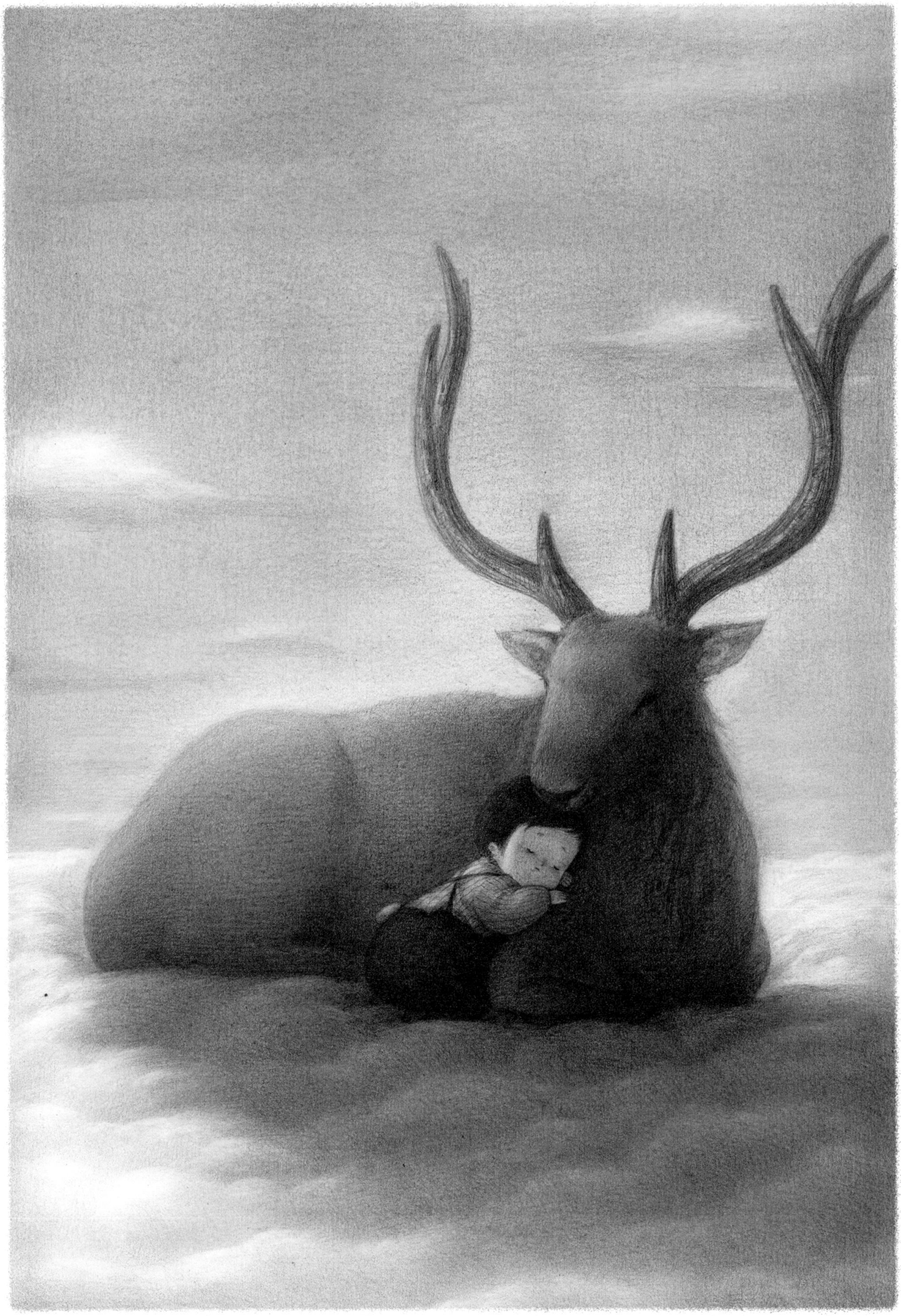

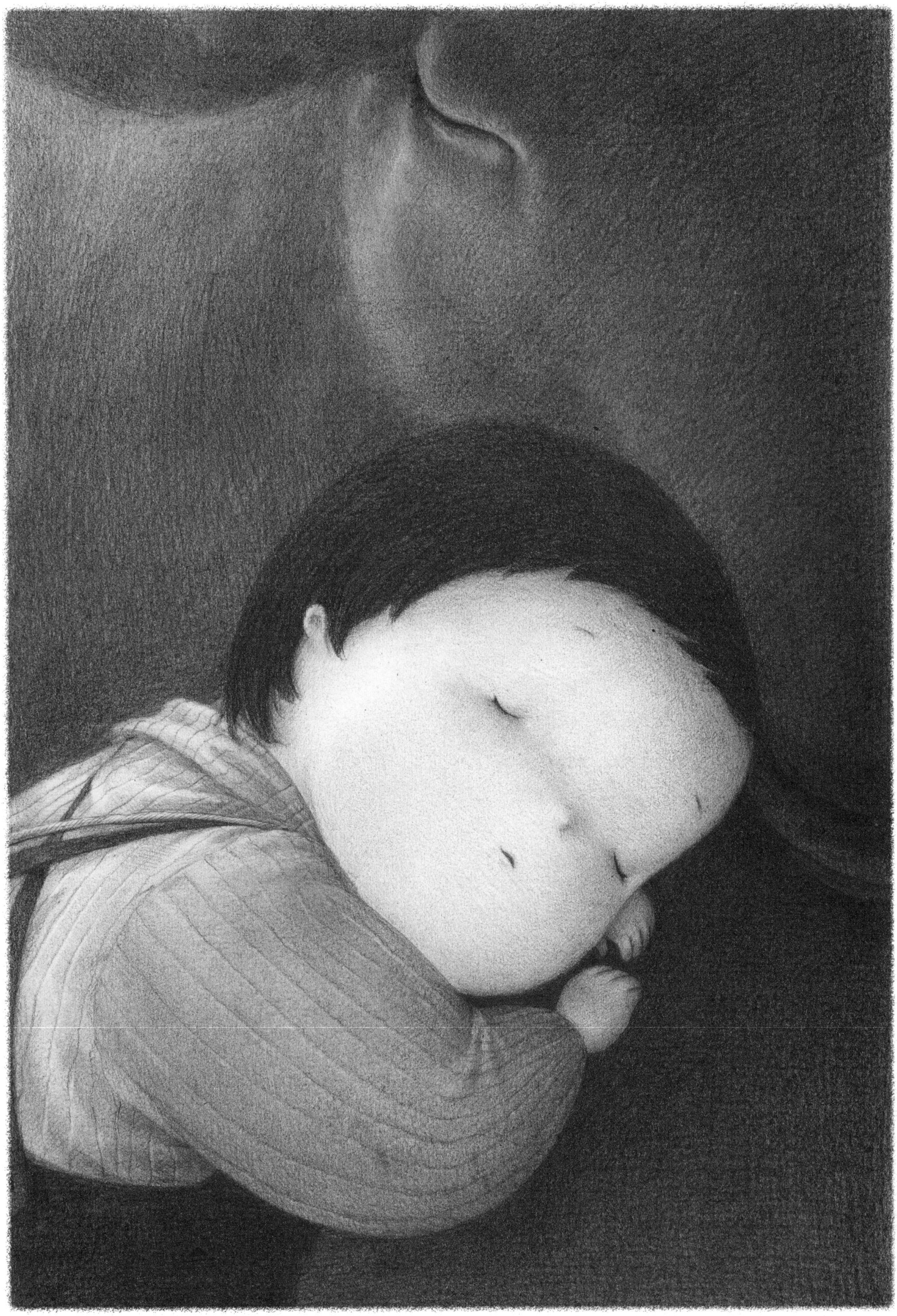

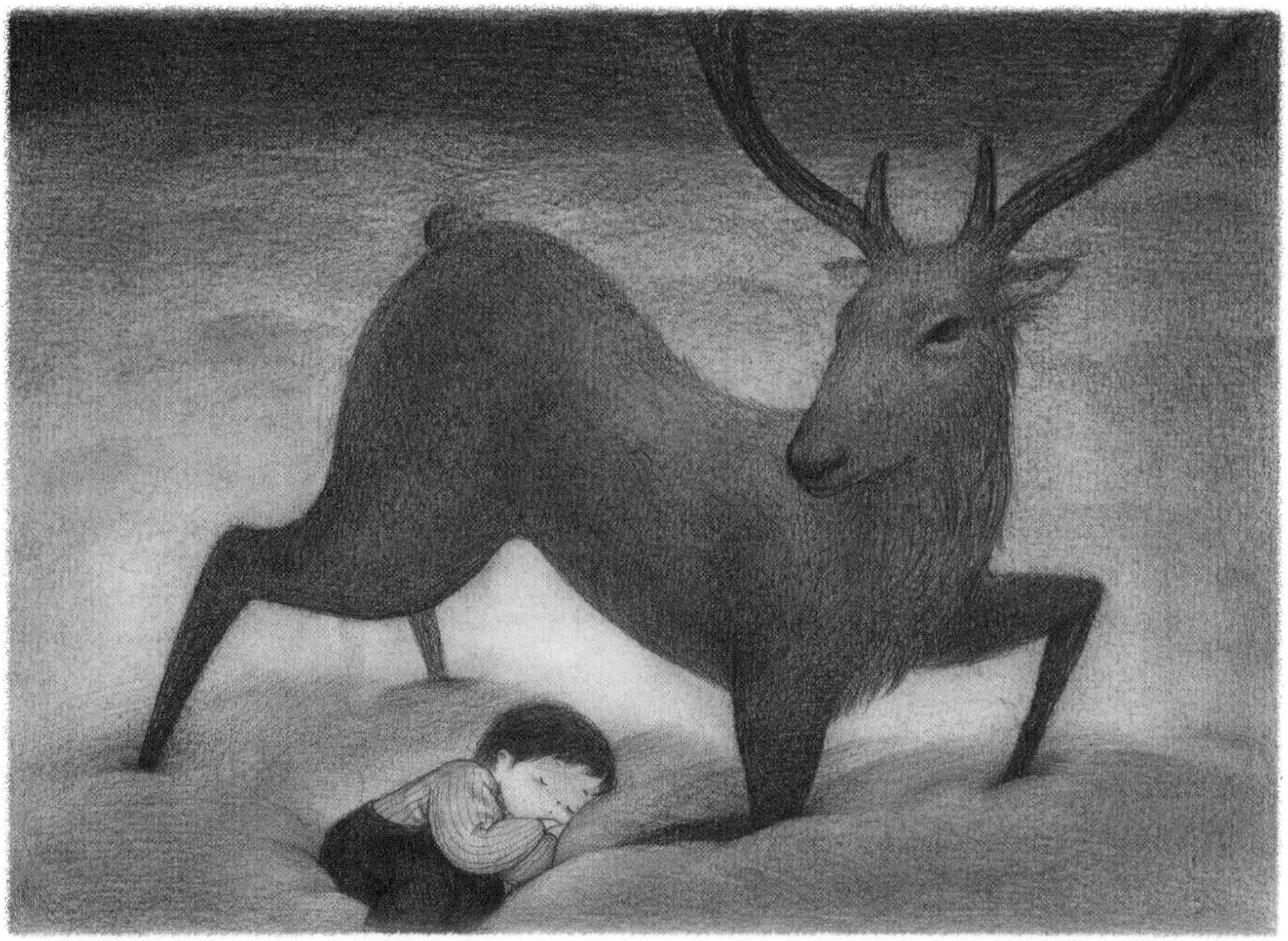

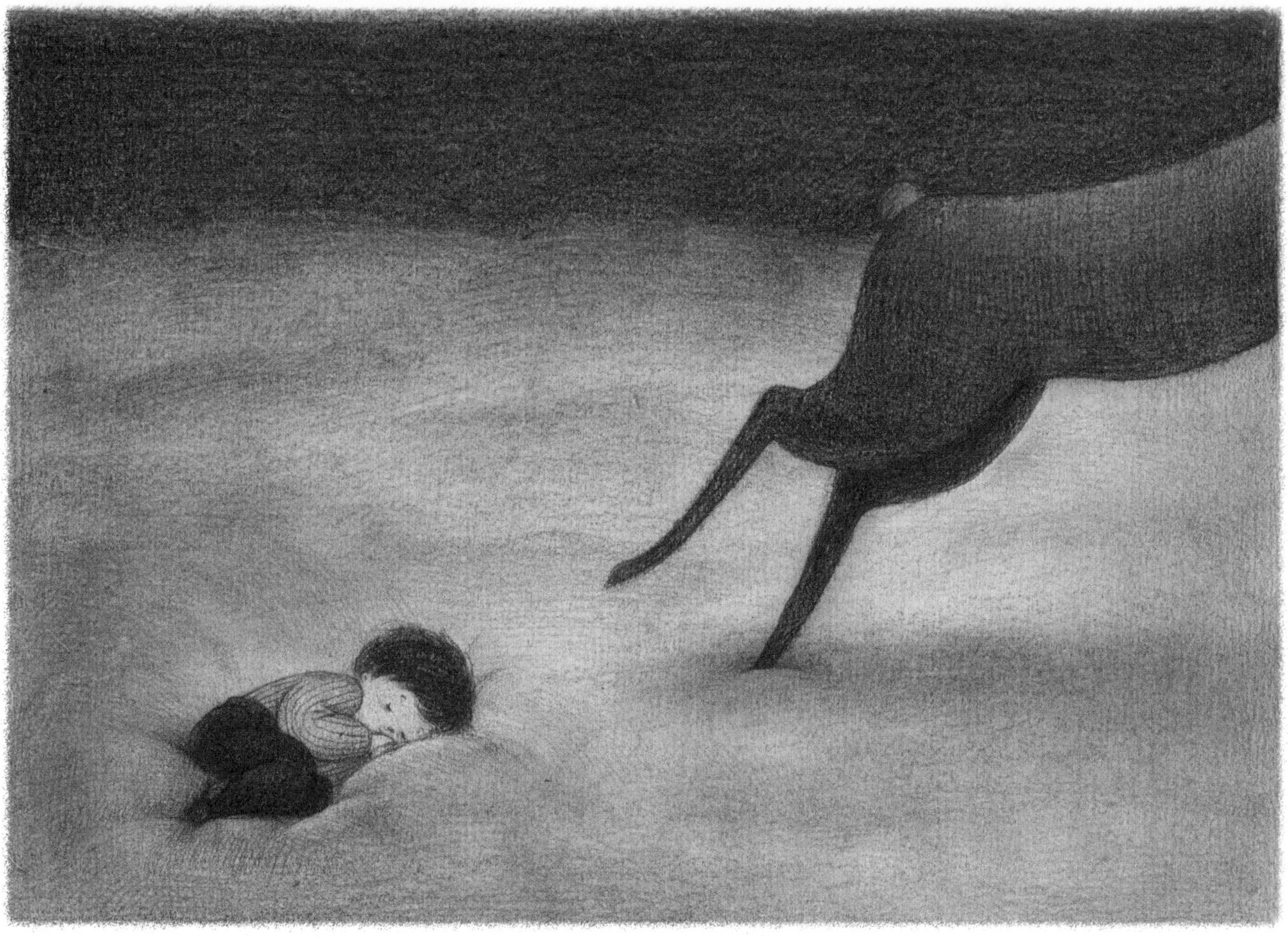

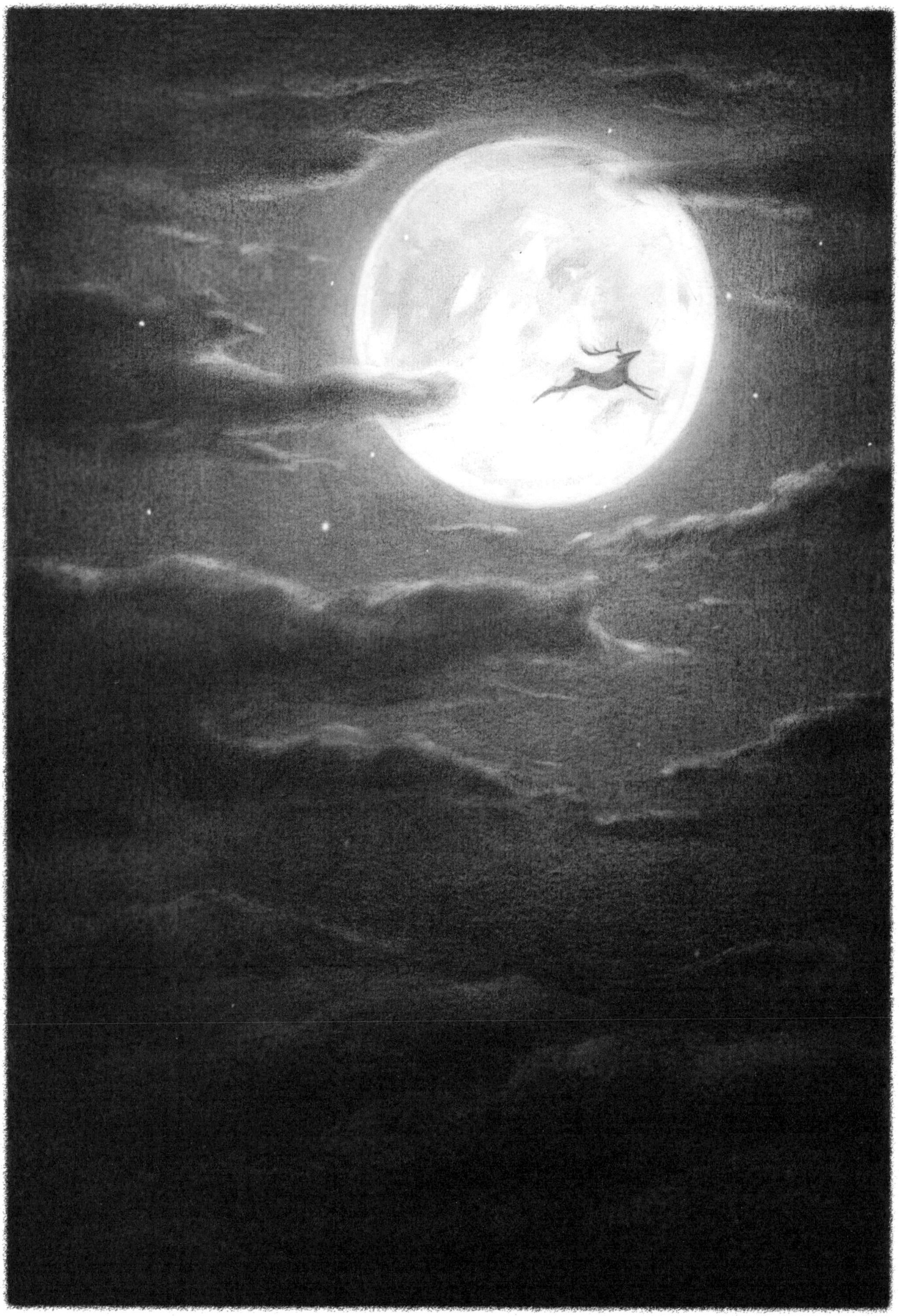

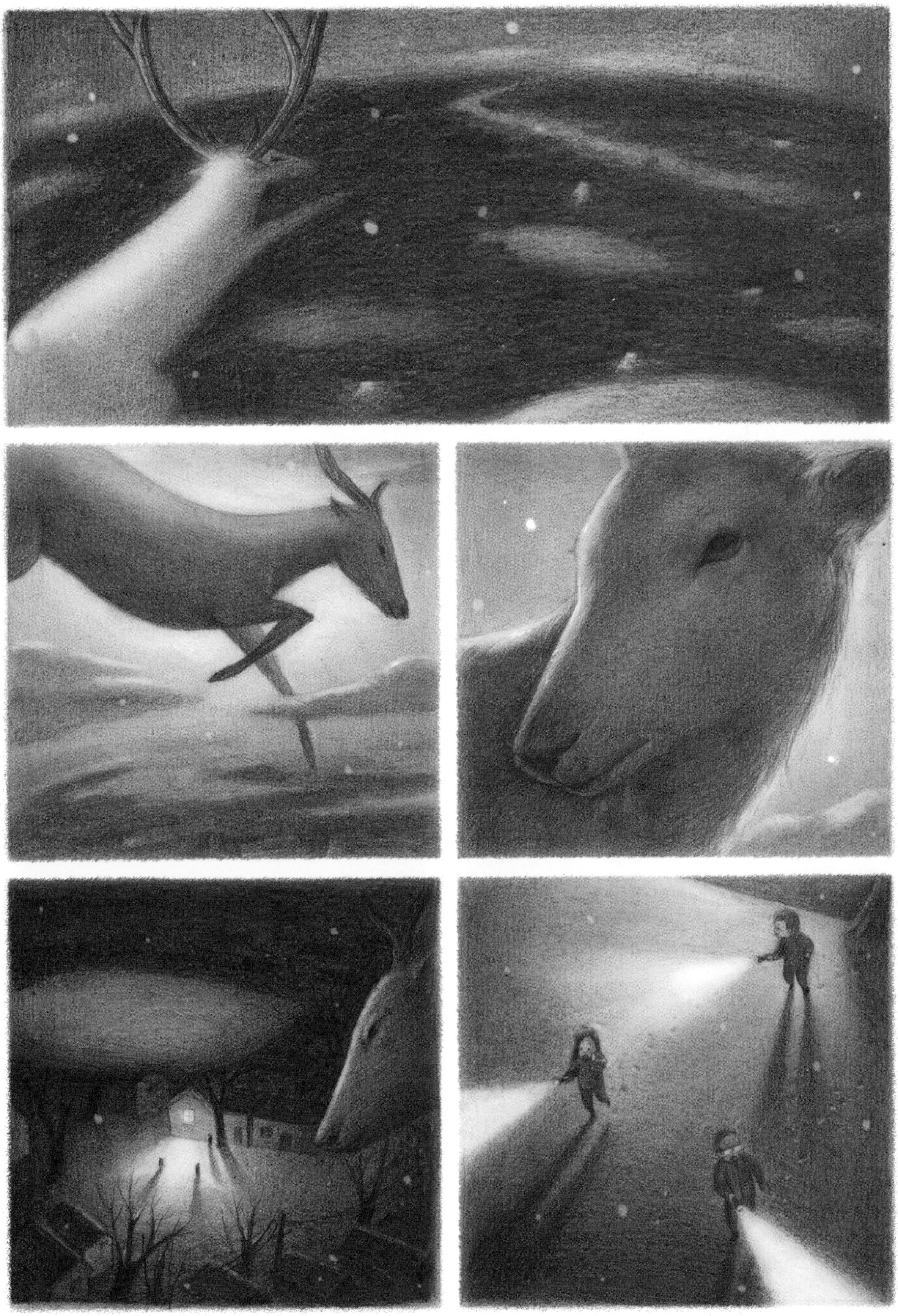

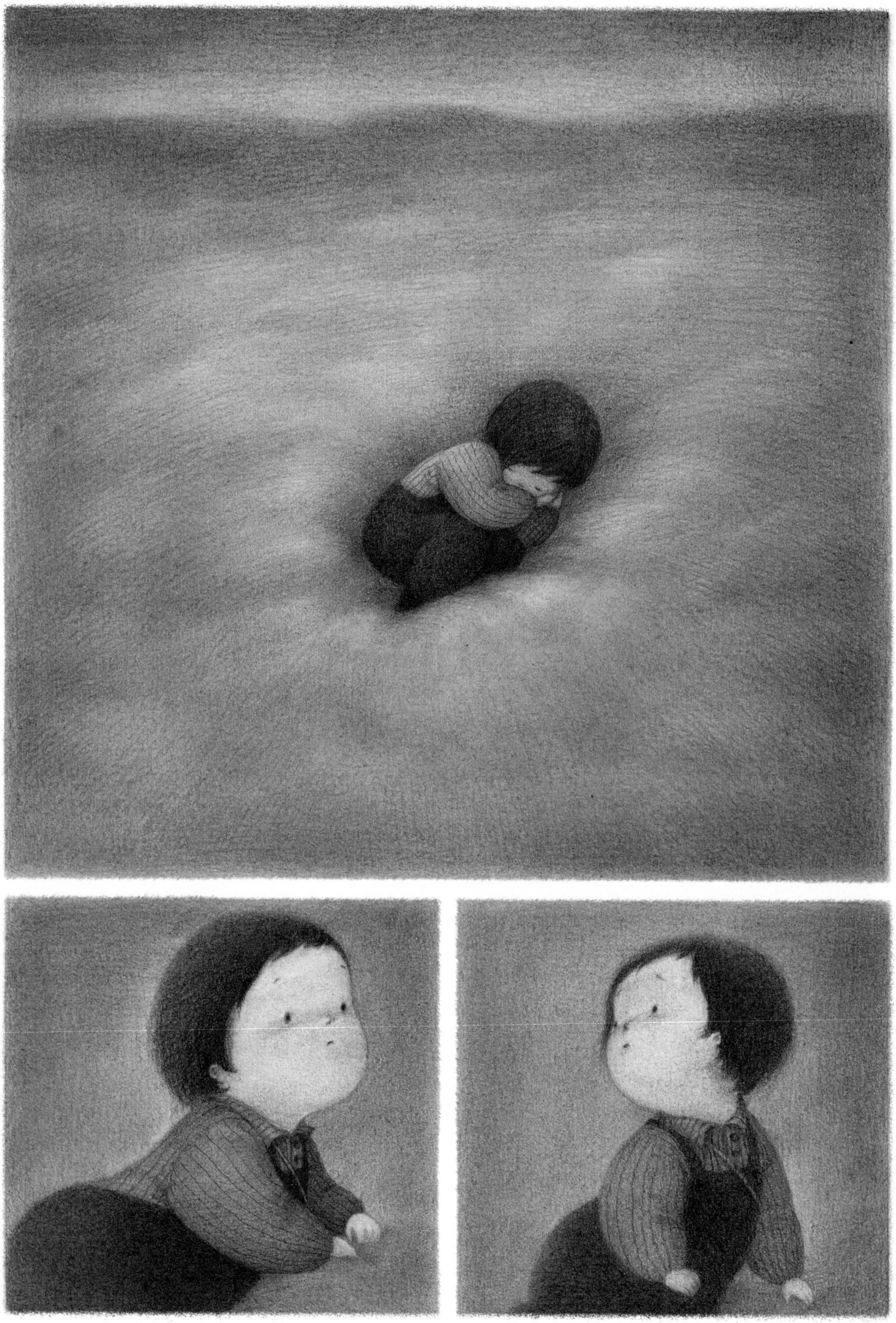

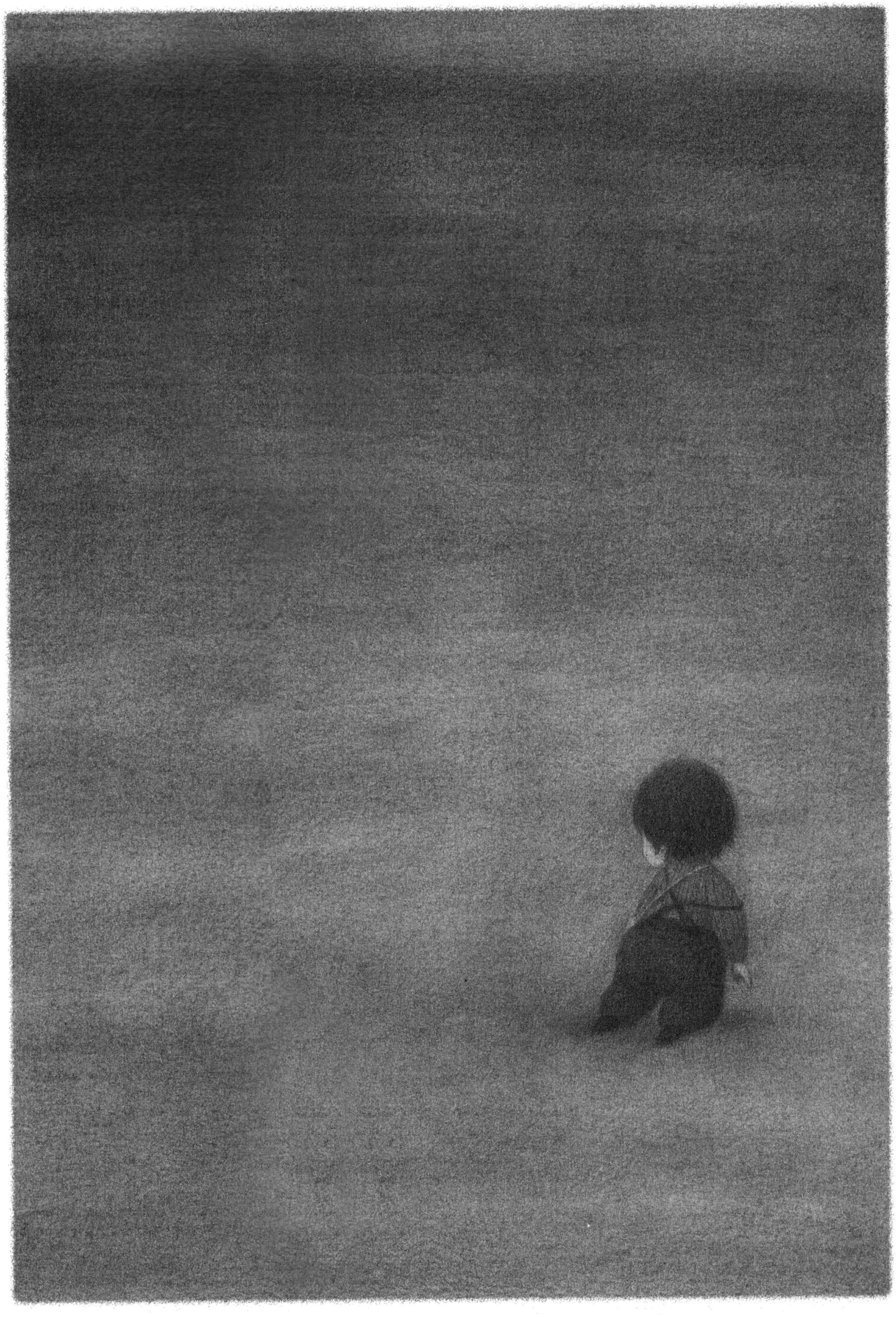

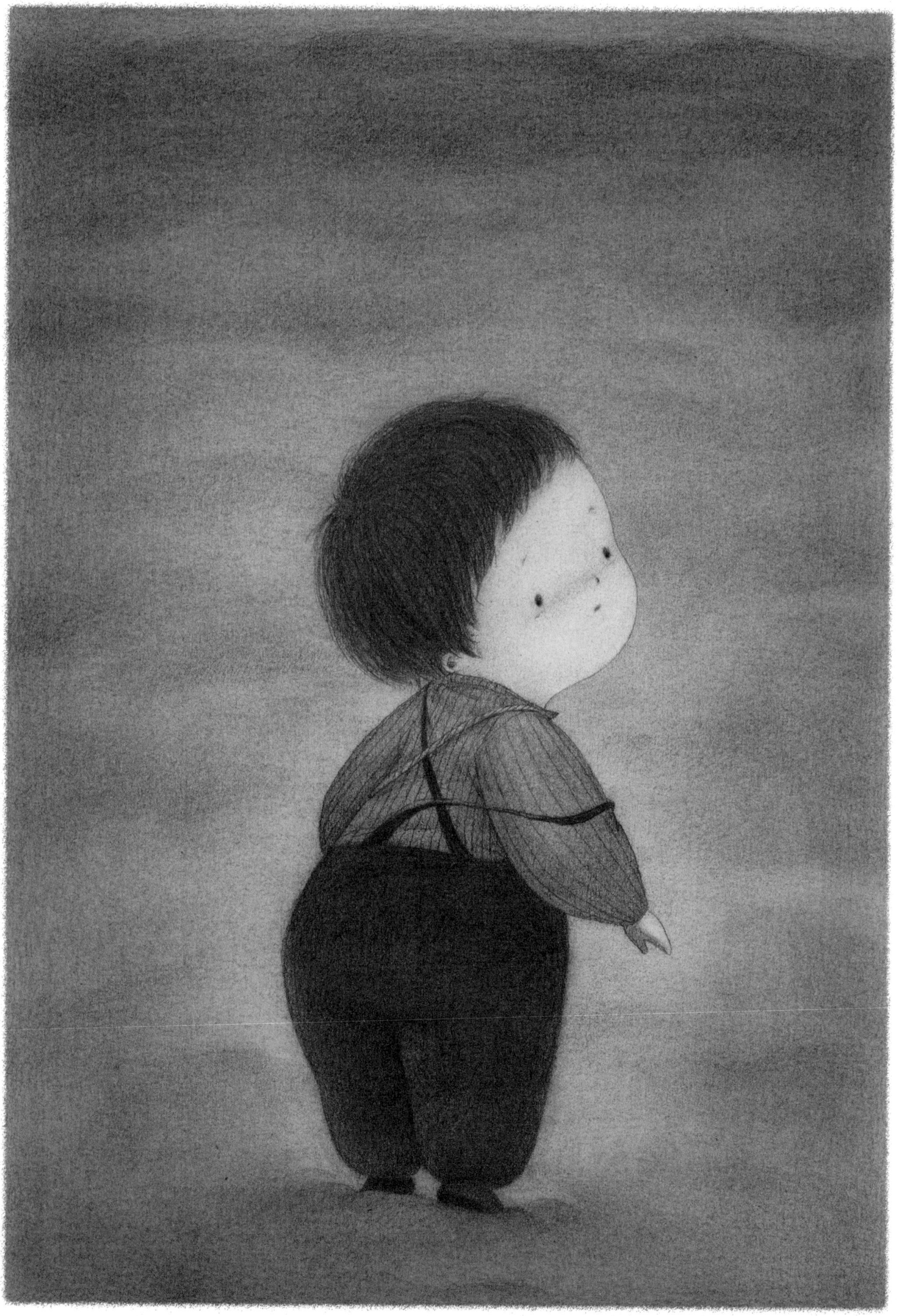

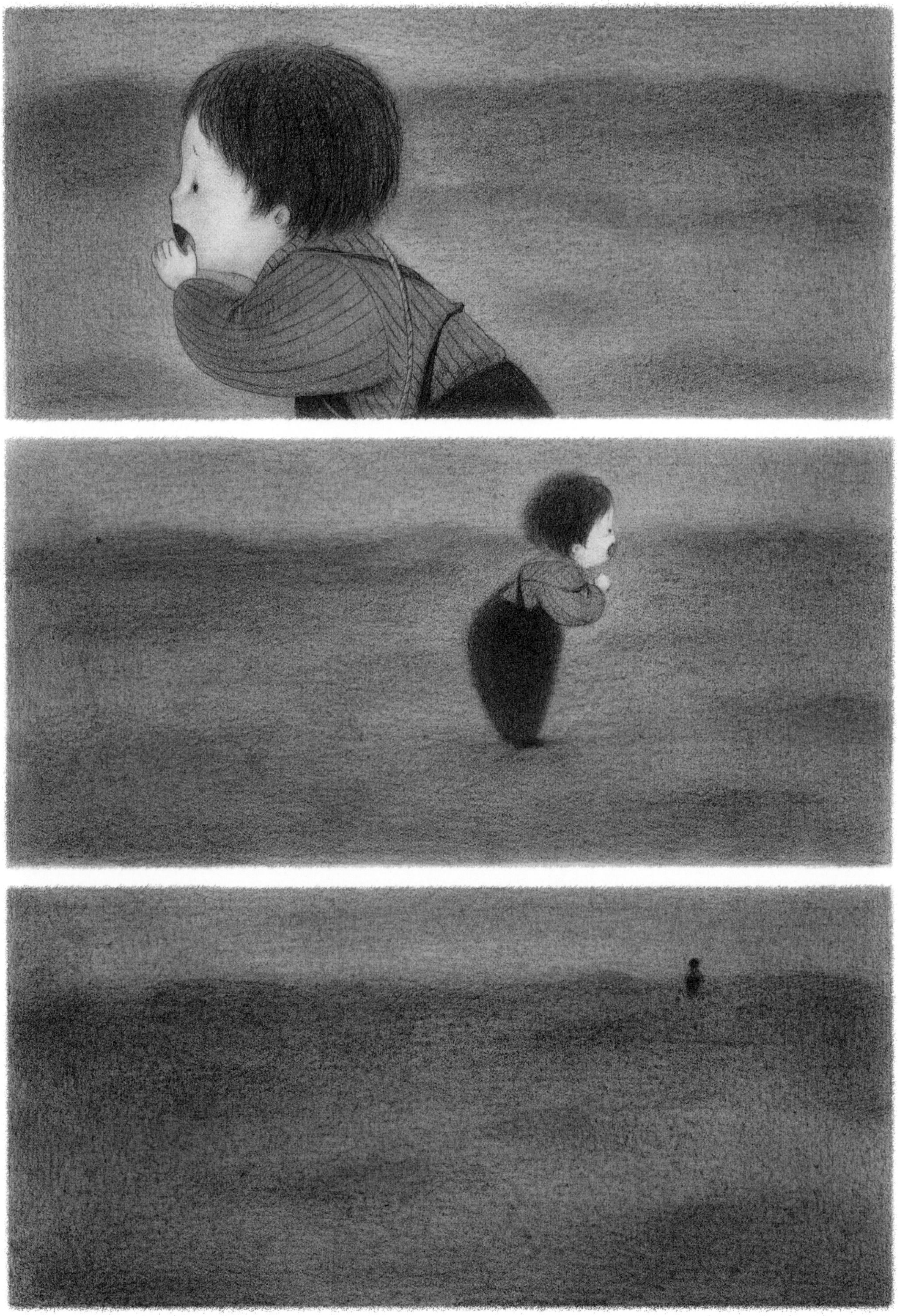

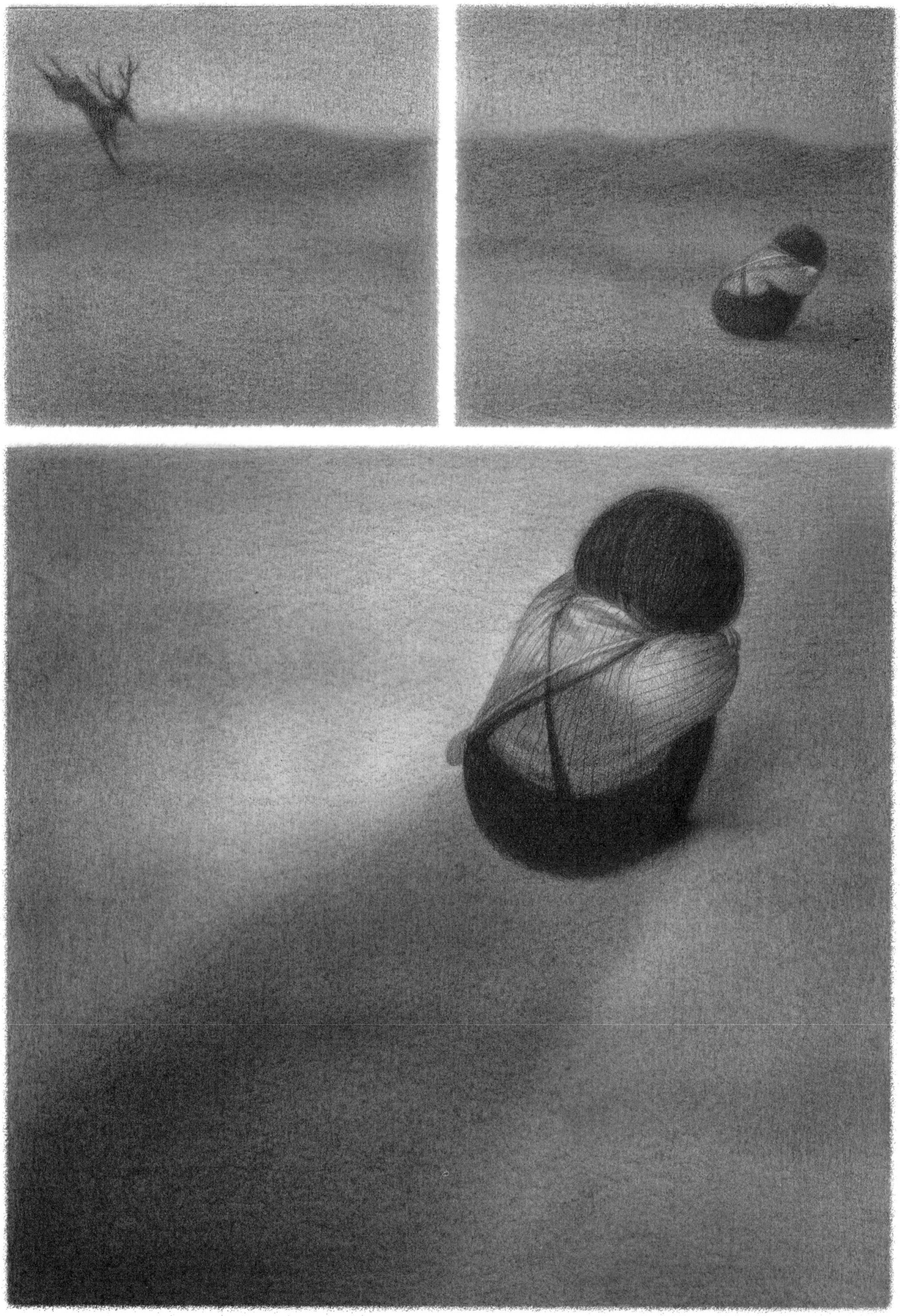

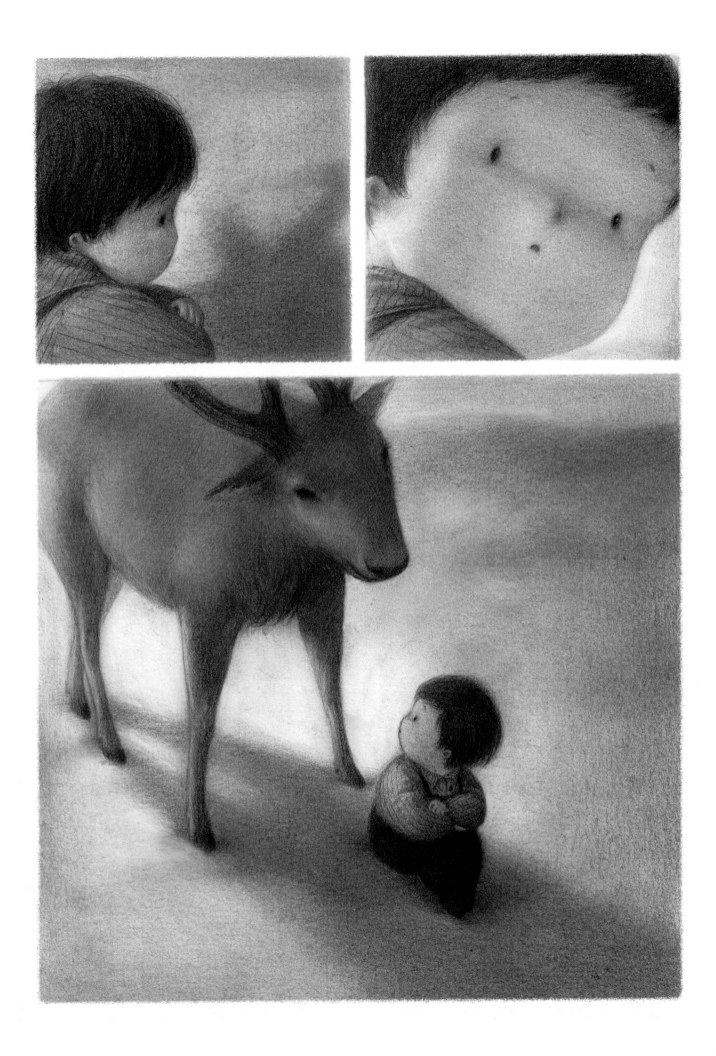

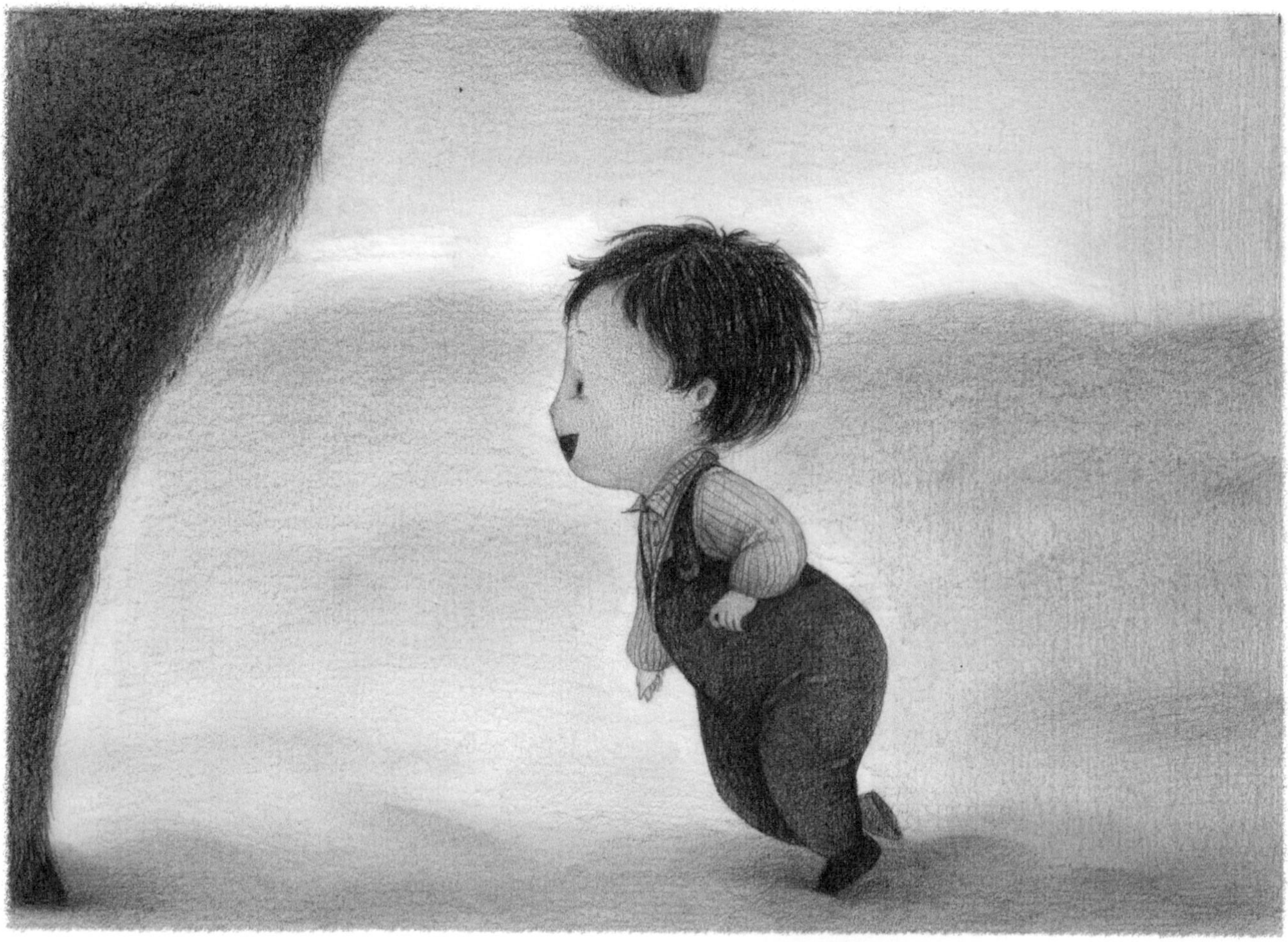

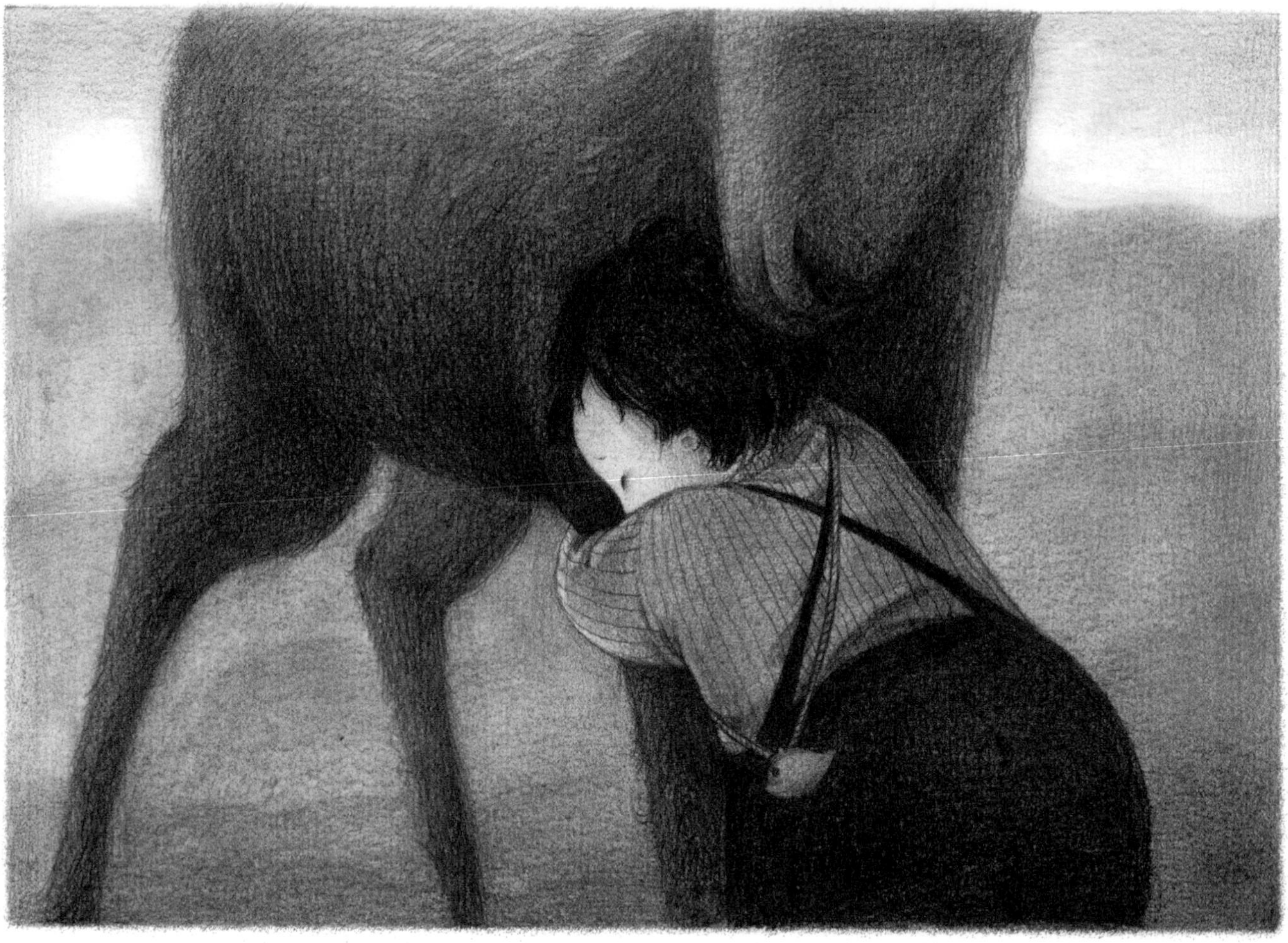

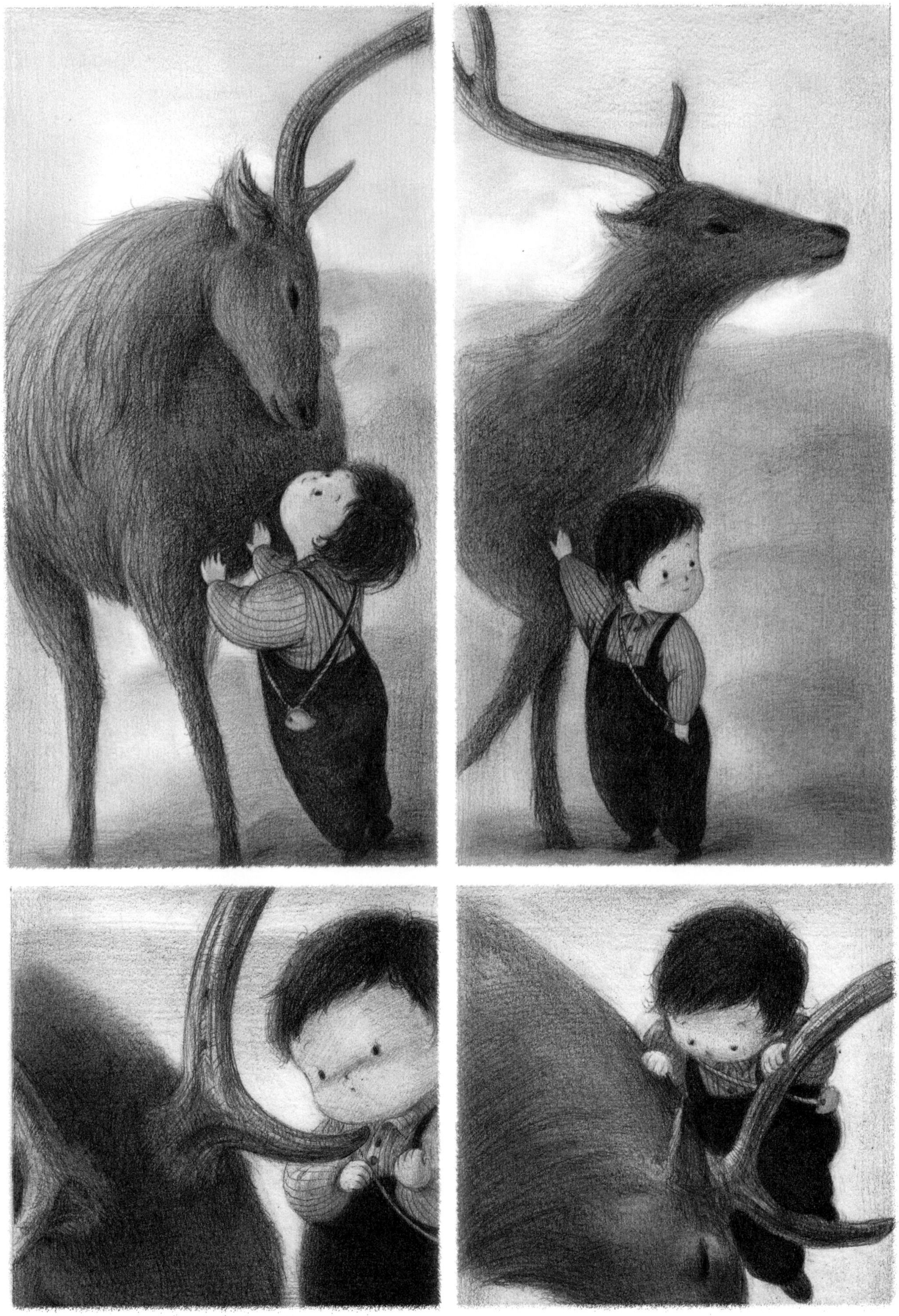

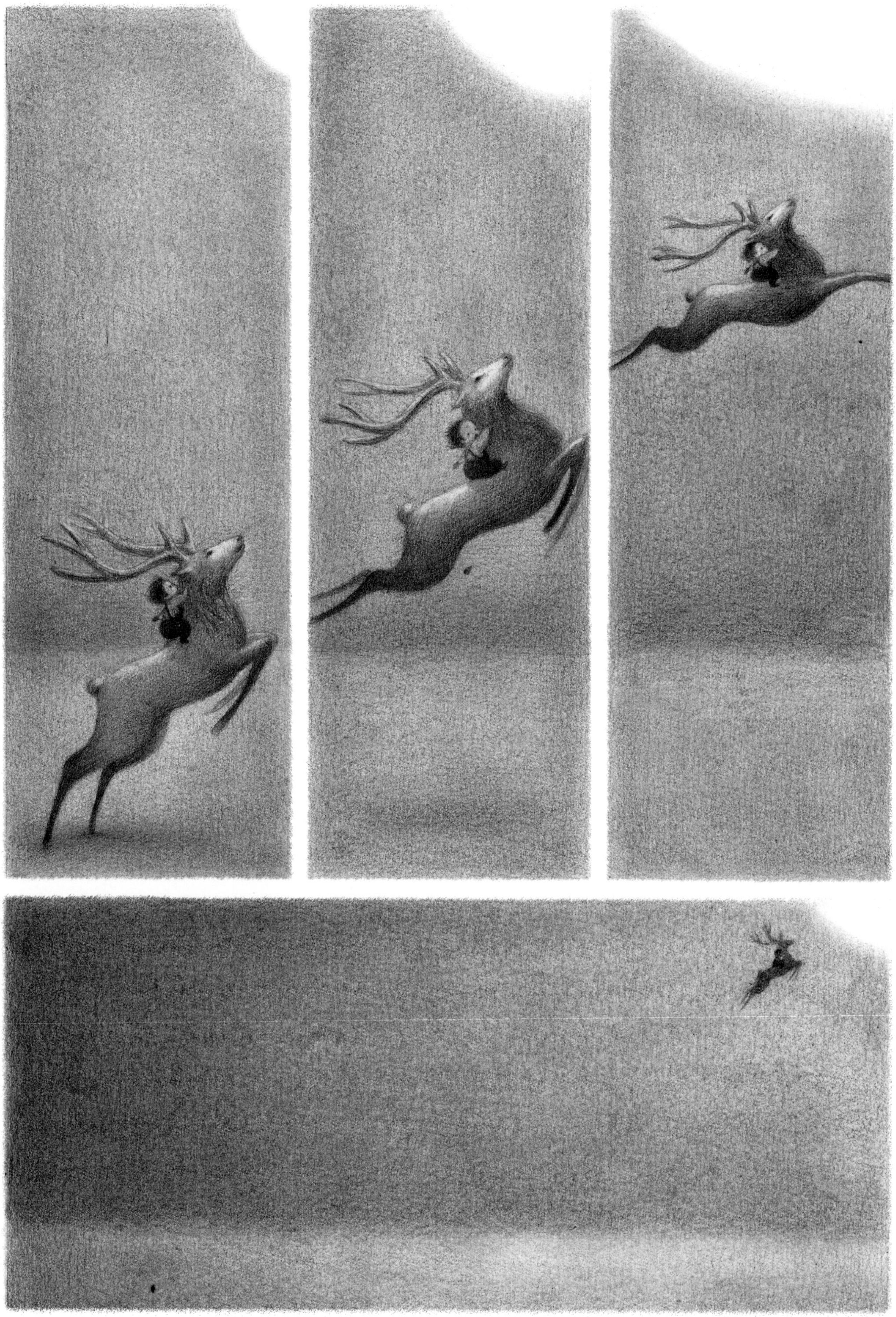

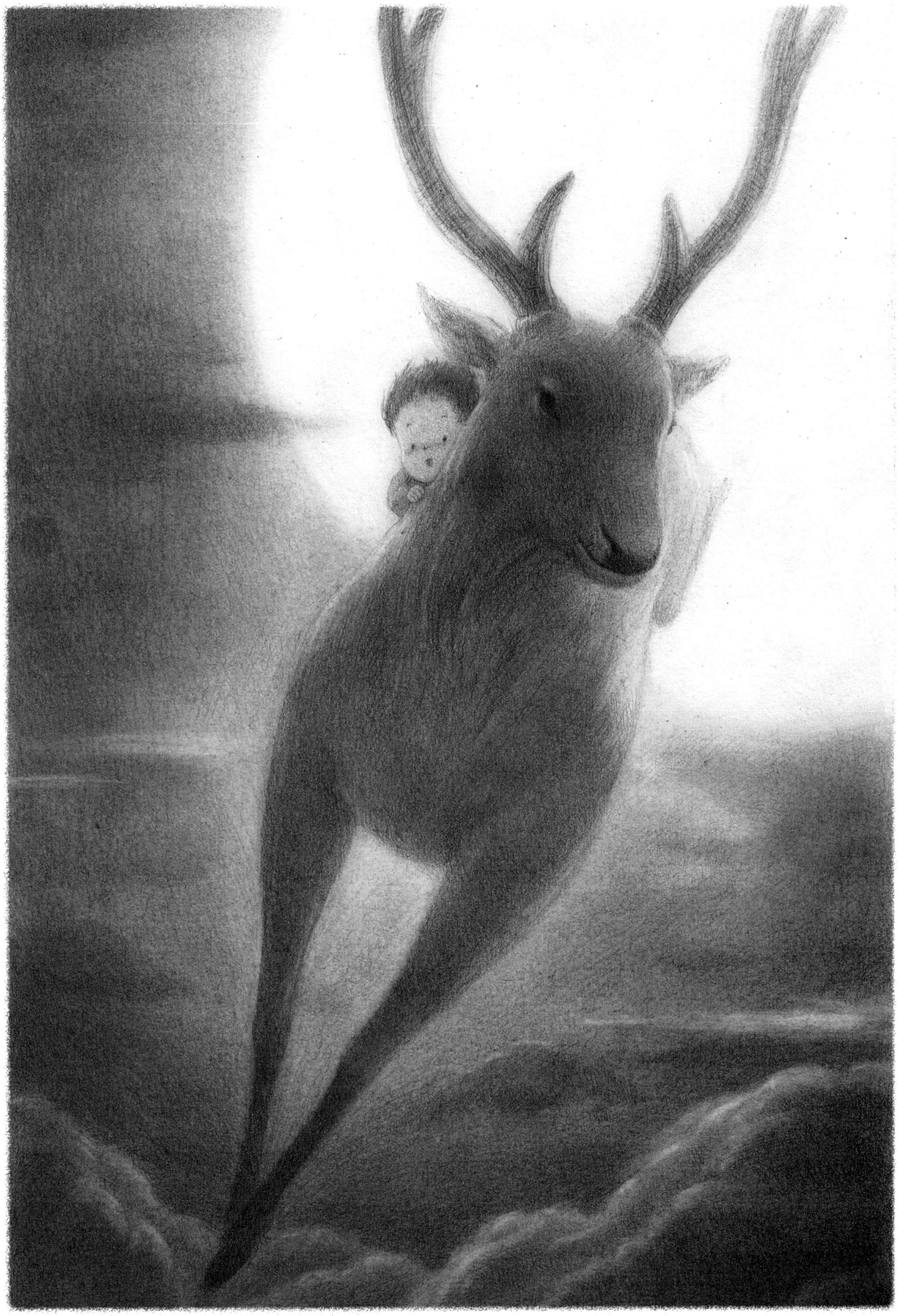

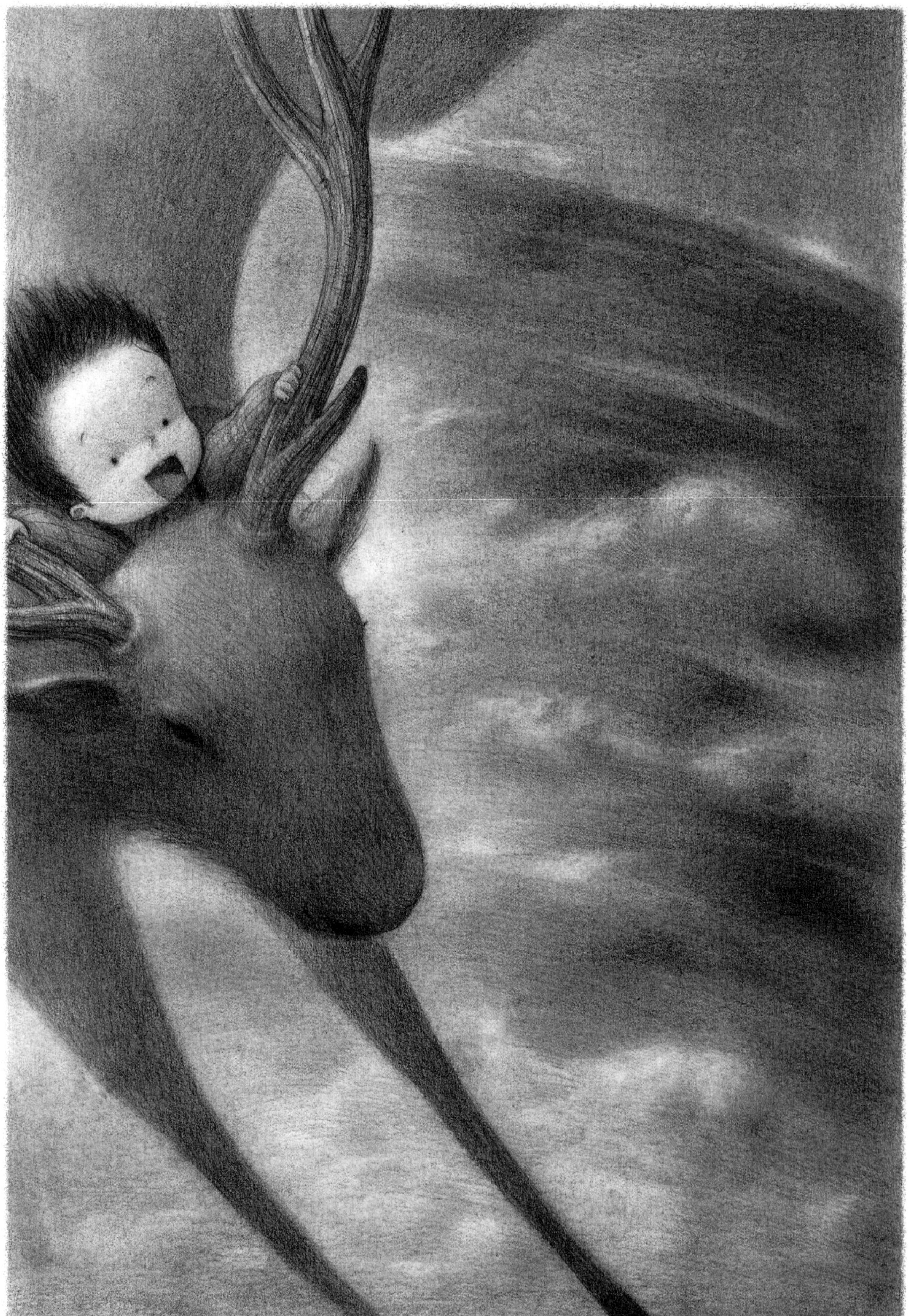

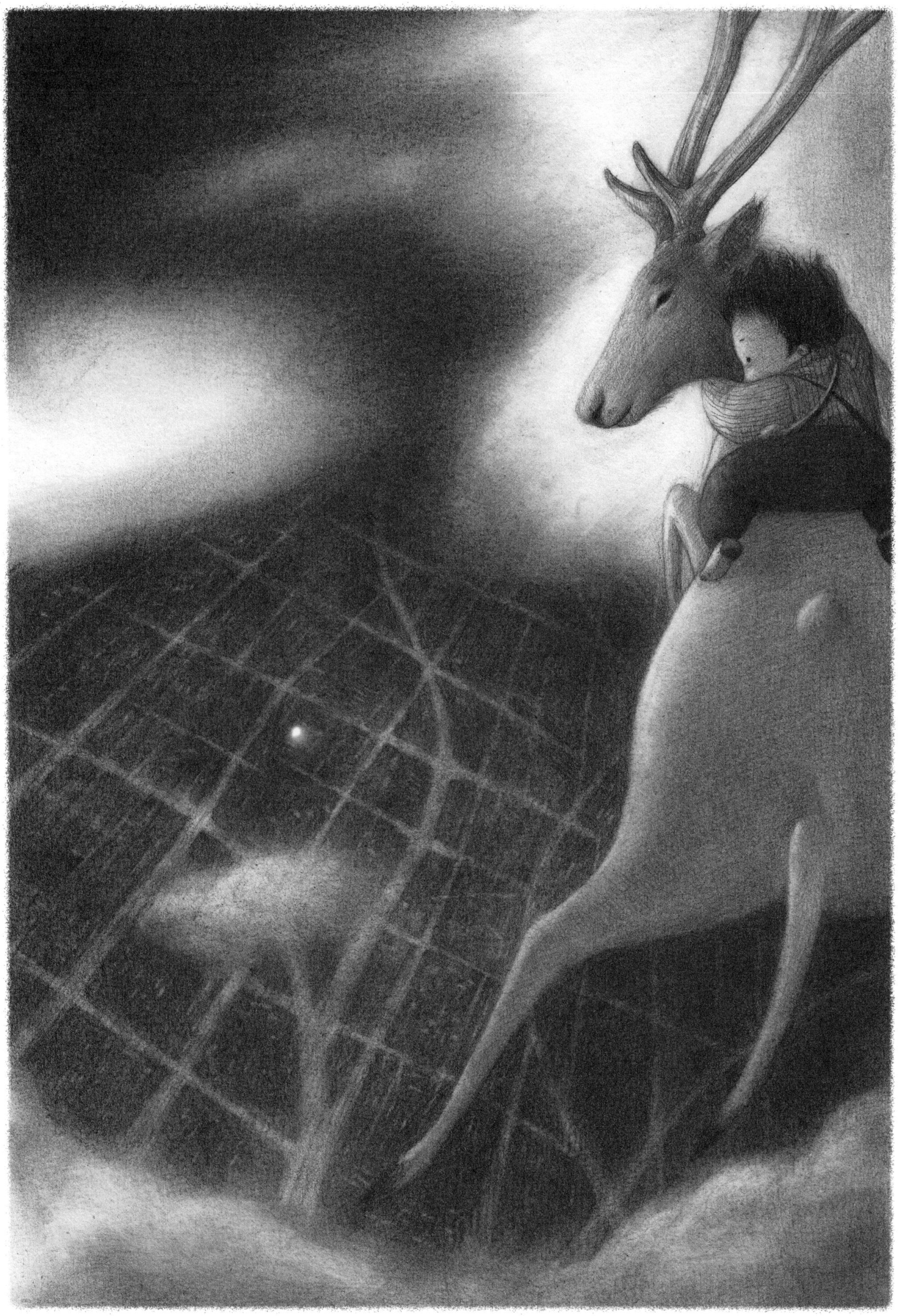

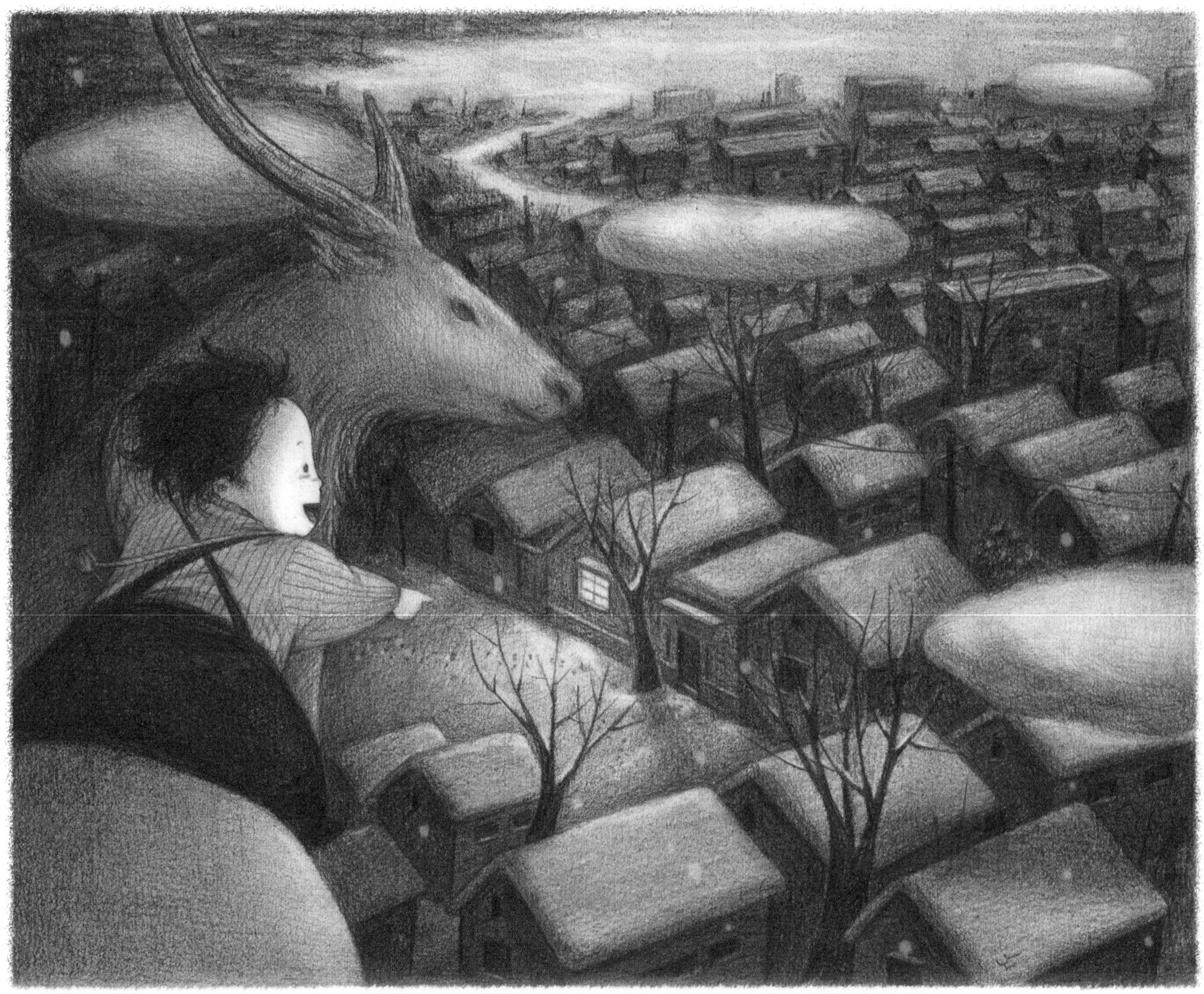

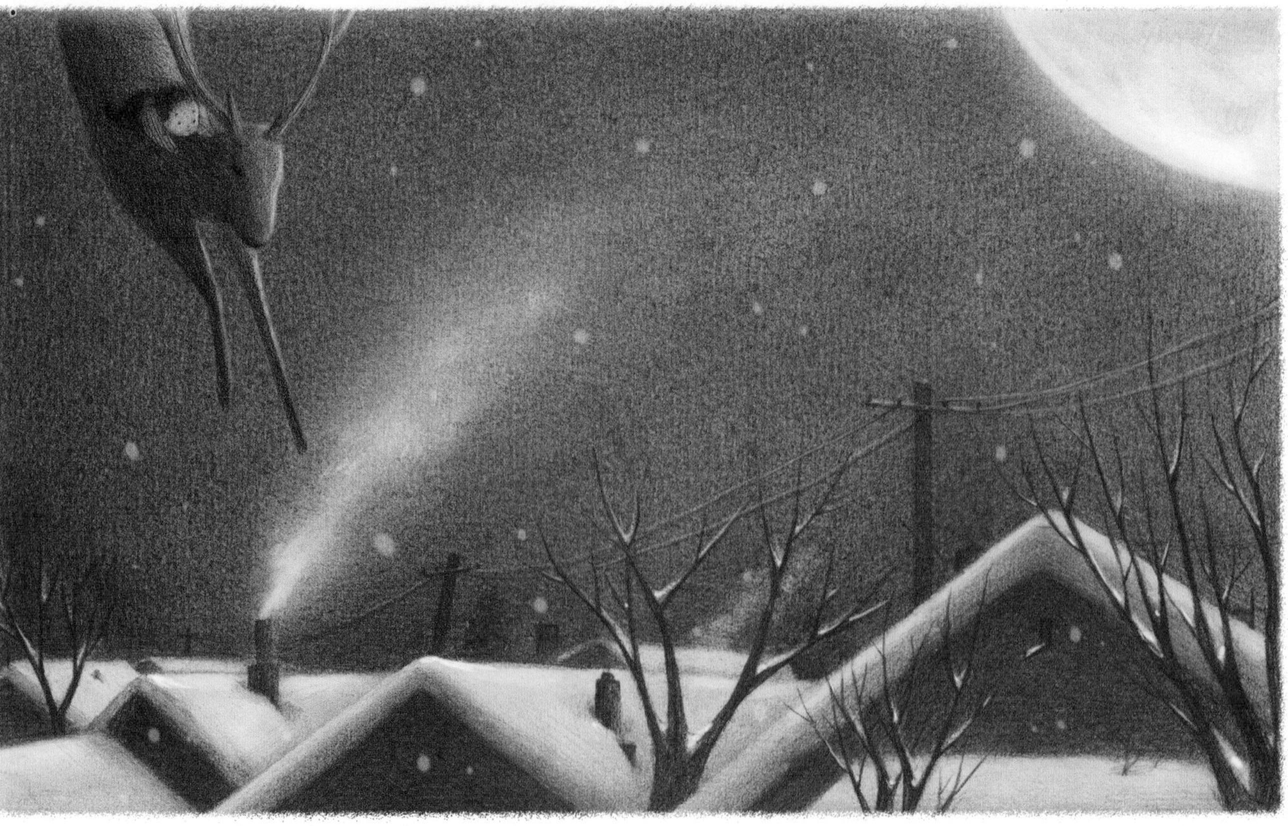

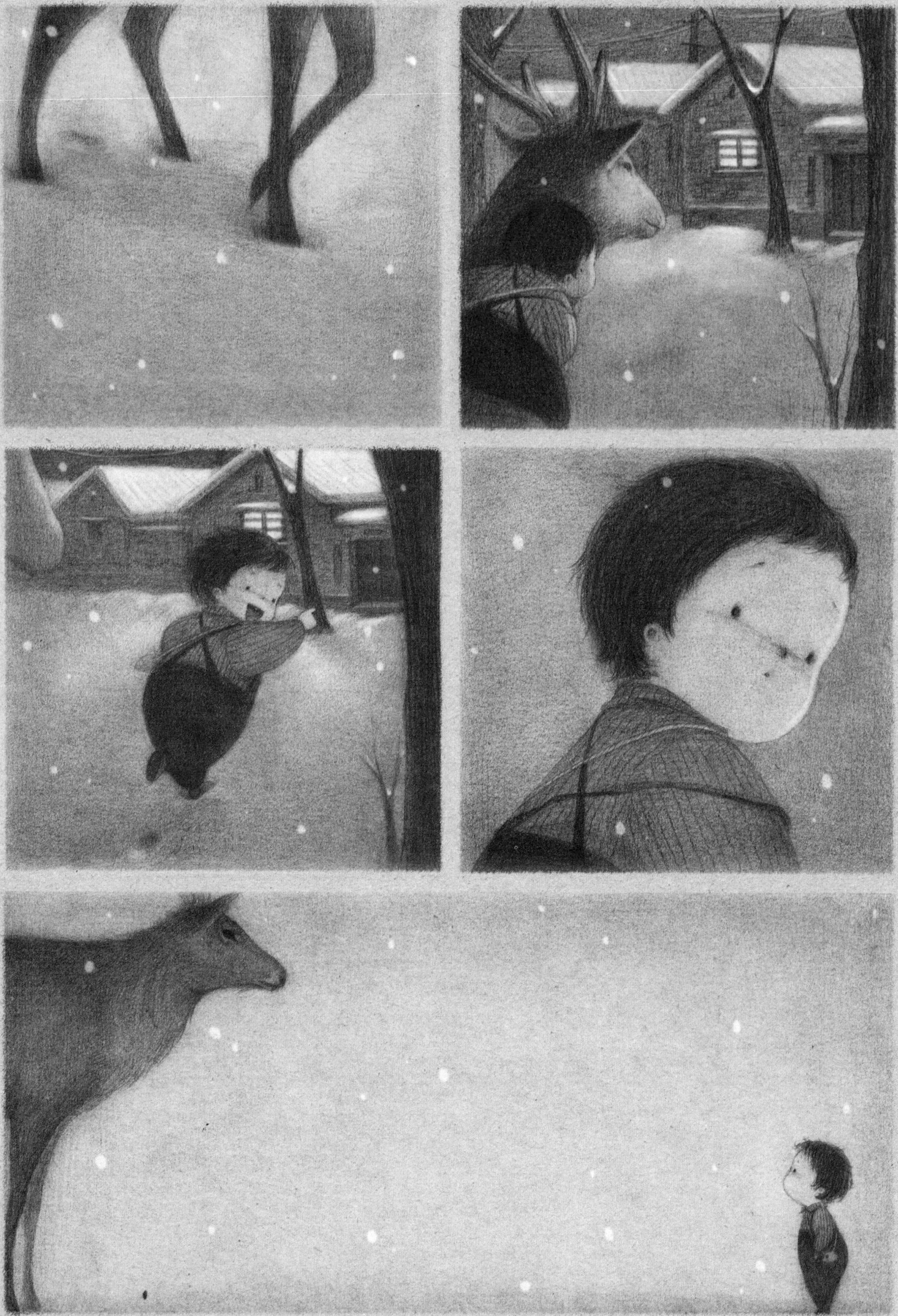

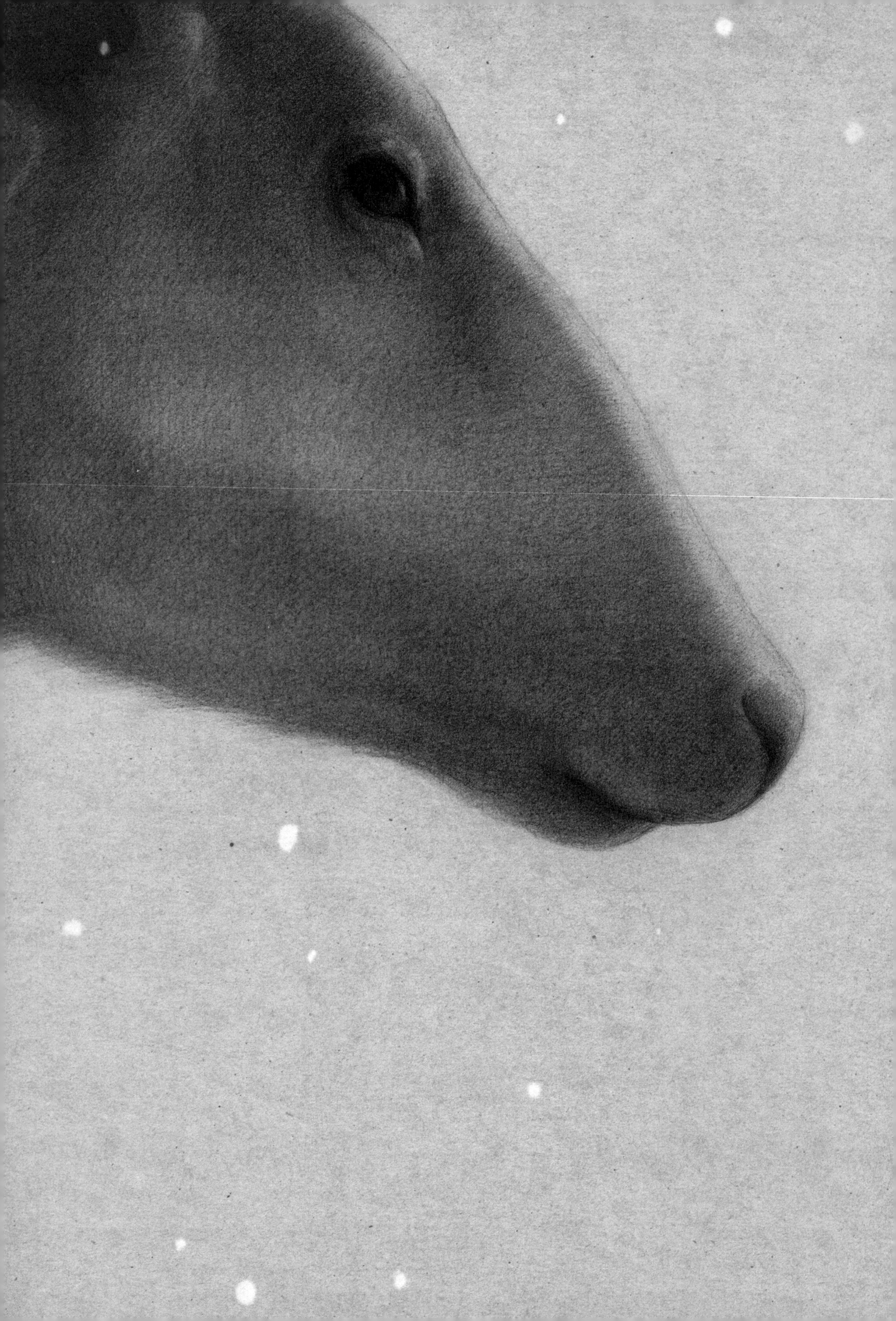

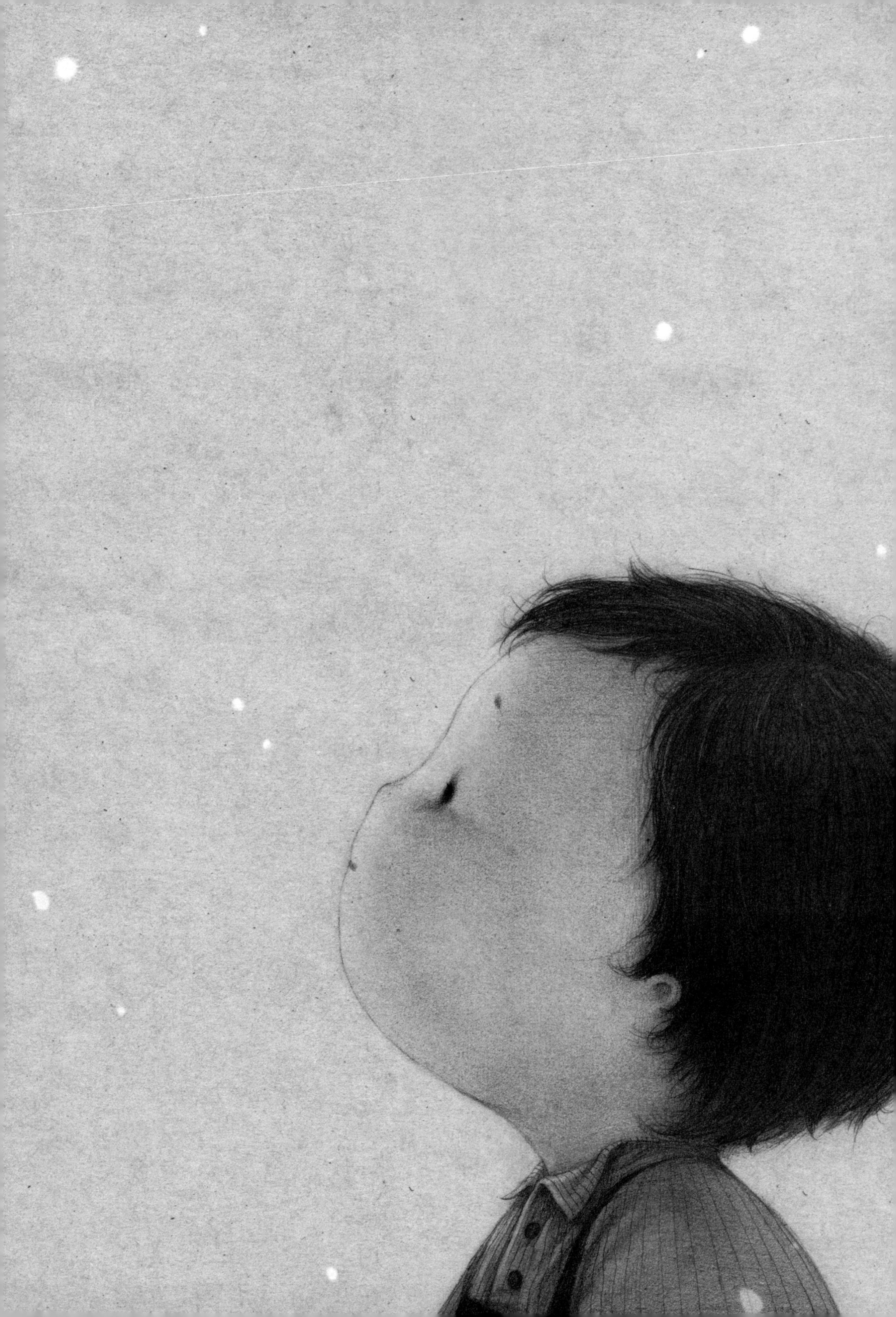

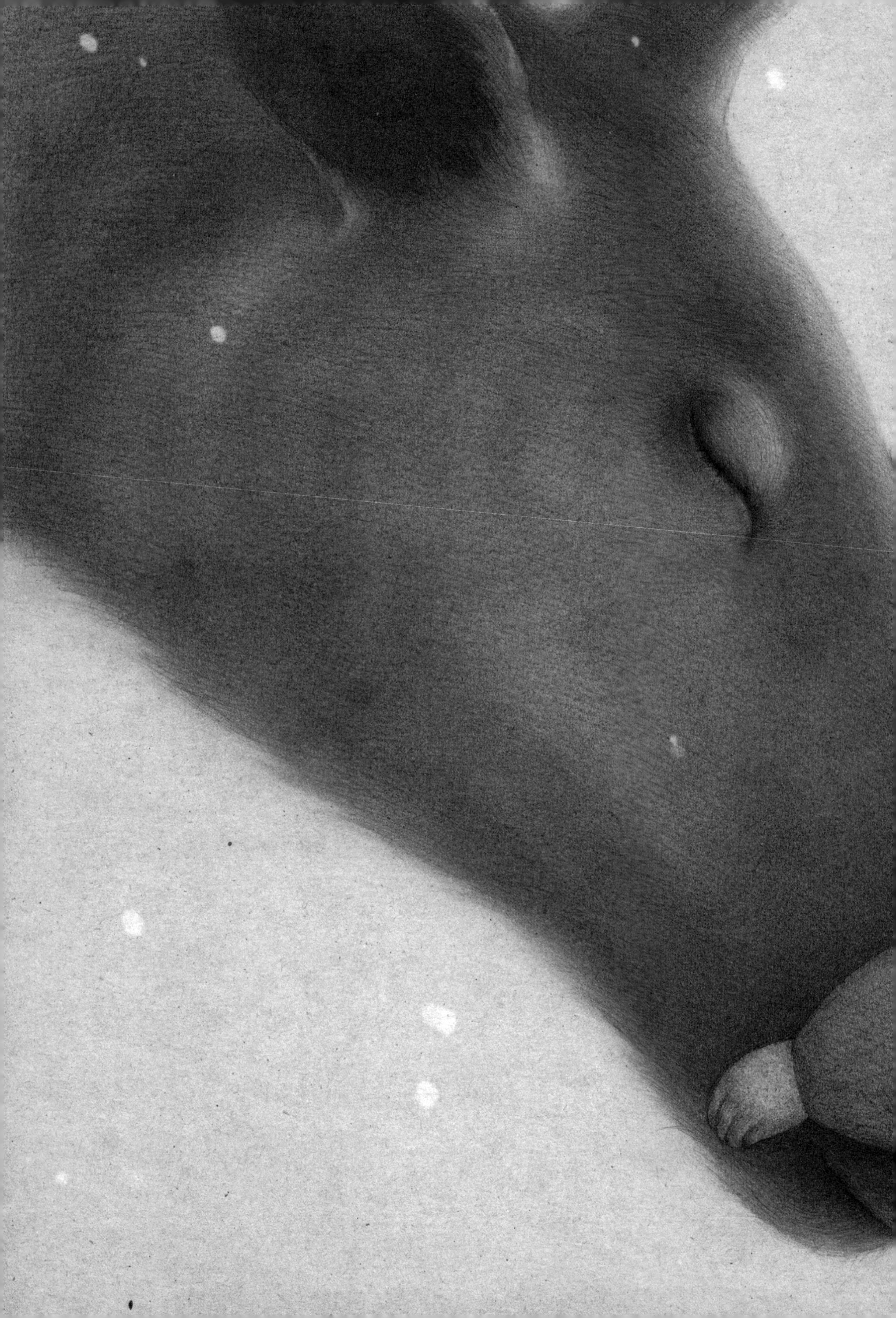

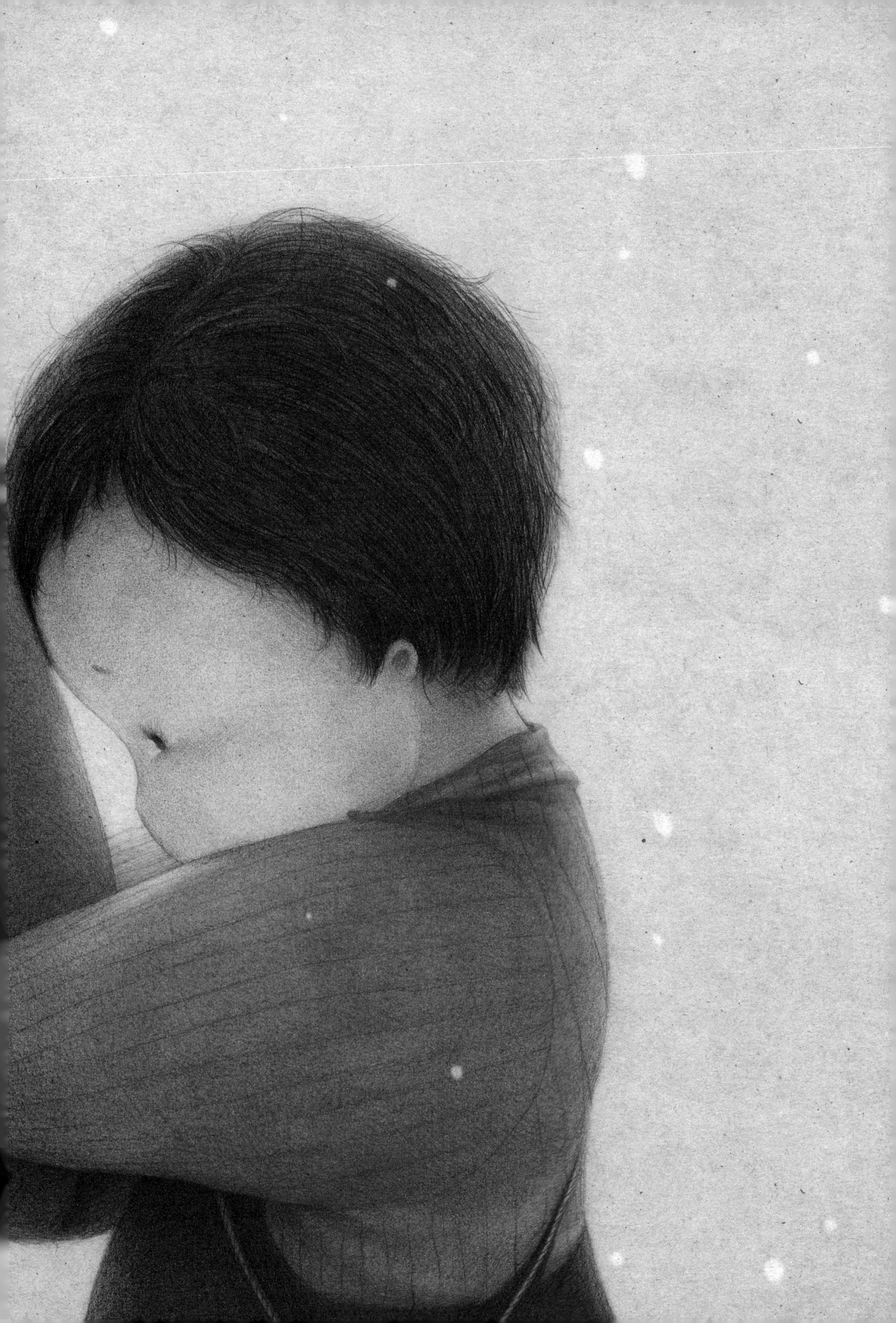

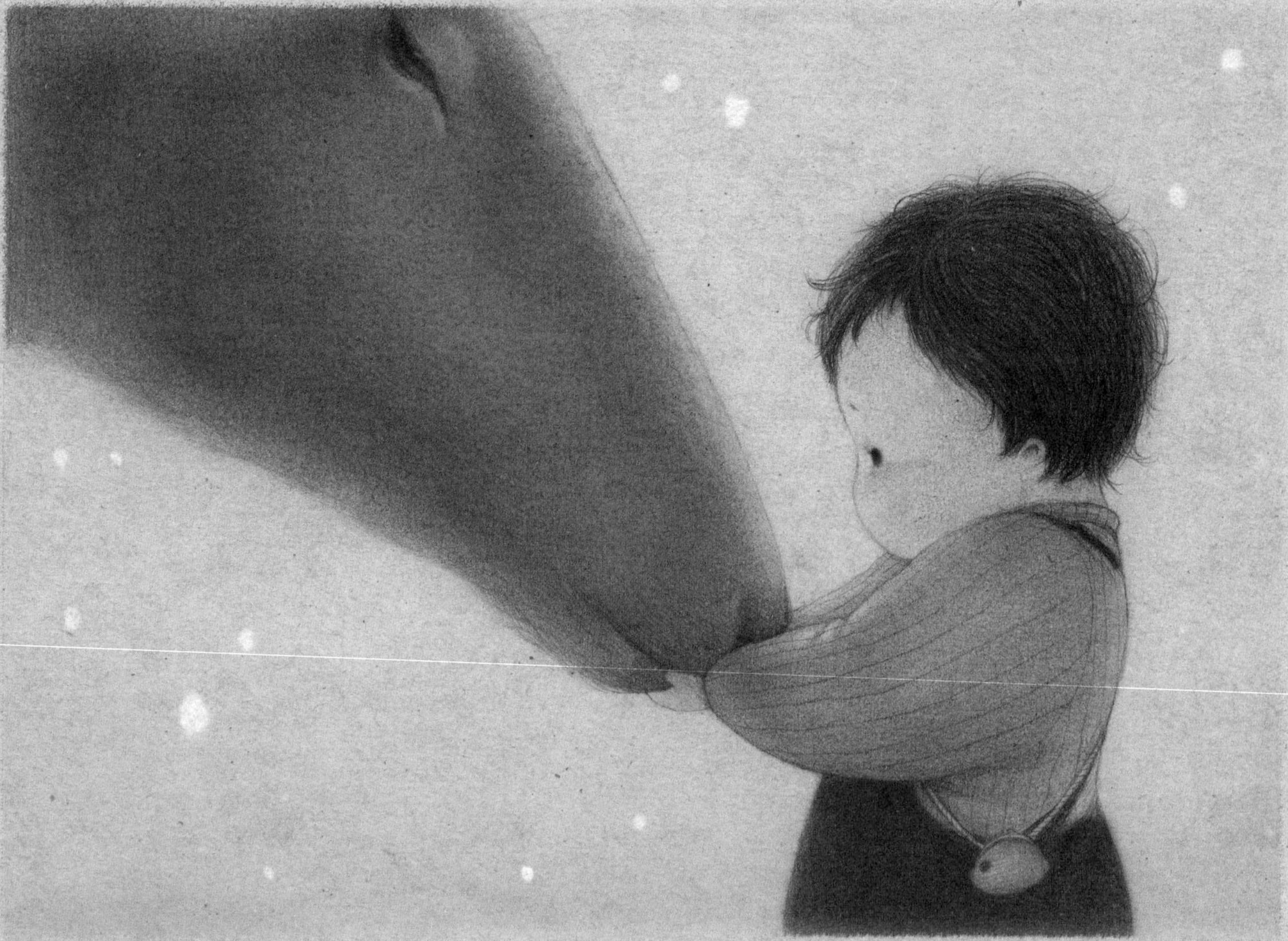

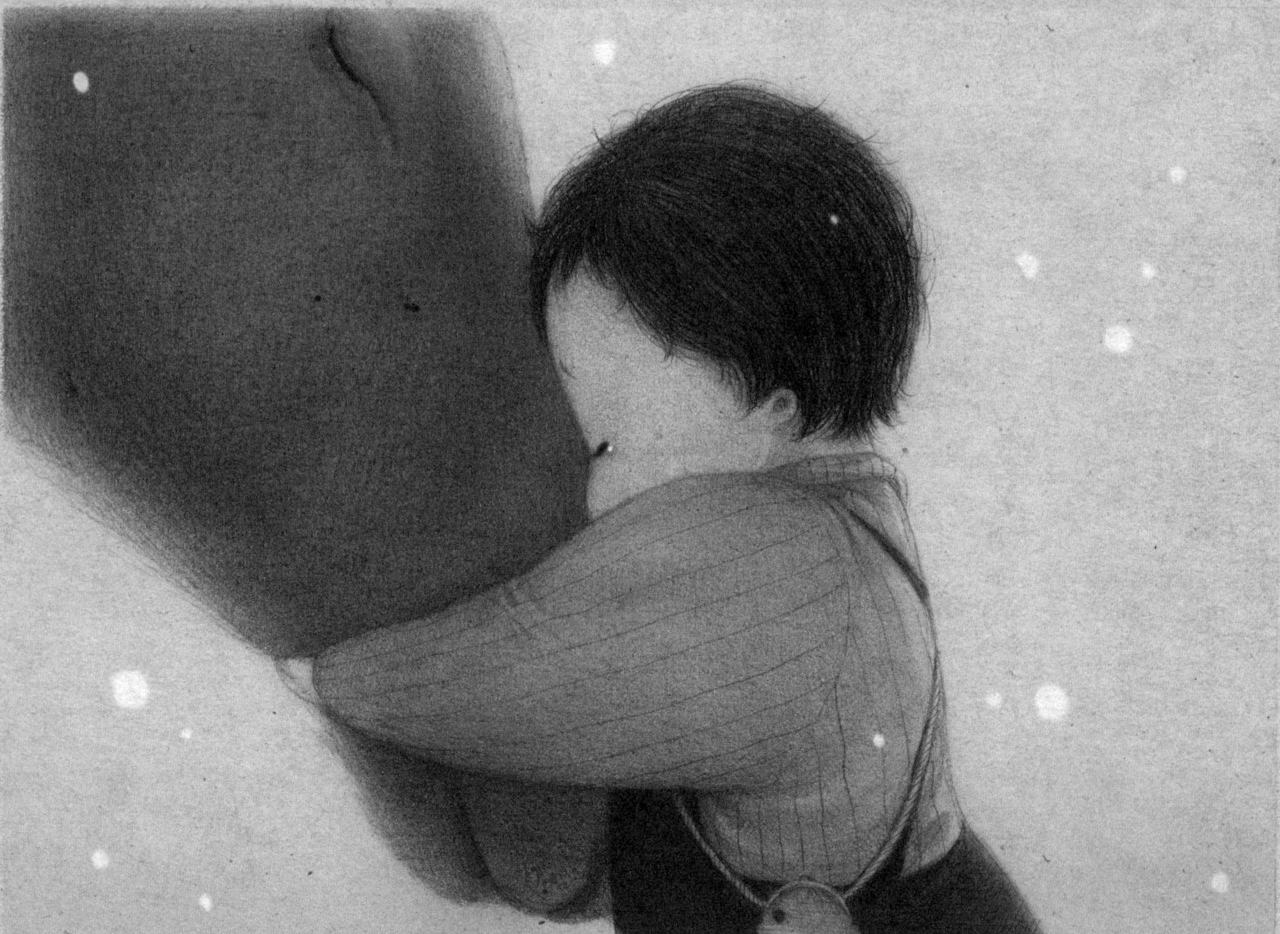

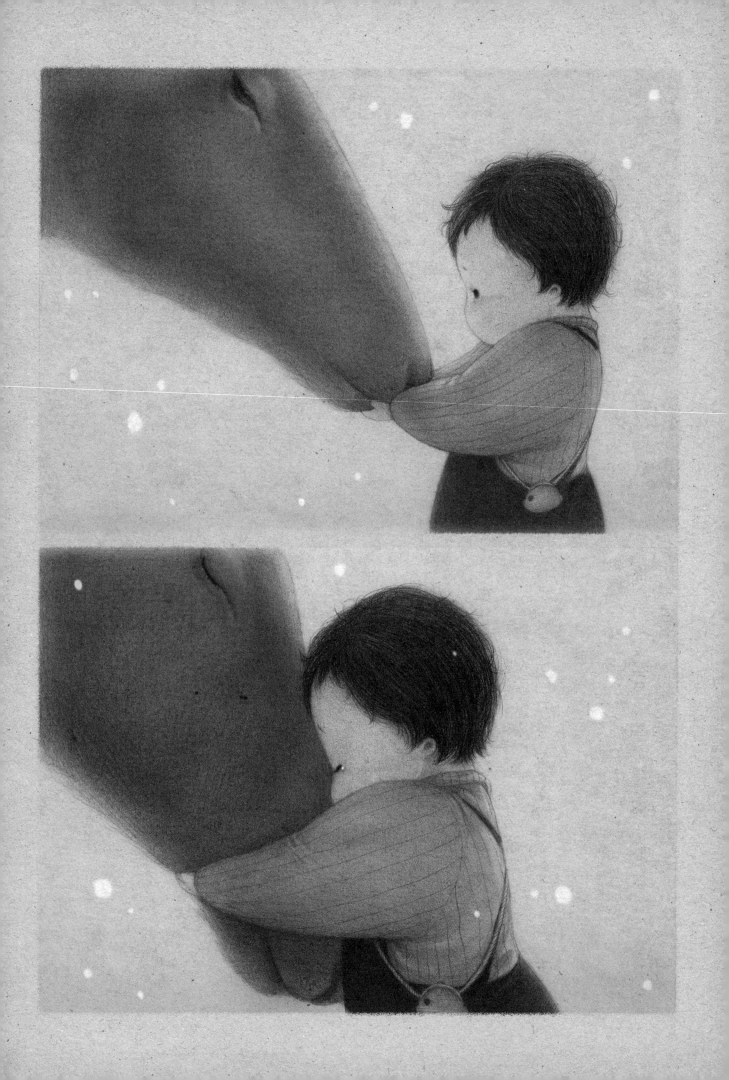

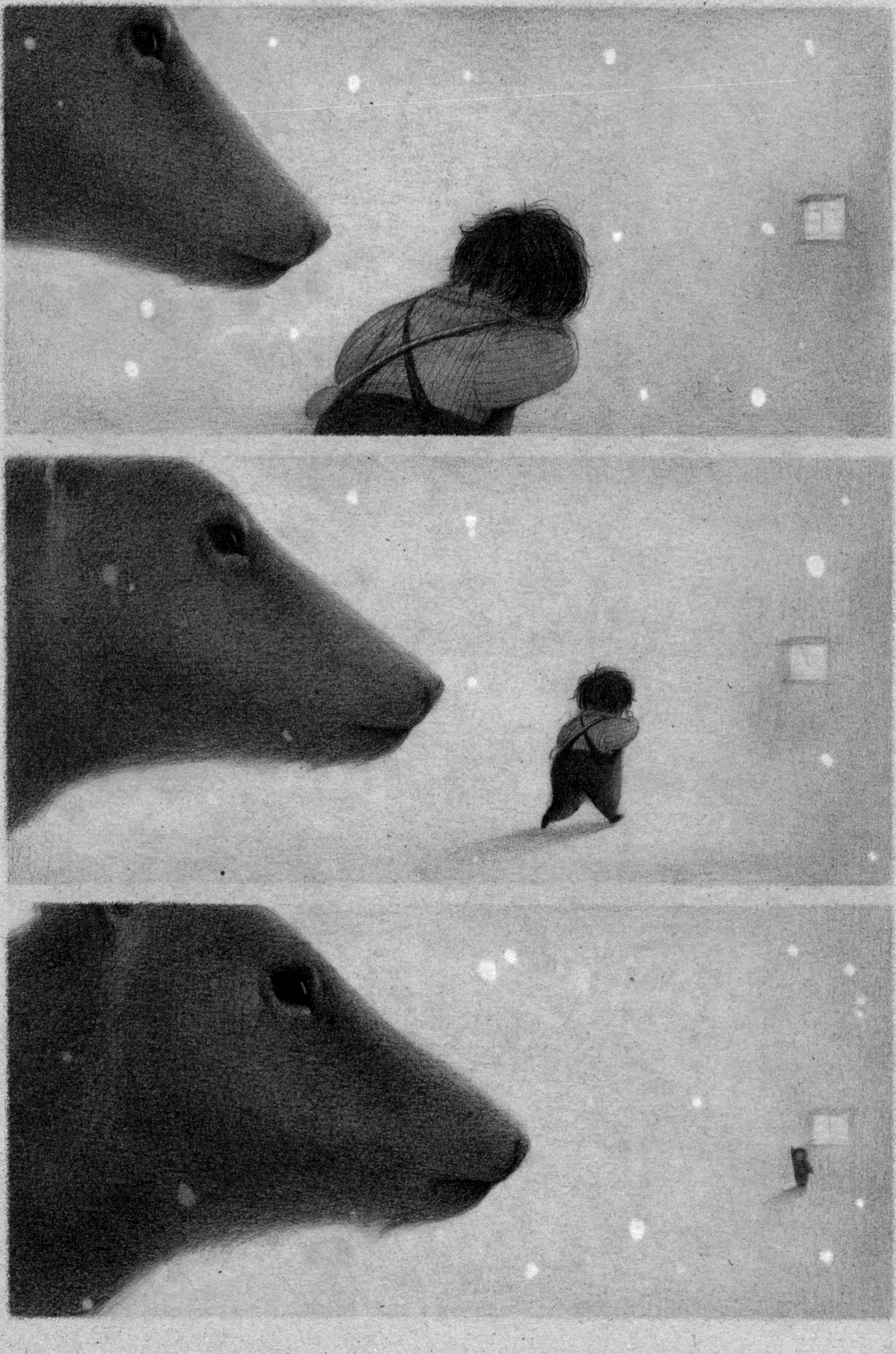

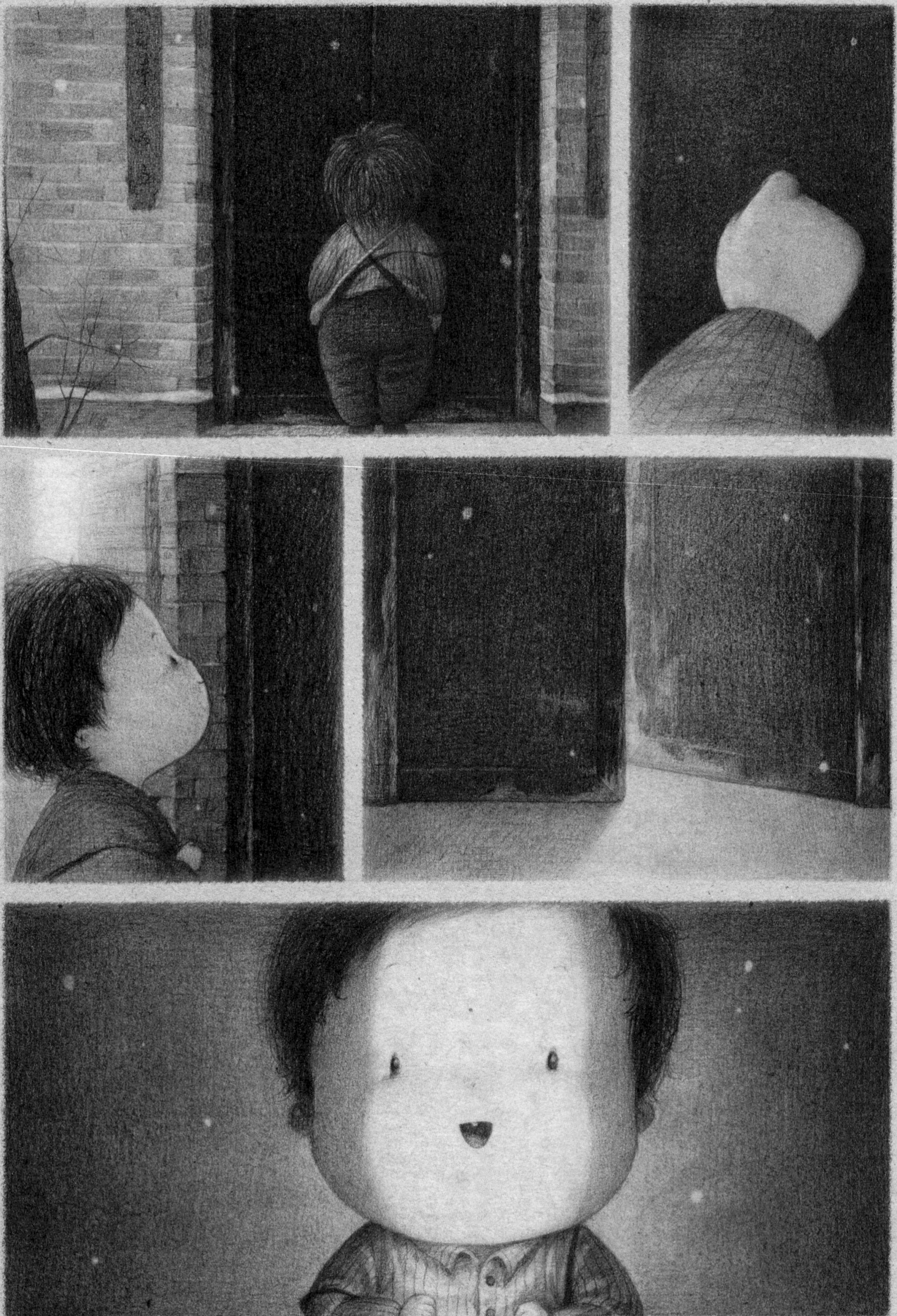

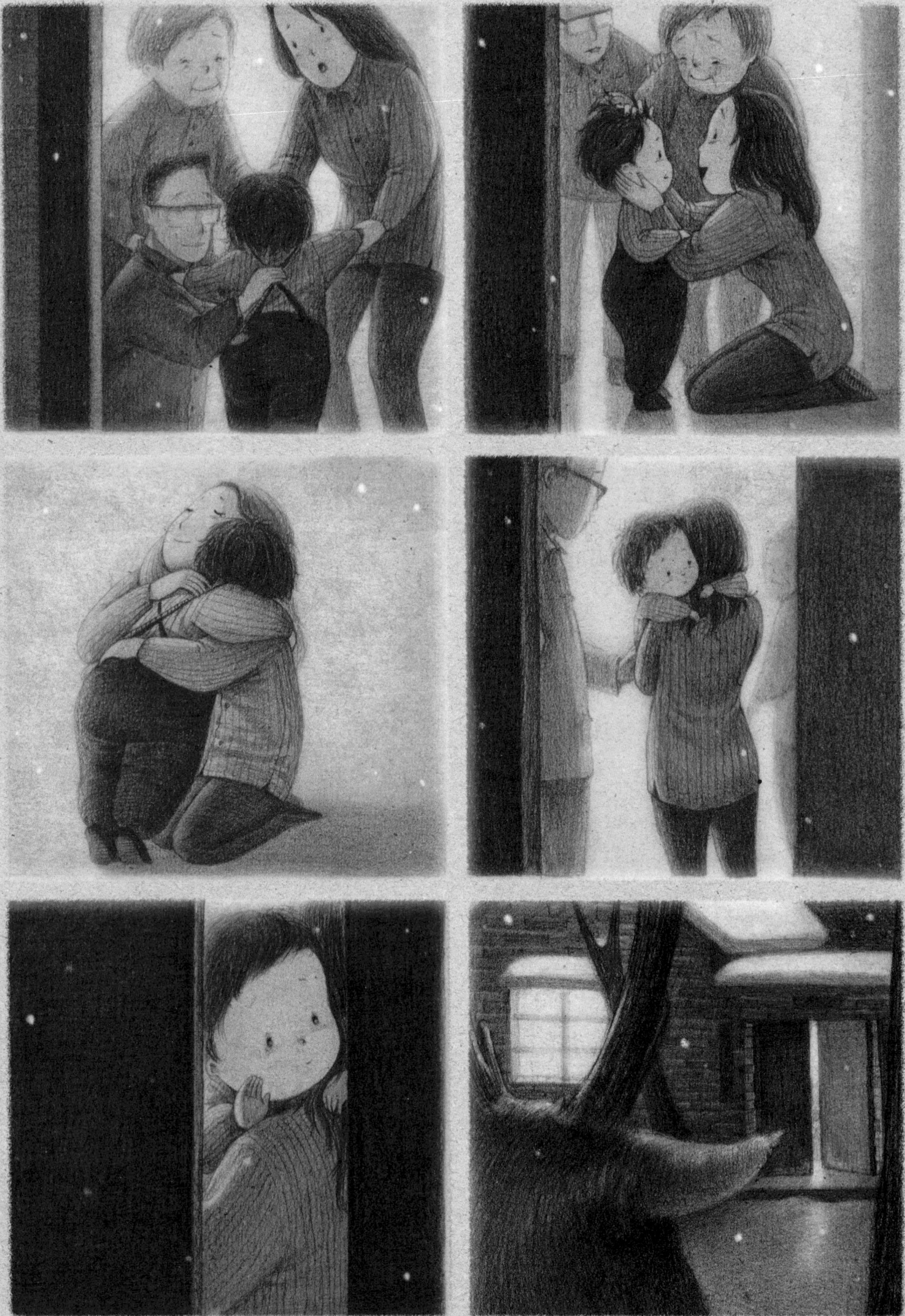

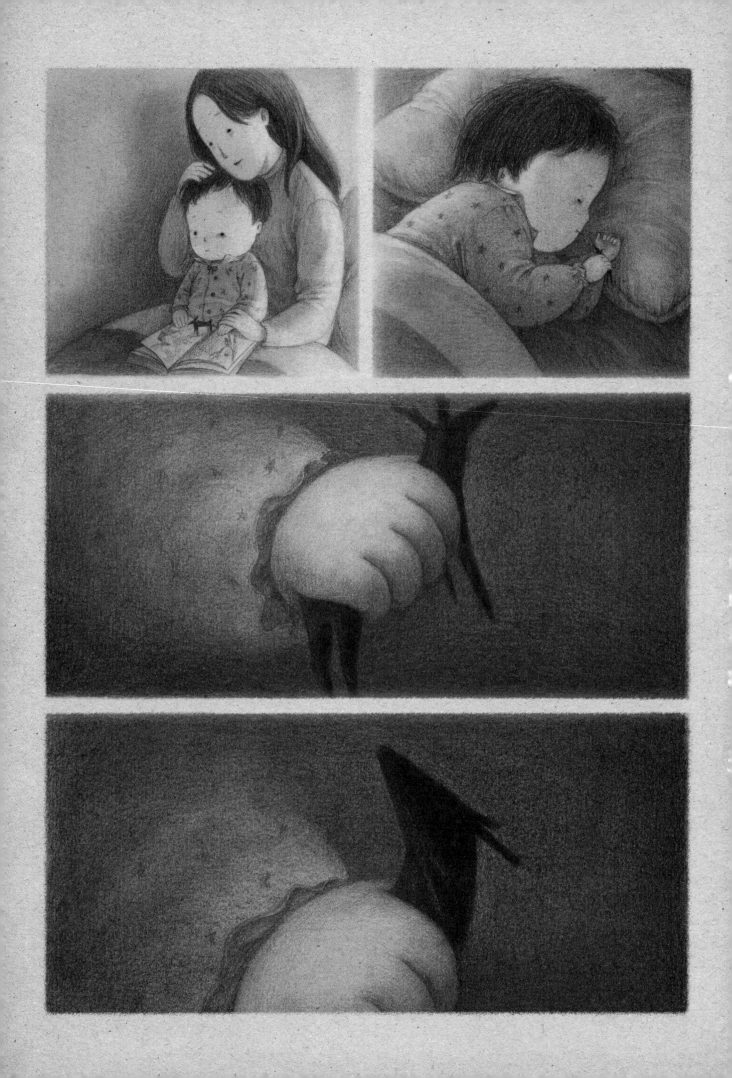

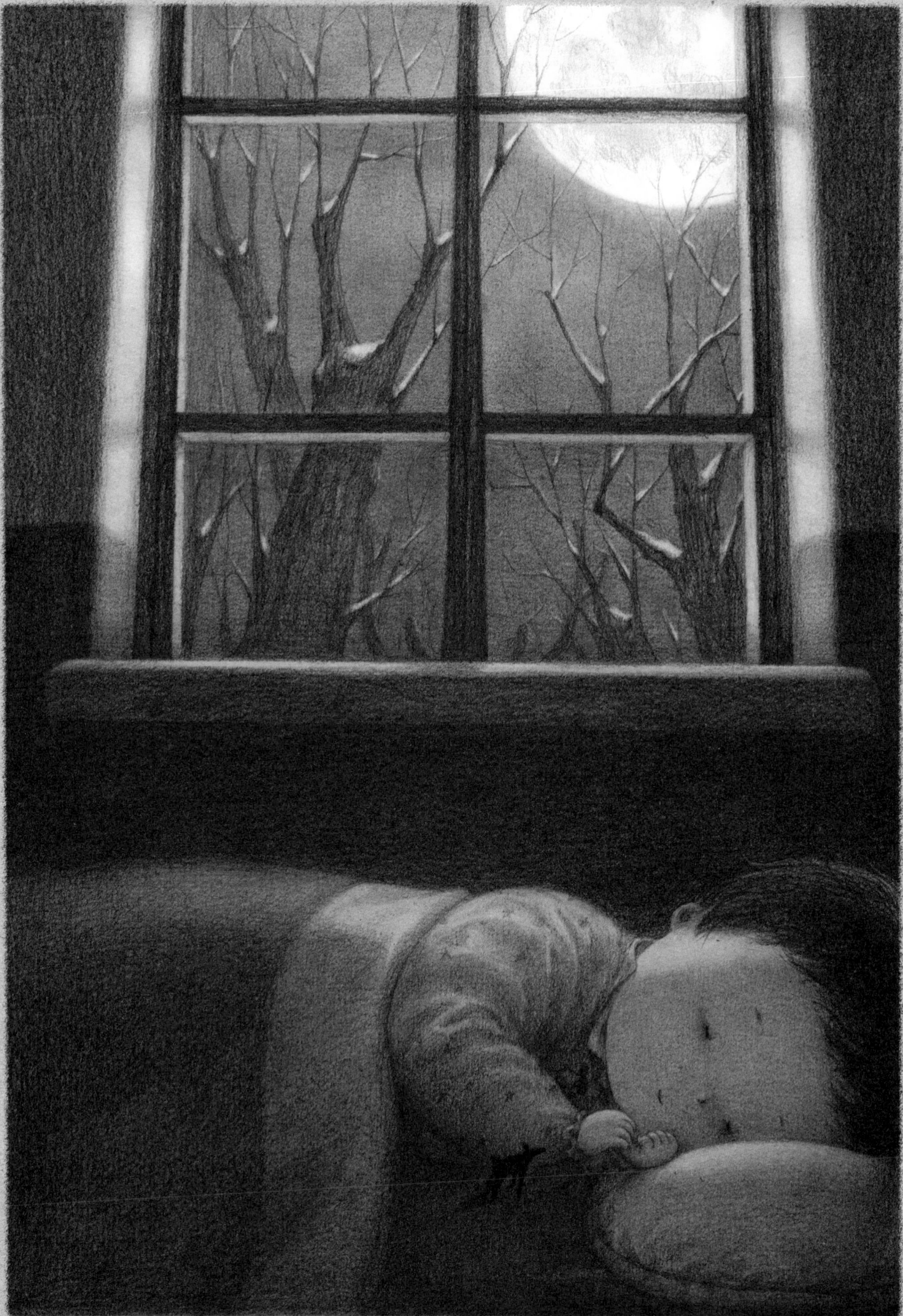